WITH THIS RING

A Lexie Starr Mystery

Book Four

Jeanne Glidewell

Cover and Book design by eBook Prep
www.ebookprep.com

First Edition, January 2014
ISBN: 978-1-61417-517-9

ePublishing Works!
www.epublishingworks.com

DEDICATION

Dedicated to Sheila Johnston Davis who has been my co-conspirator, my confidant, my partner-in-crime, and my closest and dearest friend since Junior High School. Sheila is someone I can count on to always have my back, and to be there for me when I need a true friend. Thank you, Sheila, for being my best friend forever.

ACKNOWLEDGMENTS

I'd like to thank my talented editor, Alice Duncan, for being such a pleasure to work with, and eBook Prep and ePublishing Works for their expertise and commitment to excellence.

CHAPTER 1

No one ever told me getting married would be easy. All I wanted was a short, simple ceremony, performed in the gazebo Stone built in the back yard of the Alexandria Inn. And I wanted this ceremony in the presence of as large a crowd of family and friends as I could muster. I was thrilled to be marrying the second love of my life, and I wanted to share my happiness with everyone I knew.

I didn't want the ceremony to be as elaborate and expensive as my first wedding, but I wanted it to be every bit as meaningful. We wouldn't be shelling out hard-earned money for champagne, caviar, a catered rehearsal dinner, or a dress I'd wear once in my life, that cost five grand. It would just be a day full of family, friends, love, happiness, and fond memories that would last a lifetime.

The wedding party would be small and intimate. My twenty-nine-year-old daughter, Wendy, would be my maid of honor and Stone's nephew, Andy, would serve as his best man. There wouldn't be any ring bearer or flower girl, nor any bridesmaids and groomsmen. Only the two people dearest to our hearts would stand up with us.

Andy, who was a little older than Wendy, had just moved back to the area from South Carolina to become a rancher and part-time pilot. He wanted to be closer to Wendy, whom he'd become attached to, and also near Stone, with whom he'd always been extremely close.

Andy looked more like a movie star than any movie star I'd ever seen photos of—tall, dark, handsome, blue eyes and perfect white teeth. He was even blessed with the same type of warm, loving personality his Uncle Stone possessed. I couldn't think of anyone I'd rather have as my future son-in-law. But first I had to get his uncle to the altar.

For the wedding I'd decided to wear a nice silk knee-length dress in muted shades of pink because, after all, it was both of our second marriages. Stone would wear his black pinstriped suit jacket over a brand new pair of creased blue jeans. After the short Protestant service, two nicely decorated sheet cakes, one vanilla and one chocolate, would be served with a cranberry flavored fruit punch. There'd be bowls of nuts, butter mints, and other refreshments at the reception on the courtyard patio between the back porch and the gazebo.

Stone and I had purchased matching wedding bands, made of Black Hills Gold, to exchange. Mine had inset diamonds in the middle and smaller inset rubies on either side. The bands were etched with a floral pattern in two-toned gold. The modest stones in my ring were designed to represent our April and July birthstones. We'd also written vows to recite during the ceremony. They were simply worded heartfelt declarations of our love for one another.

It wasn't slated to be an ultra fancy affair, but it

wouldn't be a fly-by-the-seat-of-our-pants affair either. The invitations were mailed out, the cakes were on order at Pete's Pantry, and the lily and baby's breath flower arrangements had been selected. I'd even had my nails done, and my short brown hair permed and highlighted. I looked hot—or, at least, as luke-warm as it's possible for me to look at a half-century old. It'd been nice not to turn fifty all by myself the previous month. I'd celebrated a lot of lonely birthdays since my first husband, Wendy's father Chester, had passed away from an embolism when Wendy was just seven years old.

As far as I could tell, all of our little wedding duckies were in alignment, standing at attention in a perfect little row. Our one little symbolic extravagance was our arrangement to have a pair of doves released after the minister pronounced us husband and wife.

The wedding was to take place in just ten days at the Alexandria Inn, Stone's bed and breakfast establishment in Rockdale, Missouri. We intended to close the inn down while we enjoyed a honeymoon in Jamaica; snorkeling, visiting tourist attractions, taking in the local cuisine, culture and traditions, and drinking margaritas as we soaked up the sun on the beautiful beaches.

Our plans were rock solid. We didn't think anything could go awry and upset our special day. We were more than ready for our wedding day to arrive. We felt we could finally sit back and relax, convinced everything would go off without a hitch. That's when we got the message on our answering machine. Thurman Steiner, the minister at the Rockdale Baptist Church who was scheduled to unite us in holy matrimony, was dead. Found in the kitchen of his home, deceased of unknown causes.

* * *

Stone Van Patten and I, Lexie Starr, had been together since we met on the East Coast the previous year. He'd come to my assistance when Wendy was abducted. I'd welcomed his help and grown to love him in the process. Stone, a retired jeweler and volunteer police officer in Myrtle Beach, South Carolina, had moved to the Midwest to be closer to me.

Stone had gotten the idea of owning a bed and breakfast after we'd stayed at the Camelot Inn in Schenectady, New York. Turning an old historic mansion in ill repair into a thriving B&B had been a labor of love for both of us. It was a challenge we both enjoyed. We'd lost a lot of blood, sweat, and tears making the Alexandria Inn an establishment we could take a great deal of pride in. It was a huge undertaking, as the inn and its grounds encompassed most of the block we lived on.

Having been a widow and on my own for over twenty years, I was now going to sell my home in Shawnee, Kansas, and give up my volunteer service at the small local library in my former neighborhood. It wasn't going to be a big adjustment for me, as I'd been practically living at the Alexandria Inn, which Stone had named after me, for quite a few months now.

I'd miss working at the library. Books were a passion of mine, and helping others at the library had given me something interesting to do in my spare time. I'd put in three or four hours at the library several days a week, when time permitted. If and when business slowed down at the inn during the winter months, I planned to volunteer at the small local library in Rockdale. Might as well put my experience as a library assistant to good use.

But the house I owned in Shawnee had become a

nuisance. Fortunately I employed a lawn-service company to take care of the yard, but the rest of the responsibilities of home ownership fell to me. Keeping up on home maintenance while living over an hour away at the inn was difficult. I worried a gas or water line might break while I was away, or the refrigerator would stop working and all the food inside would spoil.

The routine duties around the house kept me running back and forth from Rockdale to Shawnee every few days. I could kill a houseplant by just looking at it. Forgetting to water the plant for a week or two at a time had a tendency to seal its fate. I'd been systematically moving the houseplants, one at a time, to the Alexandria Inn.

I'd canceled the morning paper delivery, but mail piled up on the floor inside my front door—bills, sales fliers, magazines, and even an occasional chain letter. I'd recently filled out a permanent mail forwarding form at the post office, and brought my one surviving houseplant to the inn to place on the window ledge over the kitchen sink. Life would certainly be a lot easier for me when I stopped commuting back and forth between Shawnee, Kansas, and Rockdale, Missouri. I loved the Alexandria Inn as much as Stone did, maybe even more because it's what had brought him here from the East Coast. And the bed and breakfast that had inspired it, Harriet Spark's Camelot Inn in Schenectady, held special meaning for us. It's where we first met and fell in love.

Despite the fact that two murders had occurred in the inn during its first year of operation, the magnificent structure had accommodated many guests and was nearly always full. At the time of both murders, the inn had received a lot of press and media coverage, so I don't know if our booming business came about out of morbid curiosity or because of our outstanding service and hospitality, but I really didn't care. As long as Stone's endeavor was successful, that was all that was important to me. I wanted him to be as happy as I was. I wanted him to have no regrets.

I'd already called Wyatt Johnston, a dear friend and local police officer, to ask him to stop by this morning. I wanted to see what he'd heard about Pastor Steiner's death, and I now found him sitting in the kitchen sharing a cup of coffee and some oatmeal cookies with Stone.

Wyatt always seemed to dwarf my kitchen chairs and I often wondered how they held him up. He was an imposing man, probably over six feet, five inches tall, and built of solid muscle. He towered over Stone, who stood about five feet, ten inches and weighed just a tad too much for his height. But I weighed a tad too much for my height too, and misery loves company. Wyatt, on the other hand, didn't have one spare ounce of fat on his large frame. Both Stone and I had become very fond of Wyatt in the previous months. I listened in now as he spoke to Stone.

"I just finished notifying the family, which is always the toughest part of my job as a cop. Fortunately, I don't have to do it very often," Wyatt said. "I also notified several elders of the church, and they were all devastated. Perry Coleman, who you know is also the organist at the Rockdale Baptist Church, started sobbing uncontrollably. I didn't know what to do. I hadn't expected such an intense reaction to my news. The elders were pretty much all inconsolable though. It's obviously a very tight-knit group. However, Perry did assure me he'd let the rest of the congregation know about the loss of their beloved pastor. I was happy to pass the torch on to him. However, the way the grapevine operates in this little town, I'm sure they'll all know about his death before Perry can announce it at church Sunday."

Stone nodded, thoughtfully. "Yes, it will be plastered all over the local television news today, and across the front page of the Rockdale Gazette by tomorrow morning."

"I've already spoken with the paper's lead reporter, giving him what little information I'm allowed to release at this time. The reporter caught up with me while I was notifying Steiner's next of kin."

"Both responsibilities have got to be tough for the police force," Stone said. "You guys don't always get the credit you deserve. I don't know if I could notify people of the death of their loved ones. I'd probably start sobbing uncontrollably too. I guess I'm just too soft hearted. Fortunately, as a reserve police officer in Myrtle Beach, I was never asked to do any next-of-kin notifications. I usually just rode along with full-time officers as a backup. I got enough taste of it, however, to appreciate what you see and do on a daily basis. My experiences heightened my respect for police officers, and other first responders. It's the kind of occupation where you have to love what you do, or you couldn't possibly do it effectively."

"I love my job. I really do," Wyatt assured him. "Some days are fun, some are exciting, and some are tough and frustrating. But there's other days, when tragedies are involved, that are just plain sad."

"Oh, I can imagine." Stone sat his coffee mug down, while Wyatt stuffed an entire cookie in his mouth. He chewed about three times and swallowed. I felt as if it were only a matter of time before Stone would have to perform the Heimlich maneuver on him. At 5'3", I wasn't tall enough to get my arms around Wyatt's waist, but I'd seen Stone successfully perform the maneuver on a previous guest at the inn. When the guest started choking at the dinner table, Stone had popped up like a jack-in-the-box, and had his arms wrapped around her mid-section before I could even lay my fork down. He's a good man to have around in a crisis, I thought. He'd saved my bacon on more than one occasion.

"Good afternoon, Wyatt," I said, as I poured myself a refill from the fresh pot of Folgers I'd just brewed. I'd waited for a lull in the conversation because I hadn't wanted to interrupt. "I agree with Stone, Wyatt. I couldn't do any next-of-kin notifications either, and you should be commended for taking on a task of that nature."

"Well, I didn't exactly volunteer. It was a duty assigned by the chief."

"Yes, but I'm sure he knows how well you handle a situation like that," I said. "You have a kind and empathetic personality. So how did his family members take the news?"

"They were all shocked, of course," Wyatt replied. "But none of them sounded nearly as devastated as the elders did. Of the family members, I'd say Steiner's oldest son, Teddy, took it the hardest. He held his head in his hands, crying, and saying, 'Oh, no, what am I going to do now?' as if he didn't know how he could go on living without his father. I lost my dad several years ago, so I know how Teddy felt, but as usual, I didn't know what to say to him in response."

"Oh, Wyatt, I'm sure you handled it as well as anyone could be expected to. And hey, thanks for stopping by. We, too, are naturally deeply saddened by the news of Thurman's passing. He was not only our pastor, but also a dear friend and mentor. In fact, he was scheduled to perform our wedding ceremony next Saturday."

"I didn't know him well, myself, but he seemed like

a really good guy the few times I had an occasion to talk to him. Veronica and I have always attended the Methodist Church north of town. She talked me into going there when she moved back here from Salt Lake City last fall. I'd never been one to attend church before that, but I'm enjoying it." As Wyatt finished talking, he held out his coffee mug toward me for a refill as I swung the carafe his way. I poured his cup partially full, the way he liked it, and handed him the carton of half-and-half and the sugar bowl. He liberally added both to his cup. He liked a little coffee in his cream and sugar.

After expressing his gratitude, Wyatt grabbed another cookie and consumed it, again in one bite. For the buffest guy I knew, Wyatt could sure pack away the food. I figured he must do jumping jacks in his sleep to burn off the calories and stay so amazingly fit. Either that or he had a tape worm the size of a fireman's hose.

"Refill?" I offered Stone. He nodded and murmured his thanks. He liked his coffee black, like I did. Stone still seemed pretty shell-shocked by the news of the pastor's death. He turned and held his cup out toward me like an automated robot.

I was just going to ask Wyatt for an update on the progress of the crime scene investigation when Stone did it for me. "Any idea what killed Thurman? He appeared to be in amazingly good health. He mentioned in one of his sermons about having run several marathons in this last year alone."

"I thought he looked remarkably fit for his age, too, but his body was just discovered a couple of hours ago, so the investigation is still in its early stages. Until Nate Smith and Wendy finish the autopsy, we really have no clue exactly what happened to him. I assume the body is already at the morgue," Wyatt said.

"Yes, it was Wendy who left the message on our recorder this morning," I replied. "She called from work. Stone was mowing, and I was planting some spring flowers in the planter along the back porch when she left the message."

"I did hear, though, even though no forced entry was detected, the back door leading out to the rear deck was hanging open when Mr. Steiner's neighbor went over to check on him. She hadn't seen him all morning and his newspaper was still on the front lawn. Howie delivers his paper about five and Thurman usually retrieved it around seven to read with his morning coffee. He was an early riser and followed a pretty standard morning routine. After coffee, he generally went for a morning run, his neighbor told us. She noticed he didn't go out for his run early this morning either. The elderly neighbor, Mrs. Bonnie Bloomingfield, also noticed his kitchen blinds had not been raised, something Thurman did soon after rising each morning. Mrs. Bloomingfield sounded a little confused and befuddled at times, but her story was pretty consistent so we felt she had her facts relatively straight," Wyatt said.

"I'm sure she was still very shaken up by the entire incident," I said.

"Oh, of course she would have been. But, anyway, by this time the old gal was sufficiently worried," Wyatt continued. "Mrs. Bloomingfield hurried over to the pastor's house to find the minister prostate on the floor and not breathing. Even with no medical training and highly distraught, she knew it was too late to resuscitate him. She called nine-one-one just before noon and Nate estimated the time of death at around five a.m. Nate does that by jabbing a—"

"I know, by jabbing a thermometer into the victim's

liver. That's a memory I still can't erase from when Walter Sneed died in our parlor last October," I interjected. I shuddered at the vision his words brought on. "I still can't believe my very own daughter opted to become a coroner's assistant. I don't know how she can do and see the things she does on a daily basis and sleep at night. How can she look at cadavers with axes embedded in their skulls and not toss her cookies?"

"I don't know about axes embedded in people's skulls, but I'm sure she does witness some awfully disturbing things at the morgue," Wyatt said. "I guess you'd grow accustomed to such sights after awhile and not let them affect you emotionally or physically. I've seen a lot of blood and guts by being called to the scene of accidents, and I've had to teach myself not to let myself become emotionally involved. I couldn't have handled this job if I hadn't learned to do that, and I'm sure Wendy has learned to switch off her emotions too."

"I guess so, but I can't even glance at road kill without getting nauseated. What in the world could Wendy possibly have against teaching first-graders how to read and write, and, of course, keep their pants on in class? The most severe injury she'd likely encounter is a crayon stuck up one of her students' noses. You know, she did minor in elementary education in college. She could have taken a much different path than the one she chose to take."

"Well, Lexie," the detective said, "I know it's hard to imagine why she selected the career she did, but it does seem like an interesting position, and she does appear to thoroughly enjoy her job. She's always totally enthused when she tells me about a case she's involved in."

"I know. That's what bothers me. She enjoys it too

much for my taste."

"And," Wyatt continued, as Stone sipped at his coffee and listened to the conversation without speaking, "I'm sure she makes a better income in pathology than she would teaching. Teachers are like police officers, often unappreciated and always underpaid."

"We appreciate you guys, Wyatt. And her income is beside the point. I still find it a gruesome way to make a living. But enough of that! Let's get back to Mr. Steiner." I could only be sidetracked for a certain amount of time. My wedding was in jeopardy. Rescheduling it at this point would be a strategic nightmare, but we couldn't possibly get married while the cause of the pastor's death was still up in the air. Once he was put to rest, we could find a replacement for him and carry on as planned. And putting the dear fellow to rest shouldn't take more than three or four days, at the most. I was still fairly confident the wedding could go ahead as scheduled.

"No other news about Steiner's death?" Stone asked Detective Johnston. He had put his empty coffee cup down on the kitchen table, and taken the empty cookie plate to place in the sink. He absentmindedly ran a dishtowel across the top of the counter to wipe up an invisible spill. I could tell he was operating on autopilot. It was likely he still couldn't wrap his head around the fact the pastor was dead. Thurman Steiner had always been such a vivacious, energetic man.

"That's all I know," Wyatt said. "The wide open door is odd, but it could still be a coincidence at this point. He could have been just about to go out and get the paper, and it's quite possible the door has no bearing on Thurman's death. The coroner detected a good-sized lump on the back of Thurman's head, but thought it could have been the result of falling to the floor. His body was lying in close proximity to the kitchen counter, and he could have struck it with the back of his head as he fell to the ground."

Wyatt added another two teaspoons of sugar to his cup of coffee, and stirred as he continued. "He most likely had a heart attack. That's what seems to kill most guys his age. The Bloomingfields had known him for years. Bonnie's husband, Harold Bloomingfield, told the detectives that Thurman had to have two angioplasties performed when he was a few years younger, and a stent put in a couple years ago, so he's had a history of heart trouble in the past. He started his running regimen after the placement of the stent as part of his cardio rehab. According to Harold, Thurman's cardiologist encouraged him to get as much exercise as possible and to limit his fat and cholesterol intake. And Thurman wasn't old by any means, but he was beginning to get up in years, you know. His eyes were bloodshot, Nate noticed, but he could have suffered from allergies or just been extremely tired."

"No, he wasn't old, but he was no spring chicken anymore," I said. "He mentioned a few weeks ago he'd be celebrating his sixty-fifth birthday in mid-May, which is just about a month away now. He'd made a humorous reference to signing up for social security and Medicare in last week's sermon. Well, it's a shame he'll never see that first social security check. He was such a congenial and thoughtful man."

He was also the only minister at the only church we'd attended in Rockdale. Who could I get to officiate our wedding on such short notice? I was dead-set against marrying in front of a justice of the peace. It just didn't mesh well with my religious views not to be married by a man of the cloth. Who planned a perfectly respectable wedding and didn't have a perfectly respectable minister officiating at it? Would the powers that be find a temporary replacement for the pastor in the next ten days? Probably so. I couldn't imagine Sunday service being canceled, even with the presiding minister's sudden death. But would this replacement be willing to step in and fill Pastor Steiner's shoes by officiating at our wedding ceremony? That remained to be seen.

Somehow, I thought, things would work out and we wouldn't have to postpone the wedding and have a last minute change of plans. I tried to think positive. This sad turn of events would probably cause very little disruption in my life, short of having to find another minister to replace Pastor Steiner, and my sorrow at the loss of a friend and mentor. I would find out soon enough that I couldn't have been more dead wrong.

CHAPTER 2

Late that Friday evening Wendy called me on my cell phone. I was in the kitchen cleaning up after dinner. I'd just loaded up and started the dishwasher and was wiping off the counters when my phone rang. One of the services our all-inclusive inn boasts is offering two meals a day, breakfast and supper, instead of just the standard morning meal, as the term "bed and breakfast" implies. That was only one of the many things that made our establishment exceptional and tend to stand out from the rest. We paid special attention to details and those efforts paid off in the long run. We took *accommodating* to a whole new level, hauling guests to entertainment venues, restaurants, and businesses all over town. We held receptions, parties, reunions, and even an occasional wedding on the premises.

Ours wouldn't be the first nuptials to take place at the Alexandria Inn. Stone had built the gazebo in the flower garden off the back patio to accommodate the wedding of Cornelius Walker and Rosalinda Swift, two former guests at the inn. They were members of the local historical society, who'd spent opening night here at the inn, the night Horatio Prescott, III, was killed in his suite. Despite Prescott's untimely death, Cornelius and Rosalinda had opted to return to the inn for their nuptials, and we continued to encourage such occasions.

For me, the meal service was the toughest part of the accommodations we offered. As hard as we tried to pamper our guests, my cooking sometimes lacked finesse. I'd become accustomed to cooking for one, which usually involved pouring Raisin Bran into a bowl and adding milk. But I was definitely improving, and it was still too early in the season to employ a housekeeper and chef. I tried to only prepare dishes that required four ingredients or less, and four was pushing the outer limits of my cooking prowess. But as the saying goes, practice makes perfect, and I was getting a lot of practice these days.

I'd just finished serving our guests a slightly dried-out barbecued brisket with roasted garlic potatoes and succotash, along with a Mississippi Mud cake for dessert. The latter was made from an old family recipe that had been handed down for several generations. In front of the guests I referred to it simply as a chocolate cake, so as not to have our guests take offense at my choice. My cooking, at times, could be offensive enough without any help from my great-great-grandmother.

As I wiped off the glass top surface of the stove, I listened to Wendy jabbering on the phone. As usual, she was bombarding me with the same questions I'd been asking myself. She, too, wondered how we'd be able to carry off the wedding with the sudden, unexpected demise of Thurman Steiner. However, she didn't use the word "demise," I suddenly realized. She'd used the word "murder."

"Murder?" My ears had perked up at once, and I was no longer interested in discussing the wedding plans. I stopped wiping down the stove and began paying closer attention to what Wendy was saying. Had she really meant to imply the minister had been intentionally killed? How could a third murder cross our paths within a single year? It seemed to me we were involved, in some form or fashion, with every murder that took place in this small, suburban town. Three homicides in one year was a lot for a town of this size. Rockdale was situated just east of St. Joseph, Missouri, which, with a population of around 75,000, was ten times larger. St. Joseph had everything that a person couldn't find in Rockdale. It was also where Wendy worked as an assistant to the county coroner, Nate Smith.

"Did you say murder?" I asked again. I threw the soiled dishrag into the sink, and grabbed my coffee cup. Then I plopped down on a chair at the table, anxious to hear all the juicy details.

"I'm afraid so."

"Oh, you've got to be kidding, Wendy! Who could possibly want to hurt Pastor Steiner? How did you determine he was murdered?"

"First of all, we found a contusion and damage to the temporal lobe of his cerebral cortex and—"

"The what?"

"The temporal lobe is located beneath the Sylvian Fissure on—"

"Layman's terms, Wendy. You're talking to a former assistant librarian, not a brain surgeon."

"We found bruising on the brain in the area behind his left ear. It appears to have been caused by enough blunt-force trauma to knock him out, but not kill him. Had he lived, he might have experienced seizures, impaired memory, and other problems, with the brain damage he sustained. At first we deduced the pastor might have hit his head on the kitchen counter as he collapsed to the floor. However, after closer inspection, he appears as if he'd been struck with something heavy and solid, as a means to disable him. But it's not what we determined the C.O.D. to be," Wendy said.

"The C.O.D.?"

"Cause of death. The autopsy shows that Pastor Steiner died from pulmonary distress, or asphyxiation. He was asphyxiated after he was knocked out."

"Does that mean he was strangled? Was that the ultimate C.O.D.?"

"There are no obvious signs of strangulation. It doesn't appear as if he were choked. No bruising around the neck, or ligature marks of any kind. It seems more likely he was smothered, with a plastic bag over his head, or perhaps a pillow even," Wendy said. "As you know, Thurman was a small man, despite his good physical condition. He could be easily overpowered by someone intent on killing him, particularly if taken completely by surprise."

"How could you conclude asphyxiation was the C.O.D.?" I had learned a new acronym and I was determined to use it as often as possible. I was like a kid with a new toy.

"Primarily, his lungs were swollen, indicating a lack of oxygen, and he had broken blood vessels in his eyes. He didn't have any recent trauma to his heart. There was also a tiny fragment of cotton fiber found in his moustache, which looked like it could have come from a pillow. However, since he could have been in bed when he was awakened by an intruder, that is not significant in itself," Wendy said. Once again I was troubled by how smug Wendy sounded when describing what she and Nate Smith had discovered during the autopsy. How could this cold-hearted woman possibly have come from my womb? But I couldn't dwell on that thought now. There was more to be learned about the pastor's death.

"Yes, I see. According to Wyatt, Nate determined the T.O.D. to be around five in the morning," I said. I wanted to parade one of the latest acronyms I'd learned in front of my daughter.

"Yes, that's correct. And I'm impressed, Mom. I can tell you've actually been paying attention to some of what I tell you about my job. That is, at least, when you don't have your hands clamped over your ears to shut out all the gory details," Wendy said with a chuckle. I was too single-mindedly fixated on the fact our pastor had been intentionally murdered to laugh at Wendy's words. I couldn't help that I was not fascinated by blood and guts like Wendy was. I was beginning to wonder if my baby hadn't been switched with someone else's at the hospital when Wendy was born. Not even her father, Chester, could be blamed for this gruesome trait my daughter exhibited.

"Are they officially classifying his death as a homicide then?" I asked.

"Yes, since that's what our findings indicate. It's difficult, but not impossible, to asphyxiate yourself, Mom. There's easier ways to commit suicide."

"Oh, the poor man. What a terrible thing to happen. I really adored him."

"Yeah, I liked him a lot too. He gave uplifting and interesting sermons the few Sundays I was there to attend church with you and Stone. And he seemed like such a gentle soul. I can't imagine anyone wanting to kill him. Can you?"

"No, not at all, Wendy. This couldn't have happened to a nicer individual. And as far as Stone and I are concerned, it couldn't have happened at a worse time.

What are we going to do? This is even worse than I'd first thought. If the pastor had died from natural causes, it'd be one thing, but this is something else entirely. We can't possibly carry on with our wedding plans in the midst of a murder investigation. Or can we?" I asked, hoping in vain for a positive response from my daughter.

"I wouldn't think so. It might appear to be in very bad taste. Particularly to everyone in the congregation at your church who knew he was set to marry you two soon. They're apt to think you're being very selfish, only interested in yourselves and unconcerned about the death of the dear pastor."

"I was afraid you'd say that. And, of course, you're right. But once the suspect is identified and apprehended it might be a different matter altogether. If an arrest happens in the next day or two, the funeral could be done and over with by the weekend, and then it might not appear to be too callous and unfeeling to go ahead with the ceremony," I reasoned. I wasn't normally so self-absorbed, but a lot of planning had gone into this wedding and I didn't want to have to start backtracking at this late date.

"Well, I still think—" Wendy began. I knew she still had her reservations, and I didn't particularly want to hear her elaborate on them, so I quickly changed the subject.

"Gee, I wonder if there might be some way to speed up the process of identifying the perp," I said. "Perp" was another bit of slang I'd picked up from my daughter. I used it now to impress her. She used the term as if the word "perpetrator" was just too unimaginably long to use in a casual conversation. Four syllables did waste a lot of time when just one would suffice.

"No. No way, Mom. I already know where this is

heading. You want to once again stick your nose in where it doesn't belong. You want to interrogate his family and friends, don't you? You want to pry and snoop and possibly put yourself into dangerous situations. Well, neither Stone nor I are going to sit by and let you get involved in another homicide investigation."

"Well now, 'involved' is a bit much. I could just show a little interest. Maybe 'encourage' is a better word to use. With a little encouragement, our local homicide detectives might have Pastor Steiner's murder solved in no time at all. They might already have an idea who the killer is. This entire conversation might be just a waste of both of our time."

"Yes, it probably is. I'm sure they'll have someone in custody soon. Just another reason for you to stay plum out of it. Do you remember what has happened in the past when you have 'shown a little interest' in murder investigations?" Wendy asked.

"Yes, I know there were a couple of unfortunate incidents, but—"

"But nothing, Mom," Wendy said, exasperation evident in her voice. "You are lucky to be alive. Repeated attempts on your life are not 'unfortunate incidents' by any stretch of the imagination."

"Okay, darling," I replied, hastily. "I've really got to get busy. I've got a few chores to get done around the place and it's getting late. I'm sure we can continue this conversation at a later date."

"I don't trust you, Mom. I'm going to have a word with Stone. Andy's due in town tomorrow, arriving with the U-Haul trailer in the afternoon. As you know, he's moving into his new ranch property just in time for the wedding. Maybe among the three of us we can restrain you from putting your fool neck on the line once again."

"No, please don't speak to Stone, Wendy. With the wedding hopefully just days away, I don't need any friction and turmoil between Stone and me. I have enough anxiety to deal with as it is."

"Okay, I'll give you a pass—for now, anyway. But remember what you just said. The best and fastest way to stir up trouble with Stone is to get involved in Pastor Steiner's murder case. You know how he would feel about it. You've already put him through enough stress and worry as it is. Promise me you'll stay out of it."

I always hated to make promises I wasn't one hundred percent sure I could follow up on. I didn't intend to get too deeply "involved," but I couldn't predict the future. I desperately wanted this wedding to go off as planned. Postponing everything now would be a real hassle. Asking a question here and there couldn't hurt any, could it? I would just be very clever about it, and not bring to anyone's attention the fact that I was trying to speed up an arrest.

I faked a knock on the door, and told Wendy I had to get off the phone to run and let some guests in the front door. It was past the time we usually locked all the exterior doors at the inn. Just short of making any rash promises, I got off the phone in a hurry.

Early the next morning I sat out on the back porch, sipping coffee, and reading the daily *Rockdale Gazette*, which Howie Clamm had pitched onto the front lawn just as I opened the front door. It was a nice spring morning, so I didn't mind the lengthy walk down to the end of the driveway to retrieve the newspaper. Stone expended a lot of time and energy keeping the grounds of the inn immaculate, and it never looked as lovely as it did at dawn when the dew was still glistening on the nicely manicured grass.

As expected, an article about the death of Thurman Steiner covered the entire front page of the daily newspaper. The local pastor was known by many of Rockdale's citizens. After all, for years he'd led the congregation at a large church located in a small town. He'd participated in many other local functions, as well. The article, which included several quotes attributed to Detective Johnston, had little information about the details of the murder. It was primarily a tribute to a revered man. Many friends and church members were quoted and no one had anything but positive things to say about Thurman Steiner. He was the epitome of the term "pillar of society."

The news story went on to explain something I already knew. Thurman Steiner had always been referred to as "pastor" at his own request because he wasn't particularly fond of the monikers "reverend" or "minister," and was especially opposed to being called a "preacher." I found this aspect of his personality very endearing. "Pastor" sounded gentler and more humble, and I thought this was appropriate for the soft-spoken man we'd come to adore.

I could hardly fathom how a man of his stature and loving nature could have any skeletons in his closet, and I wondered again how he could upset someone to the point of murder. I was convinced the crime had to be a random murder, probably an armed robbery that had turned violent or the result of the pastor being assaulted by a deranged sociopath. Rockdale was not exactly littered with homicidal maniacs, but one or two in the area was not beyond the realm of possibility. Although it was difficult to imagine, we could even have a serial killer on the loose.

I did learn a few things about the late minister in the process of reading the long article. For instance, he'd served in the U.S. Navy as a Seabee during the Vietnam War. After a four-year stint in the service, he'd attended the still, at that time, relatively new Nazarene Theological Seminary down on East Meyer Boulevard in Kansas City, Missouri.

After being ordained, he began his career as a minister in a small Baptist church in Topeka, Kansas. Following a number of years there, he moved to Rockdale to be nearer to several close members of his family. He'd ministered at our church since 1990 and had no intentions of retiring any time soon, even though he'd been set to receive his first social security check the following month. Teaching the word of God was his life and his passion. Sitting on a rocking chair on his front porch hadn't appealed to him at all.

Thurman was a widower, having lost his wife, Stella, to esophageal cancer twelve years prior. I recalled he'd spoken lovingly of his late wife in many of his sermons. I was surprised to read that Thurman and Stella had produced six children—four sons and two daughters. I'd only heard mention of a daughter and two sons during the year I'd been attending services at his church. Before then I'd lived in Shawnee full-time and attended a smaller non-denominational church in my neighborhood.

Almost by accident I found a more informative article at the bottom of page twelve, as if it had been added mere moments before the paper went to press, stating no suspect had been named and little evidence had been found at the scene, save for the piece of fabric in the victim's moustache, and numerous fingerprints, all but a few belonging to Steiner himself. The fabric was cotton, but what wasn't in this day and age? And the absence of fingerprints was not altogether surprising, as the killer had probably donned a pair of gloves so as not to leave any identifying clues at the scene of the crime. Of course, it was possible some of the foreign prints belonged to the killer.

Thurman Steiner's neighbors had been questioned, and one man named Larry Blake told authorities he'd seen a small red pickup in the victim's driveway earlier in the day, and the floodlight over the parking area at the home had been lit at ten the previous evening. But he couldn't recall the very bright light being on at five-thirty, the morning of the murder when he went out to get in his vehicle and leave for work. Blake had to clock in at six at the small local community college where he worked as a janitor. Normally, in early spring, it was still rather dark at five-thirty which made the light much more noticeable when it was accidentally left on overnight. Blake didn't recall this being the case that morning.

Larry Blake also remembered hearing a voice coming from the direction of the pastor's residence early in the morning, a kind of muffled shout, but he hadn't thought much about it at the time. Blake now wondered if by chance he'd gone over to check out the odd sound he might have interrupted the murder and saved the life of his friend and neighbor, the esteemed Thurman Steiner. He had actually considered it briefly but didn't want to be late to work and be reprimanded for the same offense twice in the same week, Blake was quoted as saying.

And that was all I gleaned about the homicide from reading the morning paper. I was a little disappointed in the progress of the investigation so far. Perhaps a longer interview was scheduled with the observant neighbor, Larry Blake, and anyone else in the area who might have witnessed something. I'm sure Mrs. Bloomingfield might have more to add also, having been the one to find the body and notify the police.

Maybe I should see if I could draw any more pertinent information out of her. It couldn't hurt anything to try.

And maybe I could run by the junior college to chat with Blake on my way to the local blood drive where I'd planned to donate a pint. My blood type, the universal 0-positive, always seemed to be in great demand and I was happy to help out in any way I could. A blood donor had once benefited me following a nasty car accident in my college days, and I felt I should return the favor and help a stranger the way another stranger had helped me. In the same vein, I always made certain to check "organ donor" on my driver's license whenever it was renewed.

After I served breakfast to Stone and the guests at the inn, I'd clean up the kitchen and head downtown. The only guests staying at the inn at the moment were a college professor here on sabbatical for a few days, and an elderly couple from Colorado, in town to see a granddaughter's graduation from the community college. They were only in town for two more days and would be spending the day at their daughter and son-in-law's home.

The blood drive was being held at the VFW Hall, only a matter of two or three blocks from the college. It was scheduled to go on until early evening, so there was no rush to get there. What could possibly go wrong if I stopped by just to speak with Larry Blake for a few short minutes?

CHAPTER 3

"Going to the blood drive now!" I hollered out to Stone, who was scattering some fescue seed in a bare spot he'd tilled up in the front yard. He waved and immediately turned his attention back to sowing grass. He was really in his element when he was working on the lawn. I sometimes found it hard to believe he'd spent the majority of his adulthood as a jeweler and not a landscaper. He wore absolutely no jewelry himself, and showed little interest in the jewelry I wore. His job as a jeweler must have been a means to an end. He'd just naturally followed in his father's footsteps. His father, who had just recently passed away, had been a jeweler also.

I hopped into the little neon blue sports car I'd just traded my yellow Jeep Wrangler in on the previous month. It was a convertible and I thought it was adorable. Stone thought it was a death trap. He wanted me to wear a lot more car around me. He said with the same amount of money I could have bought a brand spanking *used* Lincoln Town Car. Because my sports car sits so low to the ground, Stone said he expected that one day I'd call him to tell him it was high-centered on a dead possum. But then, Stone, who wasn't very tall for a man, had to fold himself up like a paper airplane to get into the tiny car, with an even tinier back seat, and a trunk that could barely house the bubble spare tire and jack. According to Stone, getting out of the car took an act of God, and the flexibility of a Chinese acrobat. Even I had to rearrange my body parts in an almost inhuman position to climb aboard. I couldn't even begin to imagine stuffing someone the size of Detective Johnston into my car.

When I first met Stone, he drove a red hard-topped Corvette. While working on the restoration of the inn, he'd found the car to be impractical for the very same reasons he disliked my new vehicle. He now drove a Chevy Silverado four-door pickup and had made many trips to Home Depot to fill its bed with sheetrock, five-gallon buckets of spackle, toilets, cabinets, and other necessary home improvement items while restoring the inn.

He claimed he now felt as if he were sitting on a skateboard when he was riding in my car. Listening to advice from an ex-sports car owner was worse than listening to an ex-smoker. Still, I understood why he felt the way he did about my choice. But it was getting thirty-two miles to the gallon and I thought it was worth putting up with a little guff from Stone. He professed to only be concerned about my safety. And I knew he probably meant it, so I tried not to be offended by his disparaging remarks about my new car.

I started up the death trap and backed it out of the unattached four-car garage. It was still a little early to go to the VFW because the blood drive didn't start for forty-five minutes. So to fill a little time, I decided to stop by the community college first. Finding Larry Blake, a man I'd never met, in a large school with numerous buildings, would not be easy. I decided to ask around in hope of finding someone who could help me locate him. I'd only been inside the junior college once before, so I began my search in the administration building.

I asked the first six people I encountered who looked like they might have some official capacity at the school if they knew where the janitor, Blake, might be. But it was to no avail. Only one of the people I spoke with even recognized the name. I was just about to give up when I noticed a man dressed in gray coveralls step out of a storage closet up at the end of the corridor. I hurried down the hallway, stopping him just before he descended down the stairwell. He wasn't Larry Blake, but he knew what building the other janitor was assigned to, and pointed me in the right direction. I thanked the man for his assistance and wished him a good day.

Then I hurried over to the science building and, after searching two of the three floors, I found Larry Blake in the first room I peered into on the third and highest floor. He was throwing something that looked like cat litter down on a pile of vomit in the middle of the science lab. I had to look away or risk providing the janitor with another pile to cover up.

I thought throwing up in class was something that only happened in grade school. I remembered upchucking all over a dissected mouse in fifth grade myself. But I reasoned that even grown-ups had a propensity for getting sick on occasion, and one can never predict when or where it might happen. And God only knows what kind of chemicals and compounds the poor student was messing with in the lab at the time. It was a small wonder they didn't all

Jeanne Glidewell

get ill or blow up the building every other day. As I entered the lab, I could smell a strong scent of ammonia and wondered where it was coming from. Maybe that noxious odor was what had affected the ill student. It certainly made my stomach roil at first sniff.

"Excuse me, are you Mr. Blake?" I asked the short, slightly rotund man. His hair had receded to the point he only had a two-inch strip of hair around the perimeter of his head.

"Yep," he said, not even glancing up in my direction. "What do you need?"

"I was just wondering if I could have a word with you."

"What about?" he asked. Now he was standing up straight, looking me square in the face. Or at least as square in the face as he could with one eye pointing straight at me and the other one pointing north. I didn't know which eye to try to make contact with, assuming one must be made of glass, so I just looked over his right shoulder instead. But not before I noticed he only sported about three teeth in his entire mouth. Why bother? How could Blake chew with only three teeth when none of them even lined up with one another? Why not have them all pulled and get dentures? The man would look more intelligent and attractive and have better success at chewing food. I'm not sure why his lack of teeth bothered me so much, unless it was because I often had nightmares about all of my own teeth falling out.

Well, that was not my concern at the moment, so I tried to direct my attention to the matter at hand. I knew I couldn't portray myself as a nosy citizen and get any valuable information out of Blake, so I opted to pretend I was with the police force instead.

"I'm Natalie Wilson, Mr. Blake, but please just call

me Natalie," I said. "I work at the police station as the Witness Statements Records Collector, or the WSRC, as they like to call me. I've been assigned to ask you a few questions regarding the death of Pastor Steiner. Can you spare a couple minutes? I promise I won't keep you from your work for long."

"I reckon, Natalie. If I don't get caught goofing off, that is. I can't withstand another reprimand this soon after my last one," he said. Now one eye was pointing toward my shoes and the other one was flittering back and forth. I watched it dilate as it came to a stop, staring directly at my breasts. I suddenly had an inkling which eye was in good working order. Folding my arms across my chest, I asked, "Can you think of any observations you made around the pastor's home yesterday morning that you failed to tell the investigators at the scene? No matter how insignificant it may appear, it could prove to be valuable information and help in solving the case. And you never know, there may be a reward offered for any tip leading to the arrest and conviction of the killer."

"Really?" He asked. *No, not really, at least as far as I knew*, I said to myself. But it didn't hurt to sweeten the pot while delving for information.

"Of course!"

"Well, I told them about the floodlight and the red truck, I reckon."

"Yes, but can you remember anything specific about the truck? If you could recall what make and model it was, that information might help in the search for the suspect. Did it have a topper or shell on it? Any dents, unusual features?" I asked. Now my eyes were starting to burn from the overwhelming stench of ammonia engulfing the room. I rubbed at them repeatedly. Mr. Blake gave me an apologetic look.

"I was just stripping the floor here in the lab before the last class arrived, ma'am. I reckon that's what made the dude puke," he said, noticing my sudden discomfort. Between the smell of vomit and ammonia I was sure I'd be puking soon too. My stomach was getting more and more queasy as time went on.

"I see. Let's get back to the truck, Mr. Blake. Do you recall any details about it?"

"Well, it was kind of a faded red color, and it wasn't a full sized truck. No topper or dents that I recall. Appeared to be a fairly stripped down model, with nothing remarkable about it. I reckon it was one of those little Ford Rangers or Chevy S-10's," Larry replied.

"What year do you reckon it was?" Good Lord, I was started to talking like Larry Blake, and I'd only been conversing with him for a minute or two.

"I dunno. It must have been about ten years old or so. It wasn't a new one, anyway."

"Do you recall what time the truck got there and what time it left?"

"I dunno what time it got there, but I reckon it was getting near suppertime when it left. Maybe five or six," he answered. "It was many hours before the murder happened though."

I unfolded my arms and his one good eye immediately riveted back to my breasts. I didn't even bother to fold my arms across my chest again. If this is what it took to keep him talking, then so be it. There was more than one way to sweeten the pot. Giving him something to concentrate his one good eye on was the least I could do. It wasn't like that was offering him much. God had not blessed me with a well-endowed body.

"Any idea who owns the little red truck?" I asked. "Do you recall seeing who drove it?"

"Nope, never saw the driver, Ms. Wilson, but I've seen the truck in the driveway several times before."

"Recently?"

"Yes, and a couple other times in months past. I reckon the truck belongs to someone Steiner had known for a while," Blake said. "I know it was there last Sunday afternoon, immediately following Steiner's arrival home from church. I was mowing the lawn at the time."

His good eye was still aimed straight at my breasts while the other one wavered back and forth from my right ear to my left foot. Then with a violent shake of his head, as if to realign his eyeballs, he looked up at the ceiling before lowering his head back down to breast level again. I was beginning to wonder if anyone could believe anything this man said. He didn't seem to be completely of sound mind and body. His off-centered eyes gave me the creeps. It was hard to take anything he said seriously. But I couldn't imagine he had anything to gain by lying.

By now tears from my own eyes were beginning to run down my cheeks every so often, and I had to keep wiping them off with the sleeve of my blouse. Blake probably wondered too, if I was a nut job or just a total mess.

"What do you remember, Larry, about the sound you heard?" I asked. "I believe you told the police the noise sounded like a muffled shout?"

"Yeah, it sounded like someone hollered 'peas,' which didn't make any sense to me, cause why would anyone holler 'peas' at that time of a morning?"

Why would anyone holler "peas" at any time of day? I wondered. Maybe what Blake had actually heard was someone hollering "please." Could the pastor have been begging for his life at the time? Could he have been shouting for someone to "please" help him, or asking the killer to "please" spare him?

"I also noticed the big floodlight outside his house had been turned off sometime between ten in the evening, and about five-thirty in the morning when I left for work. It's normally still on at that time, not being turned off until after Steiner went outside and picked up his paper, which, on weekends, anyway, was around seven."

"Are you certain you didn't make any other observations as you were leaving for work?" I asked Mr. Blake. I'd already heard about the floodlight and wanted to get on with it so I could get out of the laboratory as soon as possible. My eyes could only take so much more of the intense burning I was experiencing.

"Well, nothing really, other than I saw the blinds over his kitchen sink move for just a split second before I went back inside to grab my lunch sack. I reckoned maybe old Steiner was looking out to see if his newspaper had arrived."

"You didn't think that was important enough to tell the investigators?"

"Reckon I just forgot, Natalie." Larry Blake was starting to get jittery, as if nervous he might get caught slacking off. I thought about his last recollection. Could the killer have glanced out and seen Blake going to his car and decided to wait a minute before vacating the premises? Surely he'd want to be sure no witnesses saw him leaving the pastor's house.

"That's okay. I have it all in my report now."

"Steiner was kind of a loner, when he was at his house, anyway," Blake said. "He spoke to neighbors in passing, but I rarely ever saw other vehicles in his driveway, except for the red truck occasionally. I saw him talking to some guy out on his back porch a couple of times, but I reckon it must have been someone who lives in the neighborhood, because only Steiner's mini-van was in the driveway both times. I'd occasionally go over and chat with him on his front porch, and he never turned me away, but he never walked over to my house to chat in all the years we knew each other. He'd pass by my house every morning on his daily run. He'd usually wave if I was outside, but he never once stopped to speak with me. As far as I know, he never visited with anyone in the neighborhood very much. I found this odd for a minister."

I found this tidbit odd too. Steiner seemed like such an out-going, amicable man. I would have thought he was the kind to make frequent rounds in his neighborhood, conversing with anyone who'd talk to him. Why was he so extraverted at church and so introverted at home? Why would he shut himself away in his house the way Blake said he did? Did he not want the neighbors involved in his private life for any particular reason?

I'd jotted down a few notes in the small notebook I'd brought along in my purse. I'd purchased it before making a trip back to the East Coast the previous year, and it had come in handy several times. After making another quick notation, I turned my attention back to Larry Blake. "Did Steiner ever mention having problems with anyone to you, a neighbor or otherwise? Can you recall him talking about anyone who might have wanted to harm him?"

"No, he never spoke of anything, or anyone, like that. He appeared to have high regard for everyone in his congregation and, as far as I'm aware, everyone in the neighborhood who attended Rockdale Baptist Church, was very fond of the pastor too. And most of the folks in the neighborhood did attend his church since it was so conveniently located, even though they didn't really know the pastor on a close personal basis. He never attended one block party that I can recall."

"Yes, I too think it's surprising that he wasn't very involved with the neighborhood, because he obviously was so highly thought of in the community. Well, by most people, anyway," I added. Clearly there was one person out there who didn't rank Mr. Steiner very high on their list. I didn't recognize Mr. Blake as a regular member of the congregation, but he might have rarely attended, and there were a vast number of church members. I couldn't possibly remember them all. "Are you a member of the Rockdale Baptist Church yourself?"

"No, but that's because I'm Catholic. I go to St. Mary's at the corner of Fourth and Cypress. And even then I only attend church on rare occasion—Easter, Christmas Eve, and special days like that."

"Are you married, or do you have a significant other?"

"No, I live alone, Natalie," he said. I saw his eye move quickly from my breast to my left hand. I suddenly wished I was sporting my engagement ring, but it, along with my wedding band, was at Zale's being sized. In fact, I needed to remind myself to pick the rings up in the next day or two. Blake smiled and looked back up, winking his good eye before it settled back on my breast. "But I reckon I'm available if you're interested."

"Sorry, I'm engaged," I said with a laugh, even though I don't think he was joking. Gee, what a shame I already had a partner. Blake seemed like such a good catch. Good Lord, there was a perfectly good nightmare just waiting to happen.

"Listen, lady," he said, no longer in a flirting mood. "I reckon you ought to get going now. As much as I'd like to help out, I really gotta get back to work before my boss finds me lollygagging around. I can't afford to lose this job," he said. I *reckoned* he needed every dime he could get so he could save up for a new set of chompers. I thanked him and left the room. My eyes were really bothering me now, to the point I couldn't have stayed in the science lab much longer even if Larry Blake had a whole gaggle of observations to relate to me.

"Ms. Starr, are you okay? Is there something wrong? You don't look well at all. Your eyes look a little swollen and very watery," the nurse said to me, as she inserted the butterfly I.V. into the crook of my elbow. I'd waited in line for nearly a half hour to give blood and, if anything, my eyes burned even more now than they had while I was talking with Larry Blake. I could feel them swelling as I waited. Tears were streaming down my face and I felt flushed.

"Yes, I'm fine," I assured her. "Just got these allergies to contend with."

"Okay, just checking," she said. "I've got some allergies myself so I know how it feels. With everything starting to bloom, mine are worse than usual. Let me know if you need anything. I've probably got some extra Benadryl in my purse if you'd like a tablet or two."

"I'll be fine, dear. But thanks for the offer."

Actually, the only serious allergy I was aware of other than bee stings, was shellfish. Crab legs gave me nausea and unrelenting gas, not burning, irritated eyes. And I'm sure everyone around me wishes I had burning, irritated eyes instead of the unattractive gas problem I experience after I've had a shrimp cocktail. At least that way I'd be the only one who suffered. Despite my allergy, or maybe because of it, I craved seafood and occasionally gave into those cravings, despite the consequences.

But letting the nurse think I was allergic to pollen, juniper trees, or even sunshine, was the best tactic for right now. The last thing I wanted to do was start telling everyone I met that I'd come in close proximity to ammonia at the junior college while impersonating a member of the police department and asking questions of a witness in a murder investigation. I'd rather say I was upset because I was deathly afraid of needles than to tell her the truth. But, of course, if that were so, the last place they'd find me was at a volunteer blood drive. I wouldn't be offering up a vein for a nurse to tap in to right now.

I could tell my eyes were continuing to swell. I'd be lucky if they weren't swollen shut by the time I had to drive home to the inn. How was I going to explain my current condition to Stone without letting on I'd been somewhere besides the VFW? I hated to lie, so maybe I could somehow mislead him without actually out-and-out lying to him. I gave it some serious thought as my blood drained out into a bag and my eyes drained out onto my cheeks.

"Oh my goodness," Stone exclaimed as I walked into the kitchen. There was deep concern in his expression. He set down a glass of water and grabbed the back of a chair. "What happened to you? Here sit down before you walk into a wall. Oh, honey, you look awful. You didn't get stung in the face by a bee, did you? If so, I need to get you to the emergency room. I've seen how you react to bee stings before."

"No, it wasn't a bee, Stone."

Stone pulled the chair out away from the small kitchen table and I gratefully took a seat. My vision really was greatly impaired at this stage. I was also beginning to get a terrible headache in my temples. At least the queasiness in my stomach had abated somewhat. Before I began to speak again, I pulled off a band-aid the nurse had placed over the needle mark in the crook of my arm, more to emphasize the fact I'd actually donated blood than anything else.

"There was a man stripping floors with ammonia and I guess I reacted poorly to it," I said. That was true enough.

"He was stripping floors with a powerful chemical like ammonia while a blood drive was going on?"

"Well, yes, both were happening simultaneously."

"Didn't you or anyone else complain? Why did you even stay there if it was affecting you?" Stone asked.

"I was the only one who was having a problem. My eyes didn't begin to swell this badly until I was on the way home or I would have left sooner," I said. I had yet to actually lie, but I felt a bit guilty for being so evasive with my answers. I needed to divert the conversation to a safer subject. "Listen, I need to take a couple Tylenol and lie down with a wet rag over my eyes for a spell. I tend to react poorly to all sorts of strange things. I'm sure I'll be fine in no time at all. Any news about Pastor Steiner?"

"Nothing so far, but Wyatt is stopping by later this afternoon, right after his shift ends. I'm sure he'll have some news to share. And don't worry. I'll remember what he says, and repeat to you anything Wyatt tells me after you get up from your nap. I know how interested you are in this murder case. But for now, you really need to take your medicine and go lie down."

Wyatt did stop by in the afternoon while I was asleep, and he did have news to relate to Stone. However, it wasn't the type of news I'd hoped for.

Sometimes I wondered why I even liked the human garbage disposal as much as I did. He could get me in to hot water without even trying.

I'd been napping for several hours, I realized, when I felt Stone patting me on the upper thigh. As I began to awaken I noticed my vision had improved, and the burning and swelling of my eyes had decreased somewhat. Even my pounding headache had disappeared. The second thing I noticed was that the expression on Stone's face was alarming. He was obviously upset about something, and it made the hairs on my arms stand on end. That look usually ended up with me apologizing for something foolish I'd done.

"What's going on?" I asked, with my voice barely audible.

"That's what I'd like to know, *Natalie*," he retorted. I could tell he was trying to control his temper and finding it hard to do. "WSRC? I mean really, Lexie. A WSRC? Is that the best you could come up with? I hate to inform you, but the Rockdale police department does not have a Witness Statement Record Collector on their payroll. What were you thinking?"

"Uh, well, I, uh—"

"You just had to get involved, didn't you?"

"Well, you see, I, uh. Um, I just—"

"How long were you planning on sneaking behind my back and placing yourself in jeopardy again? Did Wendy know about this?" Stone asked. He was clearly extremely displeased with me. Worrying about the wedding going off on schedule might be a moot point now. He might have decided he wanted nothing further to do with me. And who could blame him? I wouldn't want to marry me either, if I were Stone. I had to tread lightly, I realized.

"Honey, I'm sorry I misled you. I really had no

intention of getting involved to the extent I'd be putting myself into jeopardy, and, of course, I still don't."

"I've heard that before, and yet you were nearly killed because of your involvement those other times. You just don't know when to quit. 'Self-preservation' and 'self-restraint' simply aren't in your vocabulary, are they? I don't mean to sound cruel or controlling, but I love you more than life itself, and if anything happened to you, I'd be lost and extremely devastated."

"I'm sorry. Really I am, Stone. I'm just so worried about how we're going to continue with our wedding plans, and who we're going to get to conduct the ceremony. I have quite a long guest list, and they've already received invitations and marked the date off on their calendars. Postponing the wedding at this late date would be terribly difficult and inconvenient," I said.

"Inconvenient? I'm sure Pastor Steiner didn't mean to inconvenience you." He sounded sarcastic now, and irritated by my 'it's all about me' attitude. I instantly felt about two inches tall, like I could walk under the four-poster bed without bending over. Hiding under the bed sounded like a good idea right now.

"You know what I meant," I said, nearly pouting. I really can't stand it when grownups pout like four-year-olds, but Stone had driven me to the point of not knowing what else to do. Maybe I should call off the wedding and let the chips fall where they may, I thought.

"Our pastor and close friend, has been murdered! You don't think our wedding guests will understand why we've had to alter our plans? And you don't think they'd be willing to change theirs too?"

"Of course, they'd understand and change their

plans. I just hoped it wouldn't come to that. It would be so disappointing if we had to delay the wedding. I can't wait to become your wife, and I've looked forward to our special day for so long. If we don't get married next Saturday, no telling for how long we'll have to postpone the ceremony," I said. "We've got guests booked at the inn for many weeks to come after our honeymoon. I can't call and cancel out on guests who have already booked a room. It would be so unprofessional. And this is our only opportunity to take a honeymoon in the conceivable future. Who wants to go to Jamaica in the middle of the summer?"

I reached out, with tears welling up in my eyes, and stroked his hand. I could visibly see his attitude soften. He was so tenderhearted that my tears had provoked his softer side to emerge. That hadn't been my intention, but I was glad to see my heartfelt words were affecting him.

"Oh, I know you have, honey. Don't cry. I've looked forward to our wedding too. I'm not anxious to postpone it either, but I don't see that we have any choice in the matter. We had no way of predicting the pastor would be killed. Sometimes things just happen that we have no control over and we have to bend and roll with the punches."

"I know. But if they arrest the suspect and have Thurman laid to rest by next Saturday, I don't think it would be entirely inappropriate to go ahead with our scheduled plans. We'd have to find a replacement for the pastor, of course, but I'm sure that's doable," I explained. "And if we can possibly help speed the investigation up—"

"Okay, Lexie. You win," Stone said with a long drawn-out sigh. "I'm going to be pretty busy getting the grounds and everything ready for the wedding and all the guests we're anticipating at the inn. I want to put a fresh coat of redwood stain on the gazebo, weed out all the flowerbeds, and do a number of other landscaping things around the inn in the next few days. I also have some squeaky floorboards I need to replace in two of the upper suites. So I'm not going to be able to help much in your little personal investigation, nor do I think you should be intricately involved. And I don't want you going off on your own and putting yourself in any kind of danger, but I know I can't tell you what to do."

"I won't put myself in the middle of any kind of dangerous situation," I said.

"I've heard that before."

"Yes, strange things have happened in the past, but you know I'm always as cautious as possible," I said.

"No, I don't know that," Stone said. "For someone who's always cautious, you sure seem to end up in the emergency room a lot. Plus, you don't want to impede the detectives' progress or get under their skin. I hope you'll at least keep me apprised of what you're up to, and I'll help you out whenever I can, because I'd like to know you'll be protected from harm and mayhem. Unfortunately, you don't find mayhem. It has a tendency to find you. It follows you around like a shadow, and that's what concerns me. I doubt if my presence alone can prevent it, or keep your safety from being jeopardized, but I'd feel better if I were with you. To be perfectly honest, this goes way beyond my better judgment."

"I know you've got a lot to get done this week, as do I. I'm not going to go out of my way to get involved. I'm just going to keep my eyes and ears open in case I can pick up on any clues that might be overlooked by the investigators. I realize it's not likely to do any good, but I just hate the idea of postponing this wedding," I said.

"Lexie, whether or not to postpone the wedding is entirely up to you. I'm fine with whatever decision you make. I'm not overly concerned with what our fellow church members think about our decision—or anyone else for that matter. They're not the ones who have friends and family members already planning on coming in from all over to attend the ceremony. A lot of planning and scheduling has gone into this event, and if you want to go ahead with the wedding as planned, it's all right by me. Just promise me you'll be careful if you do decide to do any snooping around. Okay?"

"I promise to go about this carefully and judiciously," I said. I was ready to promise him anything. Or at least I would promise him anything but never to do anything impulsive again, because I knew there wasn't a chance in hell I could ever control my impulses to that extent. Impulsiveness was a trait I was born with and one I'd had to learn to live with. I was true to my Zodiac sign of Aries. Stone was having to learn to cope with my impulsiveness now, and not having an easy time of it.

Still, I felt so much better already just knowing I wouldn't have to sneak around behind Stone's back, or at least not as much as I would have had to otherwise. And knowing he would go along with whatever I decided to do about the wedding was a load off my mind too. "By the way, how did you find out I spoke with Mr. Blake?"

"The investigating squad interviewed him again early this afternoon and he told them about seeing someone move the blinds over the kitchen sink, and shouting what sounded like 'peas' at five-thirty in the morning. When they asked him why he was just now relating new details to them, he told them he'd already reported it to their WSRC this morning, so it should already be in their files. After he described you to the officers, it didn't take Wyatt long to figure out who'd spoken with Mr. Blake earlier this morning. He knows you almost as well as I do by now, and is as concerned about your safety as I am. You do realize that was a foolish thing to do, don't you?"

"I do now, and I'm truly sorry. Do you think I'm in legal trouble for impersonating an officer? I didn't mean to. It's not at all what I had in mind. It just sort of happened that way because I wasn't thinking of the consequences at the time."

"Do you ever consider the consequences before you act? And no, thanks to Wyatt, you're off the hook. But the chief recommended you didn't try a stunt like that again. And I highly recommend you pay heed to his advice," Stone said. "You do know that impersonating an officer is illegal, don't you? You're lucky you weren't charged with a federal offense. Trying to solve one crime should not involve committing several others. Two, or three, wrongs don't make a right, you know."

Now I remembered why I liked Wyatt so much. He could get me out of trouble as fast as he could get me into it. It was nice to have an officer of the law in your corner every once in a while when a situation like this arose. Detective Johnston always seemed to cover for me when I got myself into deep doo-doo. It would be wise of me to keep the cookies and doughnuts coming.

"Yes, I realize that. Thank God for Wyatt. Say, do you think we could go speak with Bonnie Bloomingfield this afternoon?" I asked. It was probably pushing my luck to bring this up so soon after being offered Stone's reluctant assistance, but unlimited time was not something we had in abundance. "I found a Howard Bloomingfield listed in the phone book on Cedar Street, the same block Mr. Steiner lived on. Bonnie might be able to remember something she forgot to tell the authorities when they interviewed her. By now she won't be in such a state of shock, and she may be able to remember things more clearly. She might also reiterate information Wyatt forgot to pass on to us. It couldn't hurt to ask her, anyway. Could it?"

"Why do I feel like I've been talking to myself? Did you hear anything I just said? Do I need to make an appointment with an audiologist for you?"

"Don't be silly. My hearing's just fine. But you said you'd accompany me when you could and I guess I thought you honestly meant it."

"Oh, boy," he said, shaking his head in disbelief. "What have I gotten myself in to?"

CHAPTER 4

"Mrs. Bloomingfield?" I asked the frail-looking woman who finally came to her front door after I'd knocked several times. Her gray hair was tied back in a bun, and she was hunched over. I recognized the telltale hump protruding from her back. She was a victim of osteoporosis, no doubt. I took a monthly medication and extra calcium in an attempt to ward off the bone-thinning disease, as it had a tendency to run in my family. "Good morning, ma'am. Are you Mrs. Bloomingfield?"

"Who?" She asked. She looked befuddled at the sound of her own name.

I spoke louder as I repeated myself one more time, afraid the elderly woman hadn't heard me over the sound of a car traveling up the street behind me. I guessed her age to be somewhere in the late seventies, or so.

She still looked slightly confused, I noticed, as her husband, who looked even older than she, stepped up behind her. "Yes, we're the Bloomingfields. I'm Bonnie's husband, Harold. Can we help you?"

"Good afternoon, Harold. It's nice to meet you and Mrs. Bloomingfield. My name is Lexie Starr, and this is my fiancé, Stone Van Patten. We're involved in the crime scene investigation of the murder of Thurman Steiner. We'd just like to speak with you for a few minutes, if that's all right with you. It won't take long."

"All right," Harold said, with resignation in his voice. I imagine he was already worn out from all the questioning by the investigative team. He motioned us inside as he continued to speak. "Come in, we'll sit in the kitchen. Bonnie, do you think you could fix these folks something to drink? What would you two care to drink? We've got tea, hot cocoa, or coffee if you'd like some."

"Oh, no, we don't want to inconvenience you in any way. We'll just be a few minutes, just long enough to ask Mrs. Bloomingfield a few questions," I assured the elderly gentleman. I would've killed for some coffee, but wasn't sure Bonnie was up to fixing me a cup, nor did I plan to stay long enough to drink it.

"Okay," he said, "if she's able to answer any questions this afternoon. I'm not sure she's in any shape to do so right now. And please call us Harold and Bonnie. Bloomingfield's a mouth full and sounds much too formal."

"Thank you, and we'd like you to call us Lexie and Stone," I said, as I turned to face his wife. "Bonnie, what can you tell us about what you remember happening when you found Mr. Steiner's body?"

"Who?"

"Your neighbor, Pastor Steiner. The gentleman you discovered dead in his home."

"Who?" She asked again. Bonnie was beginning to remind me of a hoot owl. All she'd managed to say so far was "who" in answer to my questions. I was sure now she was extremely hard of hearing. I nearly shouted at her as I repeated myself yet again. Maybe it was she who should make an appointment with an audiologist.

"We'd like to hear it all," I said, loudly and slowly, "even if it's repetitive of the statement you gave the authorities who interviewed you shortly after the incident occurred."

When Bonnie just looked at me in confusion, Harold spoke up to inform us his wife was having one of her bad days.

"Is she hard of hearing?" Stone asked Harold.

"Well, yes, slightly. But her real problem is that she's in the middle stages of Alzheimer's, and some days are worse than others. The trauma of finding Mr. Steiner dead seems to have affected her and caused her to be more bewildered and forgetful than normal. She's been in a state of shock and disbelief since the tragic incident. I believe her mind has shut the memories out to protect her from the psychological stress of the horrific event. You can imagine how much something like that would affect anyone, particularly someone dealing with Alzheimer's."

"Oh, we're so sorry to hear she suffers from that terrible disease," I said. Stone nodded in agreement, as his father had suffered from it too. Alzheimer's also ran in my family, and was something I was terrified of getting. Just forgetting where I'd laid my car keys was enough to send me into a full-scale panic. I decided to direct my questioning more toward Mr. Bloomingfield. I smiled at Bonnie and patted her hand, then looked directly into Harold's eyes.

"What do you recall Bonnie telling you after she'd called nine-one-one and returned to your house?"

"I'm afraid I wasn't home at the time. I'd spent the night in Knob Noster, where our eldest daughter lives."

"Knob Noster?" Stone asked. He'd only lived in Missouri for about a year and still hadn't heard of many of the nearby towns.

"Yes. Knob Noster is on Highway Fifty, west of Jefferson City. It's where Whiteman Air Force Base is located, and is the home of about two dozen B-2 Stealth Bombers."

"Oh, really? How interesting," Stone said. I could tell he was about to ask Harold something about the stealth bombers. Harold was probably a military buff, like Stone, and I didn't want them to veer off the subject of Steiner's death. We'd promised to make the visit short.

"And you left Bonnie here alone while you went to Knob Noster?" I asked, before Harold could say anything more about the air force base to Stone.

"Is that safe?" Stone added, back on track in the conversation about Steiner. He glanced over at Bonnie, who was picking absentmindedly at loose strips of vinyl on the arm of the old-fashioned kitchen chair.

"Well, you need to understand that on most days Bonnie's not this confused and forgetful. She gets along pretty well the majority of the time. She's never wandered off and gotten lost for more than a few minutes at a time, or anything of that magnitude," Harold clarified. "In fact, she's only wandered off from the house a couple of times, and both times I found her right next door in the neighbor's yard. Although the bouts of memory loss and confusion seem to be getting more frequent, this is the worst I believe I've ever seen her. But then, this is the most shocking thing that's happened to her since the onset of Alzheimer's. Had I known this was going to happen, I'd have never left her alone. Unfortunately, I can't predict the future. And I've always put Bonnie's best interests ahead of my own."

Harold sounded a little defensive, as if we'd accused him of taking poor care of his wife in her current condition. We hadn't intended to offend him, but still I was curious. "Why didn't she go to Knob Noster with you?"

"Bonnie gets carsick when we travel such distances," he said. Now he sounded very annoyed and defensive. "She also tends to get a backache, so she rarely travels with me to see the kids. Our two daughters, and the grandkids, who are grown now, come here to see her as often as they can. I traveled to Knob Noster this time to watch our youngest grandson, Nicholas, graduate from the University of Central Missouri. We felt it was important that I attend to acknowledge his achievement."

"Of course it was important. Congratulations," Stone said. "That's quite an accomplishment for Nicholas."

"Yes, we're very proud of him," Harold said, his expression softening momentarily as he thought about his grandson. "But as far as Bonnie is concerned, I'd suggest you two come back tomorrow morning. She's in no condition to answer questions right now, but she's nearly always more lucid and clear-minded in the mornings. I just don't have the answers to give you. I've only picked up pieces of Bonnie's story since I returned home this morning. I've been reluctant to ask her questions and confuse her even more. I got most of my information from the detectives who stopped by here earlier. I should think one visit from the investigators today would have been sufficient."

We thanked him for his time and promised to return at nine o'clock the next morning. He agreed. I could tell he felt he had no choice in the matter, or he'd have never let us cross his threshold again. We hadn't meant to infer we were official investigators. I really didn't want to cross that line again, but if it helped us get information from the Bloomingfields I wasn't going to correct Harold. As we stepped out onto their front porch, he shut the door rather firmly and noisily behind us. "Good riddance," I was sure he was saying on the other side of the door.

On the way home to the inn, which was only about two or three minutes from the Bloomingfields, Stone and I discussed his change in attitude. "I'm not surprised," Stone said. "I'd become upset if anyone implied I didn't take good care of you, and those two have probably been married over fifty years. I believe him when he said he'd never have left Bonnie to her own devices had he known something like the pastor's murder was going to involve his wife. I'm sure in most instances he'd feel comfortable in leaving her home alone for a short amount of time, or he'd have never made the trip to Knob Noster, not even for the sake of his grandson."

I wasn't convinced, but I kept my opinions to myself. Was he really out of town, or could he have had a feud with his neighbor and somehow been involved in Steiner's death? Bonnie probably wouldn't remember if he was home at the time or not. Feuds among neighbors were a common occurrence, even in the best of neighborhoods. The chances of Harold Bloomingfield being involved in the pastor's death were slim, but I had to make sure I didn't overlook any possibilities. I had a bad habit of judging everyone to be guilty until proven innocent. But so far that theory had worked out well for me.

Wendy called as I was fixing dinner that evening after we'd returned from the Bloomingfields. She was just checking in, and making small talk about Stone's nephew, Andy. He'd arrived with the U-Haul and was in the process of moving into his new ranch property. Being a rancher was an entirely new endeavor for Andy, having been a private charter pilot since earning a pilot's license right out of college.

In early June, he'd be taking a commercial flight to Myrtle Beach and flying his own five-passenger plane back to a nearby municipal airport where he'd rented a hangar. His Cessna 206 was a single engine aircraft, with fixed landing gear, and Andy kept it in excellent condition. He'd come to our rescue with his airplane when we were back on the east coast the previous year. He was a top-notch pilot, and I'd felt safe in the back seat of his plane.

I knew he'd missed his Uncle Stone after Stone moved to Kansas from South Carolina. I also realized he and Wendy had become closer in the last year. In fact, although Wendy hadn't said as much, I could tell she'd fallen in love with him. Andy had come to Rockdale on several occasions to visit, and he and Wendy spoke on the phone nearly every day. Wendy couldn't have been any happier when she'd learned of his decision to move to the Kansas City area. The 640-acre ranch Andy had purchased was located just outside the city limits of Atchison, Kansas, about a half-hour southwest of Rockdale.

I was very fond of Stone's nephew, the son of his older brother, Sterling. Sterling was a commercial pilot, and Andy had followed in his father's footsteps. Andy obviously enjoyed flying, and I wondered if he'd take to ranching with the same enthusiasm. He suddenly found himself with hogs, cattle, horses, chickens, and even a couple of ornery goats, to feed and take care of on a daily basis. I hoped he could easily adjust to the new lifestyle. It would be like me going from an assistant librarian to a rodeo clown overnight.

I thought about telling Wendy about Stone's decision to stand by me as we did a little prying into the circumstances of Steiner's death. I decided against it, however. I really wasn't in the mood for the lengthy and emotional lecture I was guaranteed to get from my annoyingly over-protective daughter. The guests would be down for supper shortly, anyway. I had a pot roast I needed to take out of the oven, and potatoes that weren't going to mash themselves.

"Good morning, Harold. How are you this morning?" Stone asked Mr. Bloomingfield as we stood on his porch at exactly nine o'clock the next morning. Stone hadn't been quite as enthusiastic about revisiting Harold and Bonnie as I had, but I was able to convince him to come along. I think he was afraid of the bone-chilling interrogation I was apt to conduct if I visited the Bloomingfields on my own. He knew we'd already gotten off on the wrong foot with Harold.

"I'm fine," Harold said, in a rather stilted voice. "Bonnie is much more cognizant this morning too. Come on in, folks. It's nice to see you again."

He didn't actually look happy to see us, but he opened the door to allow us into his home. Bonnie sat at the kitchen table with a cup of coffee in her hand.

"Coffee?" Harold asked. Stone declined, but I nodded enthusiastically. If there was one thing I rarely turned down, it was a cup of coffee, and I could see a nearly full carafe of already brewed coffee on the counter. If I was stranded on a deserted island and could only pick three items to have with me, coffee would be one of them.

"Good morning, Bonnie," I said, as I reached over

to pat her left hand, which was resting on the table. "How are you this morning?"

"Fine," she said. "Who are you two again?"

I knew she didn't recall our visit from the day before, so I introduced Stone and me and informed her we were going to ask her a few questions involving the murder of Pastor Steiner. She seemed to understand what I was telling her. I gave her a couple of minutes to pour some coffee, and then asked, "Can you run through, for us, just what happened that morning you found the deceased pastor?"

"Well, you see, I couldn't sleep the night before. I kept waking up and was tired of tossing and turning. So I got up and went into the living room to watch TV. An old movie, *The Day After,* was on and I didn't remember having ever seen it before. It was about the devastation in Lawrence, Kansas, the day following a nuclear bomb being dropped on the vicinity. I found it interesting, of course, since Lawrence is so near to us here in Rockdale."

"Oh, yes," I said. "It's an interesting movie. I saw the film years ago, in the early eighties. If I remember right, one of my favorite actors, John Lithgow, was in it."

"Yes, and Jason Robards portrayed a doctor in the movie," Bonnie said. I realized she was indeed very lucid and felt confident we'd get a good accounting of the way the events had unfolded the morning of the murder. I could understand now why Harold felt comfortable leaving her home alone while he traveled out of town to make a short visit with their daughter and grandson.

"Anyway," she continued, "soon after the movie had finished, I went into the kitchen to brew a pot of coffee when I looked out my kitchen window. I noticed Mr. Steiner's back door was wide open, which was odd, but I really didn't give it much thought. I often see him head out on his morning run, but didn't see him leave his house this time as I drank my coffee in front of the large plate-glass window in the living room. Later on that morning, after I fixed myself a late breakfast and was washing the dishes at about eleven-forty-five, I looked out the kitchen window again and noticed Mr. Steiner's door was still open. His newspaper was still in the driveway, which was extremely odd, since I often see him retrieving his paper at about seven. When I looked back at his house and saw that he hadn't opened up the blinds over his kitchen sink, I got really concerned and decided to go over and check on him."

Bonnie stopped to take a couple of sips of coffee, and wipe her mouth with a napkin. So far her story was consistent with the report she'd given the detectives. I was so relieved she was having a good day and seemed to be experiencing no ill effects of the Alzheimer's she was cursed with. She gazed off to a spot to the left of the kitchen table, which put her staring approximately at the trashcan for several long seconds, before Harold nudged her. He hadn't said a word since letting us into the house.

"Bonnie?" I asked. She was either reflecting back on the horrific event or gathering her thoughts.

"Yes?"

"Go on with your story," I prompted her.

"Oh, yes. Now what was I saying?"

"You were telling us how you decided to go over and check on Mr. Steiner."

"Yes, of course," she said. "As you know, I found him dead, lying flat on the floor, stretched out on his back. I could tell he wasn't breathing so I checked for a pulse and found none. He was quite pale and stiff and I knew it was too late to resuscitate him, so I called that number you call in an emergency. What's that number again?"

"Nine-one-one," I reminded her.

"Yes, of course, I called nine-one-one."

"And what else do you recall? Did anything seem out of place? Any obvious signs of a struggle, chairs overturned, broken dishes, or anything like that? Maybe a fireplace poker, or a cast iron frying pan lying on the floor, or anything else that could have been used to strike him on the back of the head?"

"Not that I recall, but I really wasn't aware at the time he'd been murdered, so I wasn't looking for any signs of Mr. Steiner having been assaulted. I just assumed he'd suffered a massive coronary, or something of that nature. And besides that, I'm sure I've already told the police department everything I can remember."

"I'm sure you have, Bonnie, but you might want to take notes as you think back and remember something, even the smallest, most seemingly insignificant, detail. Then you'll have the information to turn over to the police, or to Stone and me, if you prefer," I said. "Unfortunately, the person who calls for help is often considered a prime suspect until proven otherwise."

Bonnie looked alarmed, and Harold looked angry. I'd ticked him off again without even trying. Bonnie went back to staring at the trashcan, with her lower lip quivering slightly. I hadn't really meant to upset either of them, but I sometimes spoke without giving much thought to what I was saying. Okay, I *often* spoke without giving my words much thought.

Without turning to look at me, Bonnie, asked, "Do the police think I killed Thurman?"

"No, of course not," Stone said, giving me a look of annoyance. Jeez, I'd managed to piss off everyone in the room with just a few short words. Stone tried to ease the anxiety my words had caused both of the Bloomingfields. "I'm sure you've already been cleared of any suspicion in the murder. I'm sure the investigators no longer view you as a suspect."

Stone's words seem to have an even bigger effect on the Bloomingfields than my own had. Now Stone looked annoyed at himself for the way he'd phrased his statement to Bonnie. They were meant to be words of comfort, I knew, but had obviously had the opposite effect.

"Oh, my Lord," Bonnie said. It was evident we'd triggered the effects of Alzheimer's in Bonnie's mind. "Did I murder Mr. Steiner? I really think I must have. I don't remember it, but I have these forgetful spells, you see. Oh, my goodness! What have I done? I didn't mean to kill the pastor. How could I do such a terrible thing? What's going to happen to me now?"

Bonnie began to weep, and we left Harold to deal with her after we were escorted out of the house. The door definitely slammed behind us this time, and Howard didn't invite us back.

Wyatt stopped by the inn about an hour later. I automatically sat a platter full of cream-filled pastries down in front of him. Wyatt informed us that the Bloomingfields had come down to the police station because Mr. Bloomingfield had wanted to file a complaint against the "crime scene investigators" who'd come to their house to ask questions. Wyatt had immediately suspected me, but was surprised to hear Stone had gone along with the idea. He thought Stone had more sense than that, he said around a mouth full of cream cheese and strawberry jam. I assumed it was Wyatt's way of saying I had absolutely no sense at all, and Stone was gradually being dragged down to my level. I didn't appreciate the insinuation, but I kept quiet. I noticed Stone looked quite a bit embarrassed by Wyatt's reaction to his involvement in the matter.

"I knew better," Stone said. "I apologize for getting involved, Wyatt. I knew I couldn't prevent Lexie from going over there, and didn't want her to go alone. But, I promise you we never claimed to be crime scene investigators, per se."

Wyatt rolled his eyes dramatically and then went on to tell us that while Harold was filling out a complaint form, Bonnie Bloomingfield had walked over to the chief of police, stuck both her hands out in front of her, as if waiting for them to be cuffed. She told him she'd come to turn herself in for killing Pastor Steiner. She confessed to having no idea why she'd decided to kill him, and had no real recollection of doing so. But she seemed certain she was guilty of the crime.

Wyatt stopped chewing and turned to look me directly in the eyes. "What have you done this time, Lexie?"

"Well, you see," I stammered. "Bonnie has Alzheimer's and gets confused, and she forgets a lot of things. I'm afraid we might have accidentally misled her into thinking she was responsible for Thurman Steiner's death. It was certainly not our intention."

"Harold told us about the Alzheimer's," Wyatt said. "Do you honestly believe Bonnie could've actually had something to do with Steiner's murder? Harold stated he was out of town, attending a college graduation and visiting family in Knob Noster. The detectives really don't suspect Bonnie of the crime, but reasoned she could have become completely confused, particularly if home alone at the time, and convinced herself she needed to kill him for some reason. We can't overlook any possibility, no matter how remote and irrational it may seem. Bonnie might now have no recollection of her actions that morning. No one can fathom how she could have the strength to perform such an act. But she *was* the one who found him and reported his death, which automatically makes her a suspect."

"That's what I told her, which is what confused her into thinking she was the killer. But, no, she couldn't have killed him. I'm almost certain of that."

"How do you know that for sure? I agree I can't imagine how someone of her age, and in her physical condition, could have taken down the pastor, even though he was not a very large man and could have been taken completely off guard. Stranger things have happened and, like I said, we have to look at every possibility. So what makes you so certain Bonnie couldn't possibly have harmed Steiner?" Wyatt asked.

"Bonnie told me she'd watched the movie *The Day After* early that morning. I checked the TV guide and it really had been playing on HBO between four and six-thirty. It was during that period of time that Nate estimated Thurman had been killed. I can't see Bonnie leaving her home in the middle of a movie she's interested in to go commit a murder, and then return to her home to watch the remainder of the film. It's just not logical. If Bonnie were experiencing one of her confused and forgetful episodes, she surely wouldn't have been able to focus enough to concentrate on a movie and then remember any of the details about it at a later time. At least I wouldn't think she could."

"There are usually a lot of things that aren't logical surrounding a crime of this nature. But how do you know she really watched the movie?" Wyatt asked.

"I'm no expert on Alzheimer's, but she gave me accurate details about the movie that she most likely wouldn't have remembered if she'd watched it years ago, or even probably a week ago. Even now she may be losing memories of the movie due to the Alzheimer's. It's the nature of the beast."

"Yes," Wyatt agreed. "But Harold told us Bonnie could recite stories of events that happened forty or fifty years ago almost verbatim, but couldn't remember what she'd had for lunch by suppertime. Alzheimer's can cause a person to have a very selective memory."

I nodded. "I know that to be true, Wyatt. My grandfather had Alzheimer's and spoke in detail about a German shepherd he once owned as a child, but he didn't recognize any of us, even Grandma. As Harold told us, this entire incident has had a very adverse affect on his wife, which caused her Alzheimer's to be even more pronounced than usual. For her to relate such specific details about the movie, I feel like she had to have just seen it. And talking about seeing Thurman's door being open, his newspaper in the drive, and so on, it almost definitely had to have occurred, or she'd have been unable to give the authorities any statement at all."

"We hadn't cast much suspicion on her anyway. So, yes, I believe you're probably right."

"She is, Wyatt," Stone said. "I truly believe Bonnie Bloomingfield could no more have killed Thurman Steiner than you or I could have. She was just having one of her bad days again today, I'm afraid. As Lexie told you, we didn't mean to mislead her. I knew at the time I agreed to accompany Lexie that I would come to regret the decision. I'll use more discretion next time. I should have learned that by now."

"Don't be too hard on yourself, Stone. I know how persuasive Lexie can be. And I know you didn't intend to mislead Mrs. Bloomingfield. The conclusion you've come to is pretty much what the investigating team determined too," Wyatt said.

Stone ran his fingers through his silver hair, and continued, "I can understand why the trauma of finding Thurman's body would trigger a setback with the Alzheimer's. I sure hope this setback is reversible, and not a permanent infliction. I feel so bad for Bonnie, and Harold too, of course."

"It goes without saying that we all do. While Mrs. Bloomingfield was at the station the chief had me take a set of her fingerprints, which I personally thought was unnecessary. Naturally, this upset her again, making her even more certain she was about to be arrested for murder. It kind of irked Harold too. But her prints did match a couple of the one's found in Steiner's kitchen, which is not at all unexpected, since she was the person who found him dead and would have naturally touched a few items while reaching for the phone to call nine-one-one. That only leaves a couple of fingerprints left that haven't been accounted for yet, and no matches were found on IAFIS, the national database of prints," Wyatt said. He paused to snatch another cream-filled Danish off the pastry platter, and then continued.

"One last thing before I have to leave. A citizen on Cedar Street, just about two blocks from the pastor's house, called in to the police department to report a vehicle being parked in front of his house numerous times in the last couple of months. Most often it's parked there in the afternoon, generally around three-thirty to five-thirty or so. The concerned citizen had never seen the driver, but said the morning of the murder was the first time he'd ever seen it parked in front of his house early in the morning. He couldn't recall the exact time, but thought it could have been there at five. A noise outside had awakened him and he'd gone to the front door to look out. That's when he noticed the car, and thought it was an unusual time for it to be parked there."

"Do you think the car is connected to the murder?" Stone asked his friend.

"We have no way to determine that at this point, but we're looking for the owner of a black Ford Mustang, maybe two or three years old. Just to question him, of course. We have nothing to connect him to the crime, and it's probably unrelated, but still worth checking in to. Sometimes the most insignificant clue proves to be the turning point in solving a crime. And, like I said, we have to look at every possibility."

"Let us know if you find out anything," I said. "And I'll let you know if I happen to hear anything about the black Mustang or the driver of that car."

Wyatt nodded, rolled his eyes at Stone again, polished off his pastry in two bites, and gulped down his last swig of coffee. He turned to look at me and said, "I suppose it's a waste of time to try to convince you to stay out of this investigation, Lexie. I know how stubborn and impulsive you can be. But can you at least promise me you'll stop impersonating a member of the police squad? I can only protect you so much. The chief considered bringing you in to the station this time, but I was able to dissuade him. I might not be able to do that next time though, because his patience is wearing thin. And, believe me, you don't want to be on the chief's bad side."

I promised. It was the least I could do for him keeping me out of trouble with the police department—twice! Wyatt stayed long enough to wolf down four or five more pastries and then excused himself to go back on patrol. I couldn't believe what a mess I'd made of things where the Bloomingfields were concerned. I'd certainly never meant to upset them or convince Bonnie she'd had anything to do with the crime. Alzheimer's was such a terrible disease. I vowed to tread more lightly in the future. I didn't want to cause anybody else any unnecessary grief.

It didn't take me long after Wyatt left to get a list of all the black Mustang owners in Rockdale. I placed a call to the local Department of Motor Vehicles, and was greeted by a pleasant female voice. I knew it was illegal to impersonate a police officer, but felt sure there was no law preventing me from pretending to be a gas station attendant.

"Good morning, ma'am," I said. "I'm Brenda Burns, and I work for Rusty's gas station here in Rockdale. We just had a customer drive off without paying for his gasoline. Now we've got to try and track him down to collect the money, and possibly press charges. Can I get a list of all the owners of black Mustangs in town? I'm sure you've had to do this hundreds of times."

"No, actually I've never been asked by a gas station attendant for this kind of information before, but I'll see what I can do."

"Really? I'm shocked. Oh, and we'll also need their addresses."

"I'm not allowed to give out addresses, Ms. Burns. Strict policy. Sorry."

"That's okay," I said. I wasn't too concerned about it because I knew that was why God had invented phone books. Calling the Mustang owners might prove faster and easier than visiting them, anyway. And safer, I had to admit to myself, even though I rarely let the lack of safety stop me. I'd surely be much better off if I did.

"I can give you all the owners' names in the county if you prefer, but it would be a longer list," the lady told me. "A lot longer, actually. There are quite a few black Mustang owners in this county for some reason."

"I'll just take the list of owners in town. For now, we're going on the assumption it was a local driving the car, since Rockdale is kind of off the beaten path, not on a major freeway or anything. I'll call you back if everyone on this shorter list checks out."

"How will you know if they check out okay?" She asked, purely out of curiosity, I could tell. I hadn't thought this plan out that far so I winged it. I had the innate ability to make up crap at the drop of a pin.

"They pumped twenty-two gallons of gas, so we should be able to tell by how full the gas tanks are in their Mustangs. If they've only got half a tank, we can assume they didn't just fill their tank up. A full tank indicates a recent fill-up." Suddenly it occurred to me that a car the size of a Mustang probably didn't even have a large enough fuel capacity to hold twenty-two gallons. Hopefully this young woman did not know enough about cars to even question their fuel capacities. The receptionist's voice sounded like as if it belonged to a girl in her early twenties. I figured her to be the driver of a Volkswagen bug or Mini-Cooper, not a Ford Mustang.

"That makes sense," she replied, even though I knew it didn't. I would guess she cared more about the newest high-heeled pumps available at Nordstrom's than gas pumps at Rusty's gas station, and how much you could pump into any given gas tank.

"Of course it's only logical," I agreed. "I'm ready for that list of black Mustang owners whenever you are."

"Okay, hold on while I bring it up on my computer. It takes a couple minutes to get into that program. These antique computers are terribly slow. Someone needs to raise taxes so the DMV can afford to buy us more current equipment. I used a more sophisticated computer in my kindergarten computer lab than I use here at work."

Yep, I thought, early twenties. This gal grew up with computers. I used a crayon and construction paper when I was in kindergarten, not a mouse and a modem.

"I'd rather have to wait a few minutes than pay higher taxes. Our taxes are high enough as it is," I said. While I waited I poured myself a cup of coffee and started the dishwasher. The breakfast dishes needed to be washed before I got busy doing other chores. I'd served spinach omelets with sausage links, at around eight o'clock, but we'd left for the Bloomingfields before I'd had an opportunity to rinse off the dishes and place them in the dishwasher. I'd burnt the cheese and made a mess out of the skillet, so it was now soaking in the sink. I was pretty sure it was a lost cause. Another expensive skillet had bitten the dust.

"Ma'am?" I heard over the phone. "I have a list of five black Mustang owners for you."

I grabbed a pen and pad of paper off the counter and jotted down the names as she listed them off. I thanked her and hung up the phone. I was certain the crime scene investigators had already gotten this list, as I imagined they probably had a similar software program in their computer as the DMV. But I didn't want to ask Wyatt for the list, for obvious reasons. The entire police force was probably not too happy with me at the moment. I also figured they might be busy chasing down other leads and I could get a jump on checking out the people on the Mustang list. It was the least I could do for the police department, considering I'd been caught impersonating one of them twice in the last couple of days, even though the second time had been inadvertent.

I opened the phone book and soon had four addresses and phone numbers. One number was unlisted. I sat down at the kitchen table with my cell phone and coffee, absentmindedly swatting at a fly the size of a New York City sewer rat. Spring had definitely sprung, for the houseflies and other bugs and creepy crawlers were coming out in full force. Stone had removed a black rat snake from the shed the night before, and taken it out in the country to release it. I know black snakes eat mice, and other small varmints, which is helpful. But they also kill baby birds, and eat the eggs right out of the nests, which I just can't tolerate. I had birdhouses and feeders hanging on practically every pole and tree limb in the yard, and a big birdbath in the center of the large flowerbed inside the perimeter of the circular driveway. I'd feel guilty luring the birds in just to have them be eaten by snakes we were harboring in our shed.

After shooing away another huge fly from the lip of my coffee cup, I located the flyswatter and went on a killing rampage in the kitchen. I killed three flies and scared the hell out of another one that was a mere nanosecond faster than I was.

I couldn't bring myself to place my lips on something a nasty fly had just been perched on, so I got another cup down from the cabinet and filled it with coffee. I can be very anal retentive when it comes to bugs and bug cooties. Nothing in the world scares me as badly as a walking stick. I think they're sneaky little bastards, pretending to be something they're not. For that reason alone, I refuse to have screen doors on any house I'm living in. Screen doors are like walking stick magnets.

Before I started calling the black Mustang owners, I wanted to psych myself up. I needed yet another cup of coffee and some mindless chatter. I called my daughter to see how her day was going. I asked about the recent arrival of Stone's nephew, Andy. I listened to her rattle on for several minutes before asking if she'd heard anymore about Pastor Steiner's death.

Wendy told me his death had officially been ruled a homicide, and asphyxiation by smothering had been listed as the C.O.D. The county coroner's office had released the body to the family for burial. Because the deceased was a man of the cloth, the police department decided not to hold the body while the investigation proceeded, as they typically would have had Thurman been a truck driver, or a library assistant. There didn't appear to be any more clues to be uncovered with further examination of the body. No DNA was found at the scene or on the body, so delaying burial seemed to be an unnecessary inconvenience to the family. And exhuming Steiner's body was always a possibility if absolutely unavoidable to solve the crime.

"Have you heard when the funeral and visitation are going to be held?" I asked.

"Not yet, Mom, but I'll let you know if I hear anything. I assume you and Stone will be attending the services."

"Yes, of course. Tomorrow is Sunday, so we'll be attending regular church services, as well. Surely the elders will have arranged for someone to be there to replace Pastor Steiner. It ought to be a very interesting and highly emotional morning service."

"I'm sure," Wendy agreed. "What are you doing today?"

"Oh, just household chores and taking care of guests. I'm going to serve roasted turkey for supper, so I have that to prepare also." I didn't really want to tell Wendy I was getting ready to cold call and question total strangers just because they had the misfortune of owning a black Mustang. My daughter was well aware of my determination to have Pastor Steiner's killer brought to justice, and arrested as soon as possible so my wedding would not have to be postponed. But there was no sense, getting her stirred up this early in the morning. I was still thinking about how to go about getting the information I needed from the people on my short list. Maybe one more cup of coffee was in order while I waited for an inspiration. Whenever I felt the need to procrastinate, I wasted time feeding my severe caffeine addiction.

No one answered on the first phone call I made, but I had better luck on the second.

"Good morning. Is Rick Meier available?" I asked.

"Yes, may I tell him who's calling?" A low, raspy, female voice replied, before lapsing into a dry, hacking coughing spell. *Light another one, lady,* I said to myself. I knew my voice would eventually have sounded the same had I not quit smoking several years ago. But I never lectured anybody about smoking. I knew from experience how hard it was to kick the habit.

"My name's June. I'm just a Rockdale resident who found something in the street I thought might belong to Mr. Meier," I said, after she'd finally stopped coughing.

"Okay, hang on, June." The lady with the gravelly voice hacked a couple more times and continued, "I'll go call him to the phone."

"Hello, this is Rick Meier," a young man said a short time later.

"I hate to bother you, Rick, but I found something I thought might belong to you. I live over on Cedar Street, just off Sixth. A couple of days or so ago I noticed a black Mustang parked out on the street near my home and later on in the day I found what looks like the bolt off a motor mount in that exact same area. I thought it might have fallen off your car." I wouldn't know a bolt off a motor mount from a bolt off a lamppost, but I wanted it to be something that sounded like you could drive a car without, yet something you'd be certain to want back so you could replace it before your motor fell out while you were driving seventy miles an hour down the freeway.

"It couldn't have fallen off my car. My car's been in the shop all week getting some bodywork done on it. I got rear-ended a while back at a stop sign," Rick said. "Plus, I don't think I've ever been on Cedar Street in my life. I don't even know where it's located. I live out west of town and work in Atchison."

"Okay. Good enough," I said. "Just thought I'd tried to find the owner of this thing before I chuck it in the trash. I figured you'd want it back if it was yours."

"I sure would have, ma'am. I appreciate you calling. Take care."

"You too."

I hung up the phone and crossed Rick Meier's name off my list. Then I picked up the phone again and dialed the third number I'd located in the phone book. I got an answering machine, so I left a message about finding a motor mount bolt and hoped the caller would call back if he'd been on Cedar Street, before checking to ascertain all his bolts were in place and discovering he hadn't lost one.

One number left. I dialed the number for a Buck Webster and got another answering machine. The message said, "You've reached Coach Webster. If I'm not at home, you can reach me on my cell phone at 555-1471." I dialed the cell phone number and a deep voice answered almost immediately.

"Buck here."

I repeated my story about finding the bolt off a motor mount. He paused for a second and said, "I guess it could have come off my car. I was parked on Cedar Street recently when I stopped by to visit with a friend."

Bingo! I'd hit pay dirt, with any luck at all. The person who'd reported seeing the black Mustang the morning of the murder obviously didn't recognize the car, so I wondered why Buck Webster had parked in front of a stranger's house. I assumed it was possible there'd been no room in front of his friend's place.

"You can check it out, and if it turns out to belong to you I can drop it off at your house," I said. "I'll be out and about today anyway."

"Probably better if you drop it off here where I work at Rockdale High School during the day." That was a moot point because it was highly unlikely his car was missing a motor mount bolt. Now I knew who probably owned the black Mustang in question, but how could I find out why he was parked on Cedar Street in front of the house of someone who didn't know him? And why was he there so early in the morning on the day Steiner was killed? I didn't want to get overly optimistic, though. It was a couple of blocks from the crime scene so a connection was only remotely possible to begin with. Still, I pressed on.

"I noticed you were parked on my street early on the morning the pastor of the Baptist Church was killed. Do you remember seeing anything odd, or anyone who looked suspicious while you were parked on Cedar Street? He's our neighbor, of course, and we were very close to him," I said, as if to clarify why I was curious if Buck Webster had observed anything. I waited quite a while waiting for his response. He appeared to be reluctant to answer my question.

"No, that's not so. It must have been another car you saw parked there. It's been over a week ago since I was parked there and it wasn't in the morning. I remember it was in the evening while my wife was cleaning up after supper. Sorry for your loss, but I wasn't on Cedar Street the morning of your friend's death. Thanks for calling. I'll go check my car between classes and let you know if the bolt came off my car." Click! He'd hung up before I could say or ask anything else.

"Ever heard of Buck Webster?" I asked Stone when he came inside to grab a sandwich for lunch. He'd been out fertilizing the large lawn of the Alexandria Inn. Maintenance and upkeep of the inn kept Stone working nonstop nearly every day. He was happiest when his hands were busy. He enjoyed maintaining, repairing and building stuff. I think he broke things just to have an excuse to fix them, and he appeared unusually pleased when I reported to him that something wasn't working quite properly.

"Sure," he said. "Webster's the football coach at the high school. I met him at a game last fall. Seemed real nice. Wyatt was working security there. I went down to speak with Wyatt on the sideline and he introduced me to the coach. Why do you ask?"

I explained to Stone how I'd discovered it was possibly the coach's Mustang parked on Cedar Street the morning of the murder. I told him Buck denied being parked there the morning of the murder, even though the concerned neighbor said a car like Coach Webster's was. Stone seemed a bit disappointed, as if he had too much respect for the football coach to believe he could possibly be involved in a murder. He shook his head.

"The neighbor is probably confused about which

day he saw the car there, or it could even have been a different car. Coach Webster probably, on occasion, takes a football player, or another teacher who lives nearby, home. And Cedar Street stretches from one end of town to the other so it stands to reason he'd park on Cedar Street on some occasion or the other. I imagine the Mustang deal was just a coincidence and had nothing to do with Steiner. Webster's a stand-up kind of guy. I doubt he even knew Pastor Steiner. You know the redhead who works as a teller at the drive-through window at our bank?"

"Yeah, nice lady. Sandy something." I knew who he was referring to because she was very striking in appearance. Sandy was tall and willowy, and had perfectly applied make-up and beautifully styled, strawberry blond hair. She looked more like a model than a bank teller. She made me feel like I should dress up to go make a deposit.

"Her name's Sandy Webster. She's Buck's wife."

Now I was a bit disappointed. But Stone was right. I couldn't see how there could be a connection between Webster and Pastor Steiner. I'd have to give Detective Johnston a call and tell him what I'd found out. I was sure he'd be proud of me for impersonating someone other than a member of the police department.

CHAPTER 5

As it turns out, Detective Wyatt Johnston didn't sound too proud of me, but he assured me he'd pass the information on to the rest of the crime scene investigations team. I'd made the call to him after Stone had finished lunch and resumed working in the yard. As I talked on the phone I looked outside and saw Stone carrying a gallon of redwood stain out of the garden shed. I knew he was planning to do some touch up work on the gazebo.

Like Stone, Wyatt didn't believe there was a connection between the Mustang and the murder. He was pretty sure the crime scene investigators had already dismissed the black Mustang as inconsequential. He'd known Buck and Sandy Webster for years. "In fact, he was my coach in high school," he said.

"You played football?" I didn't have any trouble picturing Wyatt as a football player. He was big, tough, and still in top physical form.

"I was a wide receiver," he said. "We were the 4-A state runners-up my senior year. It was the year after

Coach Webster started there as a coach. His team went on to win the state championship the next two years in a row. He was always fair, but very driven and tough as nails. All his players have always idolized him. He's like a father figure in their lives."

"That's nice. Being involved in sports could only help a kid stay in school and graduate. Impressive record too," I said.

"I probably shouldn't tell you this, but you're bound to find out sooner or later, anyway."

"What? Tell me!" I could sense he was about to pass on something interesting about the murder investigation. I clumsily set my cup on the table, coffee sloshing over the lip of it. I was giddy in anticipation.

"All of Thurman Steiner's kids have arrived in town and are expected to attend the funeral services. The investigators plan to speak to each of them. The eldest son is being questioned right now. His name is Theodore but he goes by Teddy."

"Is Teddy a prime suspect?"

"Well, I wouldn't go that far, but apparently he had a very contentious relationship with his father. He got involved in drugs in high school, and was arrested twice on D.U.I. charges. A month ago he'd tried to borrow a couple of grand from Thurman and was turned down, according to one of his sisters who'd already been questioned. Thurman told him he just didn't have the money to loan out. Apparently, Teddy had never gotten along very well with any of his siblings. Neither they nor their father approved of his drug use and life style."

"That's interesting," I said into the phone. "Are you thinking Teddy might have struck out in retribution for being turned down for the loan?"

"Yes, and there's also the possibility of wanting his

share of his father's estate to buy drugs or pay off whatever debts he might have. The pastor used to have a lot of assets, such as some prime commercial property in Leavenworth, but I don't know if he still owned it at the time of his death. For all I know he might have sold the property. Also, the church carried a small, but not insignificant, insurance policy on him, listing his six children as equal beneficiaries. Beneficiaries on life insurance policies, even small ones, turn out to be the killer in more instances than you'd probably imagine. Money makes a powerful motive."

"Yes, I see what you're saying. After all, it's been said that money is the root of all evil. It sounds like Teddy had a motive. Will you let me know if anything develops from the interview with him or any of his other children?" I asked.

"I guess so, despite my misgivings on involving you in any way in this investigation," Wyatt said. "But I also know if I don't pass it on to you, you'll just find some creative way of finding the information out yourself and the very idea scares me."

"Now, don't be that way, Wyatt. You know I'm only curious and anxious to have the killer apprehended so Stone and I can continue with our wedding plans as scheduled."

"Okay, I know how much that means to you. But for now, I'd better get off the phone and back to work. I have some important paperwork I need to finish before I get off. This job is about ten percent police business and ninety percent paperwork, or so it seems at times. It's the one thing I dislike about being a cop."

"Paperwork would get old fast. Fortunately there is very little of it required here at the inn. Say, would you like to come by for supper?" I asked. "I've got a large turkey in the oven and only three guests staying at the inn right now. I plan to make some of that oyster dressing you like so much."

"What time should I be there?" Wyatt didn't turn down free food. In fact, I'd never seen him turn down any food, free or not. I knew I could lure him to the house with the mere mention of oyster dressing. And I never knew when he might cut loose with some more information on the case. If nothing else, Wyatt could always be counted on for some pleasant dinner conversation, and a little extra eye candy at the supper table was always nice.

"We'll eat about six. See you then. And thanks for the scoop, Wyatt."

The detective just groaned in response.

"Hey Mom! What's up with you guys? I tried you a few minutes ago and you didn't answer," I heard my daughter say as I picked up the house phone. I'd expected it to be Wendy, because she usually calls me on the landline. She'd probably tried to call while I was speaking to Wyatt and gotten my voice mailbox, I reasoned. I'd heard the phone click, as if someone were trying to ring through, but I hadn't wanted to interrupt the detective while he was dispersing information about the murder investigation.

"Not much going on here," I said. It hadn't been all that long since I'd spoken to her earlier. "What's new?"

"Andy's about all moved into the ranch. His remodeling crew started working a month or so back and finished up their work a couple of days ago. The place really looks terrific. There are only a few projects left and Andy intends to do those jobs himself after he gets settled in. Like Stone, he likes to keep busy."

"Really? I didn't know he was handy at that sort of

thing. But he's so much like his uncle in other ways that I shouldn't be surprised."

"He helped a friend lay tile before, so he's going to handle the new tile flooring in the kitchen and laundry room by himself. He's also going to paint several of the rooms and build on a new back porch. I think the only other projects he has in mind are refinishing some of the hardwood floors and updating the appliances. He's already ordered all new furniture from the Nebraska Furniture Mart over by the Legends shopping area in Kansas City, Kansas."

"I can't wait to see the old farmhouse when it's all completed," I said, sincerely. We had looked at the place with him last fall and found it to have a lot of character and even more potential. "Did he have a new master bath built on like he said he was going to? I know he wasn't wild about having only an old claw-footed tub, and no shower."

"Yes, the new bathroom has a tiled shower, a whirlpool tub, and Jack and Jill lavatories. He left the antique tub in there for nostalgic reasons. They also added a large walk-in closet. He's particularly proud of the new toilet. He was told you could flush sixteen golf balls down it all at one time," Wendy said with a laugh. "So if you ever have sixteen golf balls you're anxious to get rid of, just let Andy know. I'm sure he'd love to put the new toilet to the test."

I laughed along with Wendy. I was delighted to see her in such a cheery mood. She was always more upbeat when she was with Andy. I knew she'd be heartbroken if her relationship with Andy didn't result in a more permanent partnership. I would be too. I loved both of them and would like nothing better than to see them marry and produce some grandchildren for me to spoil. For now, though, I listened as my daughter chattered on.

"Anything new on the murder case?" I finally asked when she was through elaborating on Andy's move to the ranch. I didn't expect much out of Wendy. Once the C.O.D. was determined, the county coroner's office was pretty much out of the investigation.

"Not much that I know about. One of Pastor Steiner's daughters, Paula Bankston, stopped by the office here today to pick up a copy of the autopsy report. She told us it was urgent. She said she needed a couple of copies of the death certificate too, but I informed Paula she'd have to get those through the funeral director. I also got the information on her dad's services from her."

"Why would his daughter need a copy of the autopsy report so urgently? I can understand needing copies of the death certificate."

"I don't know," Wendy said. "Probably just wanted it for her own curiosity. It's not that uncommon for members of a deceased one's family to ask for a copy, particularly when a homicide is involved. We get that request fairly often. The family often wants to know every single detail involving the death of their loved one. They may even need a copy for legal reasons, because they're usually extremely keen on seeing the killer brought to justice, or sometimes just to prove to an insurance company that the death wasn't a suicide."

"Oh, of course. Well, I can understand why they'd be interested, especially in these circumstances. And there's sure to be some legal ramifications when all is said and done. So when's the funeral?"

"The visitation is Monday night, six to eight, and the funeral is to be held Tuesday morning at ten. The services will obviously be held at the Rockdale Baptist Church. Paula told me they'd found a temporary replacement for her father named Robert Zimmerman, but everyone supposedly calls him

Reverend Bob," Wendy said. "He'll be the interim pastor until a full-time one can be hired."

"And he'll preside over the funeral services?"

"Yes, and at church services tomorrow. He's from Topeka, so it's quite a drive for him, and he doesn't want to move here and take the job permanently. He actually took Pastor Steiner's job when Steiner left his church in Topeka to come minister at the Rockdale Baptist Church. So he knew Steiner personally. That Topeka church has a recently retired back-up pastor, and he'll fill in for Reverend Bob while Bob presides over the services at your church."

"So Reverend Bob will step in to fill Steiner's shoes?"

"Yes, but only for the time being. Like I said, he'll be there on Sundays until they find a permanent pastor for the church, so eventually he'll go back to his church to relieve the retired minister. Pastor Bob lives just a couple of blocks from Teddy, Steiner's oldest son, the one Wyatt told me had a drug problem. Teddy still lives in Topeka, where all Steiner's kids grew up, but he's in Rockdale right now being questioned by the police. It's a small world, huh?"

"Yes, it really is," I said. "I'm amazed all the time by how everyone seems to be connected in one way or another. I believe if you talk to anyone long enough you'll discover there's some person you both know in common. I ran into a fellow in a small café in Albuquerque, New Mexico, when I was there for the annual balloon fiesta a few years ago. We were discussing the specials that day at the café and I happened to mention my favorite taco sauce was Spanish Gardens. Turned out the fellow's grandfather owned the Spanish Gardens Company here in Kansas City. How's that for a small world?"

"You discuss your taco sauce preference with total

strangers?" Wendy asked, amused with my story.

"Safer than discussing religion or politics, don't you think?"

Wendy chuckled. "Anything's safer than those two subjects."

"Say, honey, why don't you stop by for dinner about six? Wyatt and our three guests will be at supper too. We're having turkey and dressing, like I told you earlier."

"And mashed potatoes and gravy?" She asked.

Mashed potatoes had always been my daughter's favorite food. She was thin by nature, but still too skinny for my taste. She'd picked up a few pounds in the last year, but not quite enough. Her face had a tendency to look haggard and drawn when she was tired. I tried to force food down her every chance I got. "If you come, I promise I'll make potatoes and gravy. I'll even make one of those green bean casseroles you like so much."

"How can I refuse an offer like that? I'll see you guys at six."

"Please call me Reverend Bob," the minister said, as he shook my hand at the entrance to the sanctuary Sunday morning after Stone had introduced us. "Reverend Zimmerman just doesn't suit me as far as I am concerned. You have my condolences on the loss of your former minister. It's a terrible tragedy and a great loss for both Rockdale, and the entire theological community. Pastor Steiner was highly regarded by all the other clergymen in the area. I held him in great regard myself."

"Yes, we still can't believe the murder happened," Stone said as he shook hands with Reverend Bob. "We can't imagine anyone wanting to harm Pastor Steiner in any way."

"I can't either. He was a gentleman of the highest caliber. Despite the reason I'm here, it's nice to meet you, Stone and Lexie."

"It's nice to meet you, too. Thanks for filling in on such short notice. I'm sure the congregation will all still be in shock at the services this morning. I know I sure am," Stone said.

"As I am," I added. "We can't tell you how thankful we are that you'd fill in for him the way you have. I assume you'll be taking care of all of his responsibilities and scheduled appointments until the replacement minister is hired."

Reverend Bob nodded absentmindedly, as he was turning his attention to the next couple in line. I was trying to be as polite and friendly as I could to him, hoping I could talk Reverend Bob into marrying Stone and me in a few days time. Unfortunately, I couldn't tell by his response if he felt obliged to fulfill all of the duties Pastor Steiner had lined up on his calendar, including that of officiating at weddings, of course.

We stepped forward to keep the line moving and selected one of the middle-of-the-room pews to take a seat in. I ended up next to the outside aisle, which I preferred in case I needed to go use the restroom in the middle of a sermon. I probably would need to go at least once to adjust my over-sized panty hose, which were dealing me fits.

I couldn't help but admire how handsome Stone looked in his charcoal gray suit. The color complemented his light blue eyes and silver hair perfectly. We'd dressed more formally than usual because of the circumstances. I'd even donned one of only a handful of dresses I owned. I'd probably owned the dress for twenty-five years, but it still fit, and it was such a plain and simple design, it would probably never go out of fashion. My wardrobe didn't exactly scream "fashion" to begin with. I wasn't going to get too concerned about the way I dressed until blue jeans and t-shirts went out of style.

The panty hose I was wearing were probably five years old, and I practically needed an owner's manual, and a refresher course, to figure out how to get them on. I was already uncomfortable and hoping—no praying—for a short sermon.

While Reverend Bob continued to welcome members of the congregation, I glanced around and waved at a number of people I recognized. Just as the line at the entrance was thinning, Wendy showed up. I hadn't expected her, but I wasn't altogether surprised she'd decided to attend our church on this special morning, the first service without our beloved Pastor Steiner. She'd been to Rockdale Baptist with us several times in the past year. Like all the others filing into the church, Wendy conversed with Reverend Bob for a short while before joining us.

Wendy sat down on the other side of Stone, and she and I whispered back and forth for a minute or two. She pointed out Thurman's youngest daughter, Paula Bankston, who sat in the front row on the opposite side of the room. Paula sat with another lady and two men, who I thought were probably all children of the late pastor. They all bore a resemblance to each other, and to the pastor, with their light-reddish hair, slim frames, and fair skin.

Reverend Bob Zimmerman began his sermon by honoring Pastor Steiner with a eulogy and the lighting of several candles. I fidgeted in my seat, tugging on the panty hose that kept creeping down into my out-of-style black heels. I'm sure the heels were in the height of fashion, back in the 1980s, when I still cared what everyone else thought about my appearance. But back then I must have not been too concerned about comfort, because the heels were causing my feet to hurt like crazy. My arches were cramping and my toes were beginning to go numb. I slid the shoes off and pushed them under the pew in front of me.

During the eulogy, I noticed Paula Bankston stand up and step behind the curtains that surrounded the elevated stage and pulpit. I was certain she was overtaken by grief and wanted privacy to compose herself. It was undoubtedly in very poor taste, but I wondered if this wouldn't be a good opportunity to get a word with her. I could express my sympathy, comfort her in her sorrow, and maybe even find out some tidbit of interesting information. It wasn't likely but, if there was a thread of possibility, I was willing to chance it.

I slipped my heels back on and excused myself, whispering to Stone and Wendy that I needed to use the restroom and adjust my panty hose. Fortunately Wendy didn't offer to accompany me as she frequently did. The restroom was located to the left of the stage, right behind the first panel of velvety curtain. I walked quietly up the outside aisle and ducked behind the curtain. Instead of going through the door to the restroom, I continued on around the back of the stage where I found Paula standing alone. She turned to face me as she heard me approach, but made no effort to acknowledge my presence. I could have been a stain on the curtain I was standing next to for all the attention she gave me.

I'd expected to find a sobbing, distraught woman, but instead Paula seemed to be in deep thought as she held a cell phone up to her right ear. She listened intently for a few seconds and then I heard her say her brother, Teddy, was up from Topeka and staying at the Sands Motel. She said she was surprised he'd even bothered to show up for church.

"That's what I'm thinking too," Paula spoke into the phone. Then she closed the phone and shoved it back into her purse just as I extended my hand toward her. I withdrew it once I realized she had no intention of shaking it.

"Hi, I'm Lexie Starr. Are you one of Pastor Steiner's children?" I asked, as if I'd just come across her accidentally behind the curtains and was making pleasant conversation.

Paula nodded, and then reluctantly introduced herself. She didn't appear to need comforting so I just offered my condolences and told her how fond my fiancé and I had been of her father. I informed her the pastor had been about to unite us in marriage the following weekend. "Now, of course, our wedding plans are up in the air."

"Congratulations on your upcoming wedding," Paula said. She sounded polite, but hardly interested. "I'm naturally very sorry this had to happen and upset your plans."

"I'm not concerned at all about having our plans altered," I said. *Liar, liar, pants on fire.* "The tragic loss of your father is all that concerns me."

"Thank you." She started to turn away from me, so I continued speaking.

"I think you might have met my daughter, Wendy, at the county coroner's office yesterday. She's the medical examiner's assistant."

"Wendy? Yes, I did meet her in passing," Paula said, still seemingly distracted by the phone conversation she'd just participated in. It was obvious she wasn't anxious to discuss my daughter with me. "She seemed like a nice young lady."

"Well, I think so. Wendy said you'd stopped there to pick something up. Let's see, what was it?" I was hoping to get some kind of response out of her, perhaps why she was interested in obtaining a copy of the autopsy report. Wendy had told me she hadn't simply wanted the information the report bore, but insisted on a paper copy of it. Paula remained silent, staring at me now as if she was wishing I'd dissolve and melt down into my black heels, like my panty hose seemed to be doing. Why had I bought panty hose that were three sizes too big? Had I been planning, at the time, to pack on thirty or forty pounds?

"Oh, yes, now I remember," I said, as if it had just come to me. "She said it was a copy of the autopsy report you were requesting."

Again Paula remained silent. I had to wonder why she didn't want to talk about it. Wendy had assured me it was not an uncommon practice for a family member of the deceased to request a copy of an autopsy report. Did she have something to hide? Was she afraid of what the autopsy report might show? Was she a person of interest in the case as far as the detectives were concerned? I was beginning to put her high on my own list of suspects.

"Yes, well, I've got to get back to my seat," Paula finally said. "It was nice to meet you, Ms. Starr. We're having a luncheon at my house, following the funeral service Tuesday morning if you'd like to join us. Nothing fancy, just some catered barbecue and side dishes."

I was taken aback by the offer. I would have assumed she'd only invite family members and close friends. I also hadn't realized she lived in Rockdale. She was turning to leave so I thanked her for the offer and told her we'd most likely attend, and wished her well. Then I headed back the opposite direction, toward the restroom door. I really did have to pee and adjust my hose, and I wanted to get back to my seat before Stone and Wendy got concerned about why I was taking so long. I could ask someone for directions to her house at the funeral. Nothing short of severe chest pains would prevent me from being at that luncheon. Minor or moderate chest pains could be overlooked for at least as long as the luncheon lasted.

I couldn't help but wonder if Paula had an alibi for the time of her father's murder. From watching a lot of *C.S.I. Miami* and *N.C.I.S.* shows, I knew the spouse was usually the prime suspect, unless they had a rock-solid alibi that could be verified. Steiner's wife had predeceased him. But other family members, such as the victim's children, were also often suspects until the detectives could put the smoking gun into someone else's hand. I didn't think it would hurt speaking with as many of Thurman's children as possible.

But for now I had to rush back to my seat. It was dark behind the red velvet curtains, my feet were throbbing in the too-tight heels, and I didn't see the cord snaking back from the microphone at the pulpit where Reverend Bob was speaking. Just as I reached the cord my bunching panty hose slid further down toward my knees, causing the crotch to end up about mid-thigh. This caused me to pitch forward slightly and catch the toe of my left heel under the power cord.

I swear I saw my life pass before my eyes as I began to fall in what seemed like slow motion at the time. I was grasping blindly for the curtain to grab and catch myself, when I heard a ripping sound as the fabric tore and I lurched forward, falling through the torn curtains on to the chancel. I felt something twist in my left wrist as it tightly clutched a strip of shredded velvet.

I then heard a collective gasp from the congregation,

and a shriek from the stage. I'm sure Reverend Bob felt as if he was being ambushed, and the same fate would befall him as had befallen the former minister. He probably thought there was a serial killer on the loose, who was targeting Baptist ministers. Unfortunately, the group gasp and the reverend's shriek were the last sounds I heard for several long seconds. As my foot had become tangled up in the power cord, the cord had pulled away from the electrical socket in the back wall of the stage. There was no power to the pulpit. The congregation now sat in mortified silence, still gun shy from the murder of their former pastor.

As soon as Reverend Bob was convinced I wasn't trying to attack him from behind, he rushed over to check on my welfare. I knew my wrist was injured, but I didn't want the embarrassment of an ambulance coming to collect me at the church. I told him I was fine, and apologized for disrupting his sermon. I couldn't have been more humiliated. Stone and I seriously needed to consider attending the new church in town from this point on. I didn't know if I could face anyone in the Rockdale Baptist Church again, especially Reverend Bob, who probably thought I was the village idiot. I'm sure he would love nothing better than to officiate my wedding in a few days. I decided this was not a good time to ask him.

The entire congregation was now standing on tiptoes, their mouths agape, trying to get a look at what was going on atop the chancel, behind the raised platform the pastor had been preaching from. I glanced over at the middle left section and caught the shocked expressions on Stone and Wendy's faces. I watched them slide into the outer aisle and sprint to the chancel.

It probably goes without saying, but Stone and

Wendy were not very happy with me. Stone looked disgusted, and Wendy was practically livid. I tried to explain to them I'd noticed Paula on my way to the restroom and had only approached her to offer condolences and to comfort her. For some reason they didn't believe expressing sympathy had been my sole intent.

We left the church service early that Sunday. Wendy left out of embarrassment, I'm sure. It wasn't the first time she'd wanted to be anyone's child but mine. Stone and I left to head straight for the emergency room at the Wheatfield Memorial Hospital in St. Joseph, where they put an Ace bandage on my sprained left wrist and given me a prescription for a pain reliever called Vicodin. They instructed me to keep ice on the sprain the first couple of days, in order to minimize the swelling, and advised me to keep it elevated as much as possible. They also gave me an injection to lessen the pain immediately. I was sure this day could not get any worse.

Once again, I was wrong.

CHAPTER 6

Lunchtime found us back in the kitchen at Alexandria Inn. I was feeling a bit groggy from the pain medicine they'd given me at the hospital. A shot of morphine and a Vicodin had definitely relieved the pain I'd been experiencing, but it had also left me with an out-of-body sensation. I felt like I was riding the ceiling fan and looking down at myself sitting at the kitchen table. It was an eerie feeling I didn't welcome. I had a strong urge to dust the tops of the blades of the ceiling fan too, something which hadn't been done since the inn opened for business. Out of sight, out of mind.

Very little had been said on the car ride home from the hospital. I don't think Stone trusted himself to discuss the incident with me while it was still fresh in his mind. He seemed to be mulling over important decisions, which made me slightly uneasy. With the wedding so close at hand, I didn't want him dwelling too long on my good and bad qualities. I was not sure the good traits would win in a serious comparison. At the moment I couldn't think of one admirable trait I had that would make anyone in his right mind want to marry me. My only hope was that Stone wasn't in his right mind at the moment.

Stone was busy making a couple of turkey sandwiches for us to eat for lunch, while I sat silently in the chair. I had unwrapped the Ace bandage and was holding a Ziploc bag full of chipped ice on my wrist, as instructed.

Stone put away the bread and mustard, and tossed a few Fritos on each plate, poured himself a glass of iced tea and me a cup of coffee, and set everything down on the table. He finally took a seat and reached over to grasp my right hand with both of his.

"Are you ready yet to discuss what happened this morning?" He asked. "I am extremely sorry you were injured, but when I agreed to be involved in this investigation with you, you told me you wouldn't try anything even remotely dangerous. I thought I could trust you, so I took you at your word, Lexie."

"I know. And I meant it, Stone. But how can walking behind a curtain seem like something dangerous for me, or anyone else, to do—even remotely?"

"I'll concede that point, Lexie, but didn't it seem, even to you, like an inappropriate time to question Thurman's daughter? Her father was being honored for his years of service at the church. Did you not think Paula would be more interested with what Reverend Bob was saying than listening to your words of condolence?"

"I only wanted to offer a quick word of sympathy and then proceed to the restroom," I said. "It wasn't like I was keeping Paula from listening to the sermon. She was behind the stage making phone calls. She didn't act one bit interested in what Reverend Bob was saying about her father."

"Need I read between the lines?" Stone asked.

"Don't you think it's a bit odd? I'm just saying—"

"Let's just get through the funeral before we start interrogating and pointing fingers at family members. Okay? We've got the visitation tomorrow night. You need to take another Vicodin and go lie down. I'm going back to St. Joseph, to the Home Depot, to have some paint mixed. I'd like to paint over those hideous orange walls in suites three and five before our wedding guests arrive. I thought a pale green would look nice in those rooms."

It sounded to me as if Stone was not seriously considering a postponement of the wedding ceremony. Did he think the murder case would be solved by Saturday, or did he really not care what anyone else thought? I felt a great deal of relief that he was carrying on as if nothing had happened to upset our plans.

I took the pain pill, as Stone had suggested, in case my wrist began to throb again. But I found I couldn't rest. I was too antsy and keyed up to take a nap. I started thinking about what I'd heard Paula say on the phone. This might be the only chance I'd get to talk with Steiner's oldest son, Teddy, if he wasn't out and about when I got to the motel. Speaking to all of Steiner's children at the funeral was probably highly inappropriate, but might also prove difficult, if not impossible, and Teddy was the one I had the most doubts about. He appeared to have a strong motive, and a lifestyle lacking in morals and convictions, unless you were talking about the legal kind.

The Sands Motel was just a few blocks away. Maybe I could run over there for a few minutes and be back before Stone returned from Home Depot. Stone probably wouldn't approve of my plan. Something told me he'd find me going over to a known drug addict's motel room, a bit loopy from the pain medicine and totally alone, more hazardous than me walking behind a curtain at church.

The Sands was one of only three or four small motels in town. I've noticed in my travels across the country, it seemed as if every little town had a Sands Motel, even if, like Rockdale, Missouri, it was located nearly a thousand miles from the beach. I wondered for a moment why that was so. The *Sands Motel* sounded to me like something out of a horror flick. Kind of like the Bates Motel in *Psycho.*

Well, I didn't have time to dwell on an insignificant matter such as the overabundance of Sands Motels if I was going to get to the lodging facility and back home in quick order. As I jumped to my feet, I felt a bit dizzy and had to sit back down on the edge of the bed for a few seconds. Vertigo, I told myself.

When I stood up again, I found the dizziness had abated, so I hurried down the steps, grabbed the car keys and my purse, and rushed out to my car. I didn't waste any time driving to the motel, where I parked my car along the curb and then walked into the front office. A young lady behind the counter was just hanging up the phone as I entered.

I greeted the front desk clerk and explained to her I was Teddy's aunt and had been sent over to pick up some papers we needed to give to the funeral home concerning some burial plots my brother, Thurman Steiner, had purchased years earlier. I'd forgotten to ask anyone what room Teddy was in, and could she please look it up for me. To my relief she was more than happy to help.

"He's in room two eleven. I remember checking him in," the clerk told me. "I'm sorry about the loss of your brother. It was a shock to everyone in town. I didn't know him but my aunt and uncle have gone to his church for years."

I agreed with her that the murder of my "brother" was a massive shock and thanked her for her help. As I turned away from the desk, I stumbled a bit and shook my head, trying to clear the fog that had settled over me temporarily. It was then I realized I'd probably taken the Vicodin earlier than I should have. I was suppose to wait four hours after they'd given me one in the emergency room, and it had been less than two when I'd swallowed the second one. I reacted strongly to pain medication as it was, and I could only tolerate a couple of different kinds, certainly nothing with codeine or sulfa in it. But I was already here so I'd have to tough it out and try to keep my head as clear as possible.

"Are you okay?" I heard the young clerk ask from behind me.

"I'm fine," I replied, without turning around. "I'm just upset about my brother's death, you know."

"Yes, I understand. Take care now."

Next to the front office door was a set of steps leading up to the second floor of the motel. I went up the stairs and turned right, walking straight ahead until I came to room two eleven. While I gathered my wits, I thought about what I might ask Teddy. But before I could knock, the door jerked open and a man, close to my own age, nearly fell out onto the walkway.

I caught him as best I could with an Ace bandage on my left wrist. He was clearly inebriated or strung out on drugs, even more than I, myself, was. He grabbed hold of my right shoulder and I helped him back into the room, settling him down on the king-sized bed in the room. I recognized him as the gentleman I'd seen with Paula and Steiner's other children at the Rockdale Baptist Church during the morning service.

But Teddy obviously didn't recognize me as the deranged woman who'd interrupted the sermon by crashing through the curtains down onto the chancel. Fortunately, he'd probably been already well on his way to becoming looped out of his gourd at that time.

"I don't need maid service," he said, slurring his words and thrashing his arms as he tried to wriggle himself up into an upright position. I didn't know which one of us was in the most imminent danger of passing out. I had to concentrate to make out his next words. "I need to get out of here. Right now!"

"I'm not a maid," I told him. Obviously the "Thurman's sister" story was not going to work, no matter how stoned Teddy was, so I thought for a minute before continuing. "I'm with the county. They send out a counselor to help grief-stricken people deal with their emotions after a murder is committed. It's like when a high-school student is killed in a car wreck and counselors are sent to the school."

"Oh, okay," he said. He was so out of it, I realized I could have told him I actually was his aunt, or even the center for the Boston Celtics, and he would have believed me. "What do you want? I'm pretty busy right now."

"I just want to speak with you a few minutes, to discuss your feelings and emotions about the death of your father. It won't take long. I've been sent to help you cope with your loss. It's what I do. Now why don't you sit up on the edge of the bed while I set in the chair, and then we can chat."

"I can't chat now. I've got to get out of here." His slurred words were barely coherent.

Before I could ask him why, two burly men, one black and one white, each with an array of tattoos and body piercings, came through the door that I'd intentionally left open. The larger of the two, the black guy, brushed me aside as if I were an annoying gnat, and grasped Teddy by the collar of his black leather jacket. "Were you and your girlfriend getting ready to go somewhere? I figured a low-life like you would try to sneak out without paying your debt. I'm here to pick up the money you owe, and you better cough it up right now!"

"I ain't got the money yet. But I'll get it soon. I swear on my mama's grave," Teddy whined. He looked terrified, which convinced me I ought to be terrified too.

I was thinking I'd stumbled into a drug deal gone bad and decided it was time to go back to the inn. I was headed for the door, when the other brute put his arm out to block my path. "You ain't going anywhere, sister. Your boyfriend here owes my boss, Harley, and Harley sent us to collect. Nobody gets away with stiffing Harley! Ain't that right, Rocky?"

"You got that right, Spike!" Rocky, the black goon replied.

Now I was getting scared. I was also feeling light-headed again, like I might faint, and was wishing I'd never left my bed. These guys were serious. Then I thought maybe I could pay off the debt and keep myself from getting hurt. I had a couple hundred dollars in my purse. I always carried around a little spare cash for emergencies. This was most definitely an emergency. "I've got two hundred dollars with me. How much does he owe?"

"Ten grand, lady," the white guy said.

Wow! My two hundred bucks wasn't going to impress them much. Ten grand bought a lot of drugs, I thought. No wonder Teddy was so strung out.

"Oh, I see," I said. "Never mind then. Won't Harley give him a few days to come up with the drug money? Teddy said he'd have it soon. He swore on his mama's grave. You heard him."

"Drug money?" The black guy asked. "Watcha talking about lady? Harley ain't no drug dealer, he's a bookie. Your moron boyfriend here owes him for some bad bets he placed on a horse race last week. We followed him here from Topeka, and we ain't going home empty-handed. Harley will have our heads on a platter if we do."

"Listen sir," I said, with more fear than respect. I was scared spitless and I was also beginning to feel a little "cougar-ish" with these fellows thinking I might be dating Teddy. "I can certainly understand why Harley would want his money. But I'm not this dude's girlfriend. I'm just a grief-counselor. Teddy's father was recently killed, and he's got the funeral and all to deal with. Can't you cut him some slack just this once? I'm certain he'll get you paid off as soon as he gets his father buried. Like Teddy, I'd swear on his mama's grave."

"I'm sorry his old man is dead, but a debt is a debt. His old man placed a few bad bets in his life too. The apple doesn't fall far from the tree, lady. If you ain't got the cash, you shouldn't place the bet." He turned his attention back to Teddy, who seemed to have sobered up significantly in the last few minutes. He was cowering up next to the headboard now, his hands in front of his face as if to ward off blows.

"The funeral is Tuesday, guys," Teddy said. "I promise I'll have the money by the end of the week. I'll deliver it on Friday, to Harley myself if I have to."

"Well, we'll see. I'll talk to Harley and see what he says. We'll be back later on tonight, and you'd better be here. Don't even think about skipping town or we'll be right on your ass. Hear?" The bigger guy said. "And you won't like what happens to you if we have to chase you down."

Teddy nodded. His huge sigh of relief was audible, as he released his death grip on the headboard. The two thugs left, slamming the motel door behind them.

I turned back to look at a massively relieved Teddy. "Will you really be able to pay Harley off by Friday?" I asked.

"I hope so, but probably not. It depends on how soon the money comes through."

"Swell. Well, Teddy, you've at least got a reprieve. You can hopefully get through your father's funeral before those two beat the snot out of you."

"I'll be lucky if that's all they do. And, hey, thanks lady," Teddy said. "I owe you one. But listen, I really don't need a grief counselor. I'm doing okay. Well, other than dealing with those two dudes. Really, I'm fine, so you can go ahead and leave now."

I was all for that idea. I was no longer interested in speaking with him anyway. I just wanted to get the hell out of there before someone else barged into the room. I'd learned quite a bit without talking to him much. He had gambling debts he was desperate to pay. How desperate was he? I wondered. Did the fact that he stood to inherit from his father have anything to do with Steiner's death? Was that the money he hoped would come through by Friday?

Could Pastor Steiner have also had unpaid gambling debts? Did a bookie have a score to settle with the pastor? I knew stiffing a bookie could prove deadly, or at the very least extremely painful. But with the pastor now dead, how would a bookie ever get repaid what was owed him? I still couldn't picture Pastor Steiner gambling or having any dealings with a bookie, but Teddy had not argued the case when the goon had insinuated both Teddy and his father were clients of Harley's.

"Okay, fine," I told Teddy. "I really need to get

home anyway. I may need to put on clean underwear after that little experience."

I nearly ran down to my car, suddenly feeling light-headed again as I opened the driver's side door. I managed to get home, but was having trouble concentrating on my driving. I'm not sure how many children I ran over in school crosswalks, but I tried as hard as I could to keep my eyes and my thoughts on the road. I was seeing two of everything. I felt like I was playing a video game, dodging oncoming cars the whole way home. It couldn't have taken more than three minutes to get to the inn, but it seemed like a half-hour. I was relieved to see Stone's truck was still gone when I arrived.

I could smell the aroma of coffee as I stepped into the kitchen. I saw there was still a cup or two left in the carafe. Old coffee was better than no coffee, and I didn't have the patience to wait for a fresh pot to brew. I needed something to calm me down and settle my mind, which was whirling off in a dozen different directions all at once. Even though coffee was billed as a stimulant, it always seemed to have a soothing effect on me. Well, at least the first five or six cups did. After that it was iffy.

My hands were shaking, and I was still breathing heavily. Just as I finished pouring a cup out of the carafe, I felt another wave of dizziness hit me. I reached out to steady myself with my right hand when my legs gave out beneath me and I crashed down on my left side. This time, with my second bad fall of the day, I not only felt something snap in my wrist, I heard it too. The last thing I remembered thinking was *thank God I made it home before this happened or there would have been hell to pay*!

The next thing I knew I was staring up into Stone's

blue eyes. He had a very worried expression on his face. "Lexie? Can you hear me? Lexie, what happened? Are you okay?"

When I was clear-headed enough to talk, I told him I'd gotten dizzy and lost my balance and instinctively tried to stop my fall with the left land, which now hurt even worse than it had earlier. "I think it was the last pain pill I took. I don't handle pain medication very well. I shouldn't have taken it so soon after taking the first one."

"It's my fault," Stone said. "I'm the one who told you to take another Vicodin and go lie down. I should have known better than to have you double up on the pain medicine, following a healthy dose of morphine. I'm really sorry, sweetheart."

I felt bad letting him think my condition was his fault, but at least he wasn't angry with me, as he would be if he knew the entire story. Not actually lying to Stone, just leaving out a few minor details, as I had a bad habit of doing, I said, "I tried to sleep but was too wound up. I thought I'd get a cup of coffee and relax in the parlor with it."

I looked around and saw pieces of my favorite cup, and puddles of old coffee all over the floor. "I need to get this mess cleaned up," I said, "before someone slips in a puddle or steps on a piece of the ceramic cup."

"No, you don't. I'll quickly sweep the ceramic shards out of the way, and then I'll clean the entire mess up later. Right now we're going back to the hospital to have your wrist re-examined. It doesn't look good to me. It's beginning to turn purple and swell up."

Back at Wheatfield Memorial, we passed by one of the E.R. nurses on our way to check back in. She had taken me to the x-ray room on our initial visit earlier that day. "Good grief, are you still here, Lexie?" She asked.

"I'm actually back, Terri. I've re-injured my wrist," I told her. She merely nodded, not at all surprised to see me there twice in one day. I'd been in this emergency ward numerous times in one year of being a part-time, and now a full-time, resident of Rockdale. I knew most of the E.R. staff by their first names, and they all knew mine. It was getting to be a little humiliating.

An hour and a half later we left, my fractured left wrist in a plaster cast. I'd been given another shot of morphine, to dull the pain, but I'd declined another Vicodin. That's what had brought me back to the E.R. in the first place and I didn't need both of my arms out of commission.

There wasn't much conversation between Stone and me on the way home. I sat silently while he talked about his trip to Home Depot and the paint he'd purchased. I was only listening half-heartedly, thinking more about how I was going to prepare and serve supper to our guests with my wrist in a cast and my mind still in somewhat of a fog from the morphine injection. I felt confident I could work my way around the injured wrist somehow, but the overwhelming fatigue I felt was something else entirely. Stone solved the dilemma for me.

I'd taken a frozen casserole out of the freezer earlier, and Stone convinced me to go straight to bed when we got home to the Alexandria Inn. He'd clean up the kitchen, fix dinner for the guests, and bring me some food on a tray. How was I ever so lucky as to have found a man like Stone Van Patten? I'd truly been blessed when he came into my life. How I hoped the wedding could proceed as planned. I wanted to tie this man down before my stupid impulsiveness scared him off.

CHAPTER 7

I fell asleep immediately. I didn't even recall Stone bringing supper up to me in bed. If I ate anything, it was unconsciously. I slept soundly through the night, until a dull throbbing in my wrist woke me at about seven. Stone was already up and about, probably downstairs in the kitchen debating about what to fix the guests for breakfast. I could picture them all sitting around the table over a bowl of Cheerios and a pop tart.

I got up and dressed and went downstairs for a pain pill and a cup of coffee, in that order. It was rare that coffee wasn't my first priority when I awoke in the morning, but my wrist was really starting to ache, and I wanted to keep it from getting any worse.

I was surprised to see both Wendy and Wyatt sitting in the kitchen with Stone. They all had a cup of coffee, and there was a box of store-bought doughnuts in front of them. Their chatter stopped abruptly, and all three sets of eyes watched me as I entered the room. It was clear Stone had relayed the news to them about my latest injury.

"How's your wrist?" They all asked in unison.

"I'm sure it'll be much better once I've had a pain pill," I said. Now all three sets of eyes bored right straight in to me. I could feel their glares slice through me, plum to the bone. The words "blooming idiot" seem to hang on the very tip of each of their tongues. "Trust me, the other pain medication has worn off, and this time I will wait at least four hours before taking another Vicodin, no matter how badly my wrist hurts. I just hadn't expected to have such an adverse reaction to doubling up on the medicine, along with the morphine injection."

"Have a seat," Stone said. He got up and poured me a cup of coffee. "Wyatt brought some doughnuts with him. Have one, so you don't take the pill on an empty stomach. Wendy volunteered to make some bacon, eggs, and French toast for the guests' breakfast. You can have some of that too, once it's ready."

"Oh, thank you, darling," I said to my daughter. "But I think I'll just settle for a doughnut this morning. I don't think my stomach could handle a heavy meal."

"Maybe by lunch you'll feel up to a decent meal. Don't forget we have a couple checking in around noon," Stone said, glancing back and forth from me to Wendy. "The Jacksons are in town from Texas for Pastor Steiner's funeral. Mr. Jackson's a cousin of the pastor. They'll be checking out the morning of the funeral and heading home afterward."

"I'll get suite four made up for them this morning," I told Stone. "It's the only one available on the second floor that's not in the process of being painted, and the other rooms still need a good dusting and freshening up."

"Are you sure you can handle it? I'll get started on the painting as soon as I've finished my coffee. We've got a full house scheduled for this coming weekend with people arriving for the wedding, if there's going to be a wedding this weekend, and I want all the painting done by then."

"Need any help, Stone?" Wendy asked. "I've got the entire day off and nothing to do."

"Sure, sweetie. If you don't mind lending a hand, I'd appreciate you helping your mother out. I can handle the painting by myself."

"Good idea. Mom, you take the day off and let me make up suite four for the Jacksons after breakfast is over with." Wendy talked while she laid out pots and pans and the utensils she'd need to begin cooking. "After you sprained your wrist I was afraid you'd need help. Now that it's broken, you could definitely use a spare hand—no pun intended. Other than the autopsy on Mr. Steiner, work has been slow this week. I'll ask Nate if I can take a few days off so I can assist you the rest of this week. And, like Stone says, *if* there is a wedding this weekend, you'll need help getting ready for that, too."

"I appreciate your help, Wendy, but one day of assistance around the inn is all I'll need. I'm not going to milk this little injury and inconvenience you and Stone. I may have to take you up on the offer to help me prepare for the wedding, however. Sheila Davidson will be here to help out too."

"Okay, we'll see about you handling the work here at the inn by yourself until Sheila arrives, but you're going to take it easy today. We've got the visitation to go to tonight, too, remember," Wendy said. "I know you well enough to know nothing will keep you from attending Pastor Steiner's wake."

"Yes, of course I plan to attend the wake. After all, he was our pastor and friend. All I need to do this morning is run by the bank to deposit a check, and to pick up a few items at Pete's Pantry," I assured her. "I won't do anything else all day, except rest and relax."

After several leisurely cups of coffee, I went back upstairs, leaving Wendy in charge of fixing breakfast. She'd always been a good cook, better than me. Of course, that wasn't saying much. I'd once burnt up a pan just boiling eggs in water. I'd gotten sidetracked and all the water evaporated out of the pan. Twenty minutes later I smelled smoke and burning eggshells in the kitchen and rushed to the stove to find my brand new saucepan had been ruined. There wasn't enough Soft Scrub in the world to save it.

I made the bed, as neatly as I could, and then applied a little makeup after bathing in the master bath. Bathing with only one useful hand, and having to keep the other one dry, wasn't easy. Still, I felt much better after drying off and donning a pair of sweat pants and an over-sized t-shirt.

I searched through my nightstand to find the cashier's check I'd been given for the balance of a checking account I'd closed at my former bank in Shawnee. I'd almost given up when I located it inside the latest best seller I was reading. I'd been using it as a bookmark. I was usually a lot more responsible with checks, but I'd been preoccupied with all the scheduling and details that went into organizing a wedding. I now had a lot more respect for professional wedding planners.

My bookmark was worth several thousand dollars, so I was relieved it hadn't been permanently misplaced. I'd just opened a new checking account in Rockdale, having previously transferred my savings over to a mutual-fund portfolio. With us both being a little set in our ways, Stone and I had decided to maintain separate checking accounts, with a joint one used for expenses involving the Alexandria Inn. Stone was going to take care of all major expenses, and mine would be used for small personal items, such as birthday gifts and clothes. I'd also have extra cash in it for emergencies. This check would be deposited into my own personal account. It would make me feel a lot more independent to know I could buy Stone a present without having to ask him for the money to do so.

I endorsed the check, made out a deposit form, and scratched down a few things on a memo pad I wanted to remember to pick up at the grocery store. I wanted to stock up before all the guests arrived.

Fifteen minutes later I was on the way to the bank, thankful it had been the left wrist I'd broken. Shifting gears in the sports car was less of a challenge this way. There wasn't a lot of spare room for maneuvering in my little car. I feared I'd break my turn signal indicator off the column by continually banging it with my heavy cast. I was like a bull in a china cabinet under the best of circumstances.

Traffic was backed up on Main Street. The state maintenance workers were shoveling asphalt into potholes. A bad winter had taken a toll on the city's streets. Eventually the flag man let us all pass. I turned off on Locust and then made a quick right into the parking lot at Rockdale Savings and Loan. There was no one else in the drive-through lane at the bank.

Sandy, who I now knew to be Coach Webster's wife, greeted me as I pulled up to her window. She looked like she was preparing to walk the runway at a fashion show. In contrast, I looked like something the cat had hacked up, in my old stained t-shirt that had large enough sleeves to pull on over the cast. I asked her if she was doing all right, and she responded affirmatively. I put my check and deposit slip in the little drawer she slid out toward me, and waited while she printed out a receipt.

"Did you hear about Thurman Steiner's death?" I asked, just to make conversation. Sandy nodded as she slid the little drawer back out.

"Yeah, it's too bad," she said. "A lot of people who are coming through my drive-up lane are talking about it. No one can believe it happened right here in Rockdale."

"Yes, this small town has had more than its share of murders in recent months. Does anyone have any theories on who the killer is?" You never knew who that one missing bit of information would come from. It didn't hurt to cover as many bases as possible.

"There are more theories going around than you can imagine," Sandy answered. "I think my favorite one is that Mr. Nelson, the Methodist minister, killed him in hopes of converting some of Steiner's parishioners over to his own church."

Sandy laughed, and I laughed along with her. I had hoped for a more feasible answer. Maybe someone out there knew something the investigators didn't. "That will never happen. We were all much too loyal to Pastor Steiner and to the Baptist Church in general."

"Yes, I'm sure you all are. I know a lot of people were devoted to him."

"Well, if you hear anything interesting, let me know." I laughed again, but not enough to make her think I was kidding about my request. "I'm doing a little investigative work on my own, you see, as he was not only my pastor and good friend, but he was to marry my fiancé and me this coming weekend."

"Oh, what a shame this had to disrupt your wedding. Do the police know you're involved in the investigation? I'd be afraid to get involved if I were a little bitty thing like you." Sandy chuckled again, as if the notion of me conducting my own investigation was the silliest thing she'd ever heard.

"Oh, well, despite this cast on my wrist, I'm not as fragile as I look. And of course, the police have full knowledge of my involvement. I've helped them out with previous murder cases that took place right here in Rockdale, and have been pretty successful I might add." Which was true, even though they didn't necessarily welcome my help. And they certainly were aware I was involved again this time, because they'd nearly arrested me twice for impersonating a member of the police department. But for Wyatt, I'd probably be behind bars instead of depositing a check.

It was apparent Sandy didn't take my comments seriously. I wondered what she would think if she knew her husband was on my suspect list and had been on the detective's list too. She wouldn't be laughing so much if she was aware there was a possibility Buck was somehow involved in the murder.

"Well, good luck, dear," Sandy said. "Have a nice day, Ms. Starr."

After leaving the bank, I turned back onto Locust, the most prominent industrial street in town, and headed east toward Pete's Pantry. I found a parking spot right up front. It was a narrow space, but I didn't need a very wide one for the convertible. It was yet another advantage of owning a tiny car. But there were some drawbacks too. The biggest disadvantage was that I couldn't buy very many groceries at any one time and get them all loaded into my miniscule back seat, and the trunk would hold no more than a bag or two. On more than one occasion I'd had to make several trips to the store to haul home enough stuff to stock the pantry. The more guests we had, the more groceries it took to keep them fed, and the more trips I made back and forth to Pete's. Of course, I was always welcome to take Stone's truck to the store, but it felt like I was driving a school bus in comparison to my own car, and then I had to worry about door dings when parked in a too-narrow parking spot. I didn't want to be responsible for any damage to his new vehicle that he took so much pride in.

Once inside the store, I grabbed a basket and began to select a few things off the shelf. We were out of vinegar, and the mustard bottle was nearly empty. I asked the butcher to cut me a large seven-bone roast, and picked up several packages of precut pork chops. Then I filled a few plastic bags with fresh fruit and vegetables.

We always needed milk and eggs, so I headed toward the dairy isle after grabbing a package of chocolate-chip cookies off the display at the end of the row. It was on sale, after all. I couldn't afford not to buy it when it was forty cents off its normal price. Besides, I had a broken wrist and a wedding in question. I needed comfort food in the worst way. What I didn't consume, Detective Johnston would, I was sure.

Once in the dairy department, I checked for broken eggs in four cartons and found none. Then I grabbed the last two gallons of milk in the row, assuming they'd have the longest expiration dates. Last stop was the bread aisle, where I squeezed loaves of bread with my right hand, looking for the softest, freshest loaf of sourdough, after squeezing all the sleeves of blueberry bagels.

I was on the way to the checkout stand with a carload of groceries already, when I noticed a display of spaghetti sauces on the end of the aisle, where most of the sale items were usually located. A jar of Prego for $1.69 sounded like a good deal, and there was no limit on how many a customer could buy. I decided to buy six jars of the sauce with mushrooms and garlic, even though the small amount of hauling space in my car was coming into play, and I was already pushing the limit. But my homemade sauce wasn't much to brag about and Prego was so much easier and quicker to fix. It would make for a simple supper for our guests. If I used every inch of the passenger seat too, I might be able to make room, I reasoned.

As I placed the last two jars in my cart, I looked down the aisle and saw Paula Bankston pulling a bottle of ketchup down off the top shelf to place in her cart. Before I could duck out of sight, she turned to walk toward me. It was a close call. Fortunately, she was concentrating on the various items on the shelves, and stopped in front of the pickles and olives. She was probably shopping for items she'd need to put out for the luncheon after her dad's funeral service the next day. I didn't want her to see me. I was still a bit ashamed of the commotion I'd caused at the church service honoring her father and his service to the members of the congregation. I doubted she'd have anything pleasant to say to me, and I didn't want to give her an opportunity to un-invite me to the luncheon. I hadn't been this thrilled with an invitation since Leonard Rutherford asked me to the all-school dance in junior high.

I stepped back out of the aisle before she could look up and catch me observing her. As I did, I bumped into the front of my cart and felt it begin to roll away from me. I turned to my left quickly to grab the cart and my left hand glanced off a jar of spaghetti sauce about halfway up the display. The jar teetered back and forth, while I flailed around hitting jar after jar with my plaster cast in an attempt to prevent the inevitable.

Before I could react to right the jars, they began

cascading to the floor, shattering one by one. Spaghetti sauce was splattering all over my jeans and everything else in its path.

"Oh, goodness," I heard an elderly lady say behind me. I was thinking something similar to that myself, but "goodness" wasn't quite the word that came to mind.

Not knowing what else to do, I bent down and started picking out the few unbroken jars and lining them up on the floor. I looked up to see Paula staring down at me. She didn't acknowledge me, just shook her head in disbelief and pushed her cart back up the aisle. She had to be thinking I was the biggest klutz she'd ever had the displeasure of meeting.

"Clean up in aisle six," a booming voice said over the intercom.

The manager and two younger boys showed up almost instantly with mops and towels and other cleaning paraphernalia. The two teenage boys began picking out the larger shards of glass and placing them in a metal bucket. By their expressions, I could tell they were none too pleased with me. I knew they'd rather be hiding out in the back storeroom texting their girlfriends, or sneaking a smoke in the bathroom. The manager asked me if I was okay, but he seemed more angry than concerned about my welfare. I couldn't blame him. I was a menace to society.

"That's a very good price you have on the spaghetti sauce, Edward," I said, inanely, after reading the nametag on his white canvas apron. I gestured toward my cart. "See? I'm buying six jars. I'd be more than happy to pay for all the jars I've broken, too, at the sale price of course. I apologize for the mess, but it was strictly an accident. I haven't had long enough to grow accustomed to this cast."

Edward, the store manager, was kind enough to not

allow me to pay for the damage, even though he still acted upset with me. He told me to continue my shopping and to be more careful with my cast. The young men would clean up the glass and sauce and restack the few remaining unbroken jars. I apologized one last time and slinked off toward the paper goods section of the store. There I added two rolls of paper towels to my cart, so I could wipe as much sauce off my clothes as possible in the parking lot before getting into my new car. God knows I spilled enough coffee on my seats and floorboards without adding spaghetti sauce to the mix.

It was very embarrassing going through the checkout stand with red sauce dripping off my elbows and other assorted places on my body. Everybody stared at me while I pretended to read a *People* magazine I'd taken off the rack. At least I didn't run into Paula again. Seeing her at the visitation tonight would be bad enough. Why couldn't I get through just one full day without causing a catastrophe?

I walked into the kitchen with two plastic bags. One was full of used, sloppy paper towels. I'd asked for a spare bag when checking out at Pete's Pantry. I had red stains all over my blue jeans, and scattered red blotches on my pale yellow t-shirt to complement the stains and multi-colored blotches that had been already on it. Wendy looked at me briefly and turned back toward the sink. "I don't even want to know," she said. "You look like something even a cat would be afraid to drag home."

Stone came into the kitchen a few seconds later and I explained what happened at the grocery store to both him and Wendy. I didn't actually mention seeing Paula Bankston. I just told them I'd accidentally upset a spaghetti sauce display, blaming the entire incident on the unfamiliar cast on my wrist.

Stone and Wendy couldn't keep themselves from laughing out loud at my expense. I was glad they could find humor in my humiliation. I felt a bit betrayed by the two people I loved most in life.

Stone told me to go get some clean clothes on while he brought in the rest of the groceries, which I had crammed into every nook and cranny in my car. I'd be lucky if I didn't have egg yolk stains on my floor mats.

Wendy immediately pulled out her cell phone to call Andy so she could amuse him with the story about my mishap at the store. I wondered if it was too late to put her up for adoption.

Wendy insisted on preparing dinner for everyone. She fixed spaghetti, salad, and garlic toast, with an upside-down pineapple cake for dessert. The spaghetti was just her way of rubbing salt in my wounds. While she was fixing the sauce, I was trying to get some of it out of my jeans and t-shirt. I used an entire bottle of Spray 'n Wash. I ran the load of clothes through the wash cycle three times, just to be certain all the fresh stains were out, before I put them in the dryer. The clothes weren't even worthy enough to donate to Goodwill, but I couldn't bear to throw them away. They may have been barely more than rags, but they were the most comfortable rags I owned.

Stone set plates and silverware on the large oak table in the dining room, while Wendy dished up the spaghetti and meatballs. She has a great recipe for homemade meatballs that she learned from her grandmother on Chester's side of the family. I'd always had a great relationship with my mother-in-law. She taught me a lot about running a household when I was a new bride many years ago. But she drew the line at trying to teach me to cook. She told me she'd have better luck teaching a raccoon to crochet. I'd been a tad bit insulted at the time, but, even then, I knew she had a valid point.

After dinner, Stone and Wendy worked in companionable silence cleaning up the kitchen. Wendy was a messy cook; there was more spaghetti sauce on the counter than had been on me when I returned from Pete's Pantry. She could cook a bowl of oatmeal and use every pot and pan in the house. But as long as she cleaned up after herself, I wasn't going to complain.

I relaxed in the parlor with my standard cup of coffee and the novel I'd removed from my nightstand. Once again I thought about how lucky I was to have found a man like Stone. Chester had been a wonderful husband and father, but Stone was my soul mate. He made me want to be a better person, and the perfect wife and partner. Of course, I'd once wanted to be an opera singer and failed miserably at that too.

CHAPTER 8

"How are you feeling this evening, Ms. Starr? How's that wrist? I'm sorry to see you broke it in the fall," Reverend Bob said as he came up to greet Stone, Wendy and me at the visitation that evening. He assumed it was the mishap at the church that had caused the fracture. I didn't feel like elaborating and explaining the second fall that had succeeded it.

I pulled my cardigan tighter around my waist. It was a cool night, and I'd worn black slacks and a nice lavender top, and white ankle socks. I didn't even consider one of my few dresses, afraid to risk wearing those five year-old, over-sized panty hose again. I'd have never wormed my way into them, anyway, with a cast on one arm. I'd have a run in them before I got them out of the plastic egg. Just finding an outfit in my closet I could wrangle into with the cast on was a big enough challenge as it was.

"I'm doing fine, and the wrist isn't feeling too bad either," I assured Reverend Bob. I shook his outstretched hand without making eye contact and kept moving on into the sanctuary. I was embarrassed beyond belief about the debacle during his church sermon Sunday morning. I'd been going to ask Reverend Bob if he'd step in and officiate at our wedding the following Saturday, but was too mortified to do it after the incident at church. I'd been greatly relieved when Wyatt called earlier and told us he'd asked the minister at his own church if he'd marry Stone and me. Considering the circumstances, the minister had no reservations, but he did feel it might be a tad disrespectful with the situation being what it was.

"Wouldn't they rather postpone it, and wait to ask Steiner's replacement to officiate?" The Methodist minister, Tom Nelson, had asked Wyatt. Wyatt had replied that we felt Steiner's temporary replacement, Reverend Bob, probably had too much on his plate right now, and many wedding guests were expected from out of town. It would be difficult to reschedule this late in the game. Nelson seemed to see the reasoning in my reluctance to cancel this weekend's ceremony. Wyatt went on to give him directions to the inn and asked him to arrive there no later than two-thirty on Saturday. *Bless you, Wyatt!*

It was with a great deal of relief I'd thanked Wyatt for speaking to his minister and making the arrangements to have him officiate on Saturday. There was still a glimmer of hope the wedding could go on as planned without looking tacky and insensitive. Unfortunately, Pastor Steiner's murder case appeared to be no closer to being solved than it was at the moment Bonnie Bloomingfield had found his dead body.

Tom Nelson was willing to minister at our wedding, but obviously not without reservations about the appropriateness of doing so while Pastor Steiner's killer still walked the streets among us. Knowing this only increased my resolve to find the killer and see that he was apprehended and arrested in the next couple of days. Saturday was looming, only five days away.

When we walked into the sanctuary, we saw Wyatt and Wendy conversing up near the casket. We joined them after speaking to several of the church members we recognized. Most of them had been at the church the previous morning when I taken my ill-timed tumble onto the stage. As they glanced at my cast and asked about my welfare, I answered as nonchalantly as possible, wishing I were invisible. I took a quick glance up on stage and noticed someone had tried to temporarily mend the ripped velvet curtains behind the pulpit.

After a few minutes of pleasantries with my daughter and the police detective, I wandered off to mingle with other people in the crowd. Despite my embarrassment, I was hoping to catch and speak with some of Steiner's other children. I wanted to determine if any of them beside Teddy might have a motive to kill their own father. I didn't know if or when I'd get another opportunity to talk to them.

I avoided Teddy and Paula, for obvious reasons, and because they were gathered in a group with their siblings and their families, it was next to impossible to speak to any of the other brothers or sisters. I managed to find one of Steiner's sons alone at a water fountain and offered my condolences. He introduced himself as Steve Steiner. I spoke with him briefly, just to feel him out. Steve was very solemn and withdrawn, and claimed to have been extremely close to both of his parents. I couldn't find any aspersions to cast upon him.

A real estate agent in Delaware, Steve and his wife had just arrived in town an hour ago. His wife, Julie, had already been in nearby Overland Park on a business trip the past few days and had met up with him in Rockdale. Steve told me he'd listed his father's home in Rockdale and some property in St. Joseph with ReMax Realty that very morning, and arranged to have all the furniture and personal items in the house auctioned off. Steve Steiner certainly wasn't one to let grass grow under his feet. I didn't think there was anything else to be gleaned from a conversation with him, so I told him he'd better get back to his family.

Despite my trying to sidestep her, Paula did catch up with me as I headed back to join Stone, Wendy, and Wyatt, who were still up near the casket. She inquired about my wrist, and then asked me if I was able to get all of the spaghetti sauce stains out of my clothing. I assured her I had.

"I've heard that tomato-based products like spaghetti sauce are the best things there are for getting the stench of a skunk's spray out of something," Paula said. "For instance, you can bathe a pet dog in the sauce after it gets sprayed by a skunk."

"Oh really, how interesting," I said. I wasn't sure if she was making polite conversation or trying to infer I needed something to get the stink off me, so I didn't know whether to be insulted or amused. I chose to be amused, because clubbing her with my cast didn't seem like an appropriate thing to do at her father's viewing.

Paula then reminded me of the luncheon at her house following the funeral the next morning, which came as a surprise to me. I assumed she was hoping I'd forgotten about the gathering. I told her my fiancé and I would do our best to make it. I volunteered to bring a dish with me, but Paula declined my offer. Everything had been taken care of, she told me. She was no doubt contemplating the mess I could make out of a large bowl of baked beans.

I kept the conversation with Paula as short as I could. I was certain my face was still as red as those stains she was just asking me about. On the way back to join the others, I stopped to look down into the casket. I had avoided it up until now because the very idea of an open casket at the funeral of a murder victim gave me the creeps. I might need closure, but I didn't need nightmares too.

However, Pastor Steiner did look very handsome, and as if he were at peace. He didn't look like someone who'd been the subject of a brutal murder. I had to admit the mortician had done a fine job with him. One would never know my daughter had sawed his body apart like a jigsaw puzzle while searching for the cause of his death.

I looked at Steiner's hands resting on his abdomen, one atop the other. His nails were nicely manicured, and I noticed they'd left on what I assumed was his wedding ring, even though he now wore it on his right hand. I admired a widower who wore his wedding ring to the grave, even years after the death of his loving spouse. The wedding band was unique, a flower blossom and a leaf, in different shades of Black Hills Gold. Very nice, I thought. Very similar to, and almost as attractive, as the ones we'd purchased for Stone and me for our upcoming nuptials.

"Well, hello again, Ms. Starr," I heard a female voice address me. I turned to see Sandy Webster, and a stocky man with a military crew cut who had to be her husband, the high school football coach, Buck Webster. He looked like a football coach, or more precisely, a drill sergeant. He didn't look like a man you'd want to cross. If he had told me to drop and give him twenty, I would have probably done it right then and there, in spite of my fractured wrist.

I was surprised to see them at the visitation, not expecting the Websters to know the pastor. I was pretty certain they weren't members of the Rockdale Baptist Church congregation. But then, it was a small town, and everybody seemed to know everybody else in town, particularly a man who was as intricately involved with the community as Thurman Steiner.

After a few minutes of pleasantries, I excused myself and rejoined the others in my group. I listened as they discussed the season-opener baseball game for the Royals. When there was a pause in the conversation, I turned to point out the Websters to Stone and Wyatt, but they were no longer looking down into the casket. I glanced around and didn't see them anywhere else in the sanctuary either. They must have paid their respects briefly and left.

"I just ran into Buck and Sandy Webster," I said. "I wonder how they knew Pastor Steiner."

"Like us, they probably banked at the Rockdale Savings and Loan, where Sandy works," Stone said.

"Yeah," Wyatt agreed. "And Steiner's youngest son, Quentin, played football at the high school before he moved away from Rockdale a number of years ago. He was a sophomore on the team when I played for Coach Buck my senior year."

We chatted with fellow church members, and I reluctantly walked through the receiving line with Stone to give our condolences to the family of the deceased. I stopped for a couple of minutes and spoke with the Jacksons, the relatives staying with us at the inn, and then continued on down the line. When a good-looking young man in his upper thirties introduced himself as Quentin Steiner, I asked him if he'd seen his old coach.

"No, I haven't seen him. Is Coach Buck still here?" He asked.

"I think the Websters left already."

"Darn, I'd have liked to have seen Coach Webster," Quentin said. "He was like a second father to me back in high school. I haven't seen him in years. Anyway, it's nice to meet you. Thanks for coming."

"It was nice to meet you too, Quentin, " I said, sincerely. "We thought very highly of your father. I'm so sorry for your loss."

The line was still moving ahead of me and people behind me were waiting for me to move, as well. There was no way I could continue to converse with Quentin at this time, so I stepped forward to offer my condolences to his brother, Steve, who in turn introduced me to his wife, Julie. She had an air of sophistication about her, like her husband, Quentin, and beautiful long blond hair and sparkling blue eyes. They both had a very polished, upper crust appearance, and an authoritative demeanor.

On the way home I congratulated myself for getting through the visitation without incident. Even Stone seemed to breathe a sigh of relief as we pulled into the driveway. Now if the funeral tomorrow could go just as smoothly, I'd be happy. And then if a murder suspect was identified tomorrow afternoon, I'd be even happier.

At nine-thirty Tuesday morning, we were getting into Stone's truck to head to the Rockdale Baptist Church for Pastor Steiner's funeral. I had on a gray and pink pantsuit that hadn't been easy to get on. As it was, I popped a button off the cuff of the blouse, and ripped open a seam up the sleeve that I could mend later on. Stone had on a navy blue sports jacket over a new pair of jeans. I'd ironed creases in them to make them look more dignified. Wendy, who was riding with us, wore a strapless tan and brown trimmed spring dress. I feared she'd be a little chilly in the outfit, but had to admit she looked fresh and youthful.

"Mom," she had said, while getting dressed. "Do you think I should cut my hair? I'm getting tired of this style."

I'd worn the same short curly hairdo since I was a senior in high school, so I was hardly the person to ask about trendy new hairstyles. But I thought it was time Wendy updated her look to something more flattering to her thin face. Her straight, dark brown hair hung down to just below her shoulder blades. It had a tendency to look stringy, but I didn't think cutting it was the answer. All it really needed was some waves to look fuller. "Have you considered getting a perm wrap, or something like a spiral perm? I like the length, but I think it might look better with a little more body to it."

To get an idea how a spiral perm might look, Wendy had borrowed my curling iron and added some waves to her hair. I thought it looked terrific now, as we headed down the driveway. She seemed to be pleased with the results too. She even wondered out loud about how Andy would like the new style.

Finding a parking spot was next to impossible. We ended up parking two blocks from the church. As we walked down the sidewalk, we noticed a small faded red truck slowing down and pulling over to the curb in a spot Stone had thought was too narrow for his full-sized truck.

"Look, Lexie," Stone said. "I'll bet that's the truck that was parked at the pastor's house earlier in the afternoon the day Steiner was killed. It looks like Perry Coleman, the organist at the church."

"Yes, it is Perry. He's also an elder. Wyatt said he

was highly emotional when notified of Pastor Steiner's passing."

"I should think if he'd been at Steiner's house just hours before the pastor was murdered, Perry *would* take it hard. The killer could have come earlier in the day and killed both of them, not wanting to leave any witnesses. I'm sure the thought crossed Perry's mind," Stone said. "Or, it's even possible that Perry's presence might have thwarted the murder altogether. Overtaking two grown men would have posed a bigger challenge than just overpowering the pastor himself. Perry isn't a large man, but he's taller and heftier than Steiner was. And probably ten years younger."

Wendy and I both agreed. I felt certain the crime scene investigators had spoken with Perry. He was probably the last person to have seen Steiner alive except, of course, for the murderer. I wondered what he and the pastor had discussed that day. Could they have had a disagreement of some sort? Did Steiner seem anxious, worried, or out of sorts for any reason during their visit? I hoped to get a moment to speak with Perry before the funeral service.

Stone must have been thinking the same thing. He stopped on the sidewalk and waited for Perry Coleman to exit his car. Naturally, we stopped too. "Good morning, Perry. Would you care to walk with us?" Stone asked. Perry nodded and fell in to step with us. "It looks like there will be a huge crowd here this morning. The church grounds are already teeming with people."

"I'm not surprised," Perry said. "Thurman was a fixture in town and loved by everyone."

Well, not exactly *everyone.* There was someone out there who hadn't placed the pastor high on his or her list of favorite people. Would that someone be attending the funeral this morning? I'd heard it was not unusual at all for the killer to show up, pretending to mourn the deceased to help ward off suspicion.

"Are you playing the organ at the service this morning?" Stone asked.

"Yes, I'll be playing 'The Old Rugged Cross' and 'In the Garden' with Frieda singing the vocals. The hymns were selected by Thurman's children."

"Good song choices," Stone said. "I heard the family also selected a casket made of solid oak. Those are beautiful, but quite expensive."

Enough small talk, I thought. We'd be at the church in a short amount of time. Before they started discussing the types of flowers in the casket spread, I decided to jump in with some questions of my own.

"Detective Wyatt Johnston, who's a good friend of ours, told us you were at the pastor's house, making a social call, earlier on the day of his death. With that being so, it must have been a terrible shock to you to hear he'd been killed just hours later."

"Yes, I was shocked and quite devastated. I just broke down at the news," Perry said. "But it wasn't strictly what you'd call a social call. We were deliberating on whether or not to add a Bible study class for teenagers and young adults. We'd argued about this many times before. Thurman told me we couldn't afford it at this time because the church was experiencing some financial troubles. But I thought, and still think, making the church attractive to youth is essential to the future of the church. We need to draw young people into the fold anyway we can."

"So what did you decide?"

"We couldn't come to a compromise, so we decided to put the matter on the shelf for the time being. We chatted about other church matters over a couple of glasses of wine, and then I left, never expecting it to be the last time I'd see Thurman alive."

How badly did Perry want a new Bible study class? Had he taken it back off the shelf and decided to settle the matter once and for all? I couldn't imagine an elder of the church committing cold-blooded murder, against the pastor of all people. But nobody could be ruled out until a suspect was apprehended and convicted. How spirited had their discussion about the class been? Had it elevated beyond a civil debate? Could Perry possibly be that passionate about a Bible study class for the youth in town? I knew Perry and his wife had several teenagers in their family, but it still seemed like a stretch to me. A Bible class was not worth killing over, for God's sake!

"Perry, do you know why the church is having financial problems? It seems to me with a congregation the size of ours, money would not be an issue. How much can supporting a Bible study class cost? It seems to me it would be a nominal expense."

"I don't really know the details, because, although Thurman expressed a concern to me about the money problems, he didn't go into any details about the cause. He said the money seemed to be going out as fast as it came in, with nothing substantial to show for it. I'd like to talk to the treasurer, Betty Largo, to see if she knows what could be going on, and where all the income is going. I haven't given up on the Bible study class if we can get our spending under control. Whatever we can do to help keep our kids off the street would be a blessing."

I'd like to talk to Betty Largo too. Was something corrupt going on behind the pastor's back? Was someone on the financial side of things misappropriating the money? Had the pastor caught wind of it and been offed by the person involved in the misappropriation, maybe out of self-preservation?

I suddenly had the feeling that if you could find out who was behind the money problem, you could find out who killed Pastor Steiner.

We were almost to the front steps of the church. I had just one more thing I wanted to ask Perry Coleman. "Were you questioned by the police, Perry? I know they expressed a concern about who was driving the little red truck that was parked in Thurman's driveway hours before his murder."

"Well, yes," he replied. "And I was fingerprinted too. I was told it was routine, and that I was not considered a suspect in the investigation."

"No, I'm sure you're not. I was just curious."

"As it turned out, my fingerprints matched two that were found in Thurman's kitchen, but the detectives weren't surprised by that after I explained to them that I'd been to see him just hours prior to the crime, and had gone into the kitchen to pour Thurman and me each a refill of wine."

"Of course," Stone said. "I'd expect your fingerprints to be found in his kitchen, too. Well, here we are at the church. It was nice to see you this morning, Perry."

Now all the fingerprints found at the scene seemed to be accounted for. As far as I knew, none were deemed suspicious. That indicated to me that the killer wore gloves while murdering Pastor Steiner. If someone entered his house already wearing the gloves, it stood to reason the murder was premeditated. Of course premeditation had been assumed all along; otherwise the killer would not have shown up at the house at such an early hour. Could the presence of Perry's fingerprints have been prematurely dismissed? Had he discussed the argument he'd had with Steiner with the investigators? Had the treasurer, Betty Largo, been questioned by the police?

Surely Betty Largo would be at the funeral. I'd never spoken with her, but I knew who she was. She sang in the church choir, I recalled. Maybe I could find some way to speak with her and worm out a little more information on the church's financial situation. Talking to Perry Coleman had generated more questions than it had answered. I needed to find some answers to those questions.

CHAPTER 9

The place was packed. Mourners spilled out into the hallways, and out on to the front lawn of the Rockdale Baptist Church. It seemed as if everyone in town had come to pay their respects. There was no way this many people would be able to partake in the services if held in the inner sanctuary. I wasn't surprised when Reverend Bob Zimmerman stepped out onto the front steps and announced the service would take place on the large back lawn of the church. It was a beautiful spring day and the perfect solution to the problem. Chairs were being placed in a section near the front for those who were unable to stand throughout the funeral service, Reverend Bob informed the crowd.

Wendy, who had ridden with us, pointed out Detective Wyatt Johnston on the front steps of the church, just to the left of where Reverend Bob had just stood to make his announcement. Wyatt was speaking with the chief of police and two other detectives. I would have loved to be an ant standing in the middle of that foursome, listening with interest to their conversation. There had to be facets of the investigation Detective Johnston wasn't passing on to Stone and me. I'm sure he had some kind of protocol he had to follow, and I know he didn't want to encourage me in any way if he could help it. With my luck, however, if I were an ant I'd probably end up squashed beneath the heel of one of their shiny black boots.

We mingled on the front lawn with fellow parishioners, family, friends, neighbors, and local businessmen who had attended the funeral. Harold and Bonnie Bloomington were there and I spoke briefly with them. Bonnie seemed to be very alert and cognitive. She was having a good day. She told me she was still very upset over finding her neighbor's body, and wished she'd had the opportunity to do something proactive to prevent his death. I assured her that hindsight was 20/20 and no one could have predicted what would happen early that morning. I told her she'd reacted to the situation with due diligence, and should be commended for her actions. She beamed at my words of praise.

When asked how she herself was feeling, Bonnie told me she felt very good and had been working in the flowerbeds alongside the front porch. Harold merely nodded to acknowledge my presence. Apparently he was holding a grudge against Stone and me for insinuating Bonnie might be viewed as a suspect in the crime. We hadn't really meant to convince Bonnie she was a killer. In fact, we hadn't intentionally meant to upset either of them. I could have pointed this out but chose to ignore him. At least Bonnie didn't appear to be holding a grudge or resent me in any way. Of course, it could be that she either didn't remember me, or couldn't recall the anguish I'd put her through.

Stone was busy talking to Cornelius Walker, a

previous guest at the inn who worked as a manager at the local farm and ranch supply store. Cornelius and his wife, Rosalinda Swift, had been the first couple to marry in the gazebo Stone had built behind the inn. Pastor Steiner had officiated the wedding and couldn't have done a finer job. I so wished he were still alive and healthy and preparing to officiate at ours. His presence would be sorely missed.

We hoped to host other weddings in the gazebo and receptions in the parlor in the future. Part of the reason Stone and I had decided to wed there was to promote the idea around town. There was nothing more productive than word of mouth advertising. A photo of the Walkers, toasting with their fluted champagne glasses in the gazebo, ended up on the front page of the *Rockdale Gazette,* and was even more beneficial to our cause. Later that week, we received two requests to rent the grounds for future weddings.

While Stone was chatting with Cornelius, I walked over and greeted Larry Blake. I tried to ignore the fact he was staring at my breasts with one eye while checking out cloud formations with the other. "I barely recognized you in a suit, Mr. Blake. You sure do clean up nicely."

"Thank you," he said. "I did wear my nicest jacket. Natalie, did you know the Rockdale Police Department didn't even realize they had a Witness Statement Records Collector, or a WSRC, as you called it, on their staff?"

"Imagine that," I replied. Okay, this little chat was over with. I didn't want to have to explain my little ruse to gain information from Larry Blake. "It was nice to see you again. Got to run, Mr. Blake."

"The offer still stands," I heard him say as I walked away.

Mourners were beginning to file back to the rear lawn of the church. I hurried over to Stone and Wendy and found that Wyatt had joined their little group. He was explaining to them the recent developments in the police department's crime scene investigation. So far every witness and possible suspect they'd interviewed had been cleared of any wrongdoing, but there were still a couple of people they were waiting to speak with. I assumed the murderer was none of the people they'd cleared, or was a very good liar. If someone was devious enough to commit murder, he or she was surely capable of telling bald-faced lies to investigators. What would the killer have to lose at that stage of the game?

Wyatt assured me that Perry Coleman had been questioned and cleared of any suspicion. He reiterated the fact that the two remaining fingerprints had belonged to Perry and dismissed as inconsequential. He didn't believe, however, that Betty Largo had been questioned.

The detectives had spoken to all of the church elders, most of Steiner's neighbors and family members, and a few of his closest acquaintances. No suspects had been named, few additional clues had been found, and none of those few clues found had been productive in finding the killer. A number of tips had come through the hotline, but none of them proved to be viable. In other words, no progress had been made by the Rockdale Police Department, and, most likely, none would be made in the near future. I was very disappointed by this accounting. Wyatt tried to assure me it was only a matter of time before a suspect was apprehended. The investigators were being very thorough, he told me. "As always, they're doing the best they possibly can, given the circumstances, and the lack of evidence."

"Oh, I'm sure they're doing the best they can," I said, unconvinced. Their best was not proving to be good enough to get the job done. Of course, the Rockdale detectives were seldom called upon to investigate a murder, but they seemed to be getting more and more opportunities the longer the Alexandria Inn was in business.

"How are you doing this morning, Lexie?" Wyatt asked, after he'd finished with his update. "How's the wrist feel today?"

"Well, I'm still looking at the grass green-side up," I said, without thinking. Oh my God! Did I really just make that morbid off-hand remark at a funeral? Why couldn't I ever think before I opened my mouth and let words start spewing out? I needed to have my lips sewn together and be fed through a tube in my stomach. "I'm so sorry. I didn't mean to say such a terrible thing at such an inappropriate time and place."

Wyatt gave me a sly little smile, while Stone and Wendy just rolled their eyes and shook their heads. I hung my own head in mortification and followed them silently to the back lawn, vowing to keep my pie-hole shut the rest of the morning.

I noticed a grave had been dug and covered with a blue open-sided tent in the small cemetery located just east of the church. The mourners would walk to the gravesite following this memorial service. There would be no funeral procession through town with a long line of cars following a hearse. With the size of the crowd gathering, it was probably quite fortunate to have the cemetery located so near to the church.

Besides the obvious logistics, I also thought it was fitting for a long-time pastor to be buried on the grounds of his own church. The only more fitting final resting place would have been a sarcophagus in a holy chamber inside the church. Maybe the stone coffin could have been inscribed with John 3:16 or The Lord's Prayer, and have a golden cross at the head of it. I thought if there were ever an individual deserving of that honor, it would be Thurman Steiner. He had invested a lot of time, effort, love, and devotion to the Rockdale Baptist Church, in his many years as its presiding pastor.

Once the service began, people started crying, and some were out-and-out sobbing in grief. I took a tissue out of my purse and dabbed at my own eyes. The fourth of Thurman Steiner's sons, whom I'd yet to meet, gave a moving eulogy for his father, telling a few humorous stories about his childhood. He and his siblings had been surrounded by the love of a doting mother and father and were grateful for the good times they'd shared with their parents.

As I had filed past the casket earlier, I'd noticed Thurman Steiner still had on the Black Hills Gold wedding band he'd had on the previous night. It still rested on the ring finger of his right hand, so could possibly have represented something other than his long-time marriage to his wife, Stella. It could, in fact, represent nothing at all, other than the fact the pastor was fond of that style of ring. Either it held no sentimental value to his children, or they wanted him to be buried with a reminder of the deep love he'd shared with his late wife. I now felt a bit guilty that both my father's wedding band and my mother's engagement ring were stored in the jewelry chest at my home in Shawnee. I was touched by the devotion Pastor Steiner had still obviously felt toward his late wife and hoped my marriage to Stone was just as wonderful and lasting.

Glancing around, I saw Buck and Sandy Webster standing in the back of the crowd. Bonnie and Harold Bloomingfield were sitting in chairs up at the front of the large gathering. All of the pastor's children, and a few other close relatives, were standing directly behind several rows of fold-up metal chairs. I spotted Teddy Steiner talking to his sister, Paula. They were whispering back and forth, appearing to be engrossed in an argument. Both had determined expressions on their faces. I had to wonder what they were discussing. Teddy looked uncomfortable, but he appeared sober, at least. Paula just looked angry. Neither appeared emotionally distraught.

Steve Steiner, the real estate mogul, and his wife, Julie, stood off to the side of the casket, with solemn expressions on their faces. They waved or nodded occasionally to various mourners in the crowd. They made no effort to speak to those mourners, or to each other. They appeared almost detached from the events occurring around them.

Just as I turned to point the couple out to Stone, I saw the church treasurer, Betty Largo, slipping through the back door into the rear of the church. I pointed Betty out to Stone instead, and said, "I'd like to go speak with her for just a minute or two."

"Right now? Does it have to be done today? Is this really an appropriate time? I'm sure the detectives will speak with her."

"It's probably not a great time, but our wedding is just four days away now. I'm wondering why she is slinking back into the church. If she sees me, I can just tell her I'm on my way to use the restroom."

"Yeah, that worked out so splendidly the last time you tried that trick," Stone said. "If you have to do it now, I'm going with you to keep you out of trouble, if nothing else."

We were toward the back of the crowd, so were pretty much unnoticed as we returned to the church and followed Betty through the back door. Once inside we found we were the only ones in the back meeting room. I motioned for Stone to follow me down a hallway. Just as we rounded the corner we saw Betty looking to her right, away from us, and walking stealthily into a room with the placard "Church Treasurer" on the door. Why was she sneaking into her own office in the middle of Steiner's funeral service?

Betty wasn't an elder or anything of that caliber at the church, so it wasn't surprising she hadn't been questioned or scrutinized by the authorities yet. Maybe I could make the suggestion to Wyatt that she be questioned. An interview with the treasurer might wind up being fruitless, but, considering the financial health of the church, I felt it was justified and necessary.

We heard a drawer being opened and something being placed on a desk, and then heard Betty walking toward the entrance of her office. We ducked behind the open door of the sanctuary and waited silently for her to pass. She didn't carry anything in her arms. She opened the women's restroom door and went in. I could have followed her in, but thought better of it. I felt those precious minutes could be better spent prying in her office.

"We've got two minutes tops to see what she placed on the desk," I whispered to Stone. "I have a feeling it's something crucial to this investigation. We need to go in there just long enough to see what it is."

"I'm probably going to regret saying this, but you go and I'll detain her if she comes back out while you're in her office," Stone whispered back. "Go ahead now, and hurry!"

I couldn't believe Stone was going along with my idea. I must have caught him at a weak moment. I'd expected him to take hold of my arm and drag me back outside. Apparently, Betty's furtive actions had piqued his curiosity too. I nearly sprinted to her door and rushed in. The only thing on her desk, other than a statue of Jesus and a paperweight that had a depiction of Moses holding a long staff etched on it, were two ledgers.

I quickly flipped them both open to the last page with notations on them. I assumed these would be the most recent figures entered. Under the headings "Tithes" and "Weekly Offerings" in each book was a list of numbers. The dates on each line matched, but the numbers in the two books didn't; the figures on one were quite a bit more substantial than on the other. Was Betty keeping two sets of books? Was one ledger for the church and one for her own self-interest? It looked that way. Had Pastor Steiner been aware of this transgression? He surely had to be curious as to why the church was suffering financial woes.

"Isn't this a beautiful day for the service to be held outdoors?" I heard Stone ask, in a louder voice than the soft-spoken man usually used. He was giving me a warning. I pulled my cell phone out of my purse and quickly took pictures of the same corresponding page in each book. I hoped the pictures would be clear enough to make out the figures, so the authorities could tell they didn't match. I took two photos of each page, one close up, and one farther back.

I then closed the books, stacked them one atop the other, as I'd found them, and hurried back out the door. Fortunately, Stone and Betty were around the corner and she wouldn't be able to tell which door I'd come out of. It would appear to her as if I'd been walking through the sanctuary, most likely a late arrival.

"Well, have a nice day, Betty," Stone said as I

joined them. "What took you so long, Lexie? I thought you were directly behind me."

"I'm hurrying, Stone," I said. "It just took me a minute to put my lipstick on."

"That's fine. I didn't mind waiting for you."

"Good morning, Betty," I said. I greeted her before she could comment on the fact I wore no lipstick. Damn! Why hadn't I said "foundation," as it tends to blend in with your natural complexion? But then she'd have wondered why she hadn't seen me in the ladies' room applying the makeup, which is hard to do without looking into a mirror. I needn't have worried, however. She appeared too flustered to notice I'd even donned clothing before leaving home. "Has the service already begun, Ms. Largo?"

"Good morning, Ms. Starr," she replied. "Yes, it's only just begun. You haven't missed much. I just stepped in momentarily to use the ladies' room."

We nodded and retreated out the back door. I whispered to Stone, quickly informing him about what I'd discovered. As we reached the outside, Stone stopped me. He untied his tie and began to slowly retie it, while we stood just off to the side of the back patio. He put his finger up to his lips in a "keep quiet" gesture.

While Stone was fumbling clumsily with his tie, Betty Largo walked out a minute later, carrying the two ledgers. I understood Stone's reasoning now. He wanted to look like he had a reason to dawdle so he could see if she was intent on getting those record books out of her office, as apparently she was, as she had both tucked discretely beneath her arm. She had a knit shawl draped over her shoulders, which nearly masked the two ledgers she carried. She nodded to us again, and walked up to stand behind the Websters, who were still in the back of the crowd. We returned to stand with Wyatt and Wendy, who both gave us a questioning glance. "We'll tell you later," Stone whispered.

A couple of minutes later I looked back to where Betty Largo had chosen to stand and she was gone, as were the Websters. I didn't see Betty anywhere in the crowd. She'd made an appearance, probably spoken to a number of church members and other mourners so they'd remember seeing her at the service, and then had slipped in to retrieve the ledgers and head home with them before anyone noticed her carrying them. I couldn't wait to tell Wyatt what we'd witnessed.

I pulled out my cell phone to check out the photos I'd taken and forward them to Detective Johnston. The close-up pictures looked pretty blurry, but the other ones looked relatively clear. I think they would suffice in pointing out the differences in balances to the investigators. With the amazing equipment crime labs had these days, they could enlarge the photos and make the writing more legible, if need be.

We turned our attention back to Reverend Bob, who instructed everyone to bow their heads in prayer. After the prayer, Frieda Smith took the microphone. They'd been unable to move the organ outside for Perry Coleman to play, so Frieda sang her songs a cappella, and did a remarkable job of it. She had a strong, clear voice that carried well.

After another eulogy, and two more prayers, the group marched as one to the gravesite. As the vault was lowered into the ground, the sobbing intensified. Even Teddy and Paula were blowing their noses and dabbing at their eyes with tissues now. I saw tears well up in Stone's eyes, and I passed him a Kleenex. He was a tough guy with a soft heart, just one of the things I loved so much about him. It was one of the reasons I wanted to become his wife in four days time.

CHAPTER 10

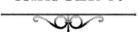

By the conclusion of the funeral, my feet were aching from wearing a brand new pair of shoes. We had an hour to spare before the luncheon at Paula Bankston's house across town, so we returned to the inn to change into something more comfortable. I put on a pair of black jeans and a short-sleeved sweater, along with my whitest pair of tennis shoes. At this point I was more interested in comfort than style. My wrist was beginning to throb, and I didn't want to dull my senses by taking a pain pill.

Stone removed his sports jacket and changed into a polo shirt. It would just be the two of us going over to the luncheon. Wyatt had to report for duty at the station, and Andy was picking up Wendy to go see some new improvements at the farmhouse on his new ranch property.

I'm the type who usually opts to be fashionably late to any social event, but today I wanted to be assured of not missing out on anything that might prove to be advantageous in the murder investigation. We were among the first to arrive at Paula's. Paula greeted us out on the large patio where the luncheon was to be held. Several tables were lined up to hold the food, and others were arranged for guests to relax and eat on. I volunteered to assist Paula in any way I could. I'd have to get past my embarrassment over the church incident if I wanted to garner any information out of anybody at the luncheon.

"There are a few dishes in the kitchen that need to be brought out and placed on the long table next to the swing," Paula told me. "Do you mind bringing those out to me while I place them on the table?"

"No, not at all. I'd be happy to lend a hand."

"Oh, yeah. I forgot you only had one hand to lend," Paula said, with a rather demeaning chuckle. "Are you sure you can pick anything up with that cast on your wrist?"

"Oh, I think so. I was carrying around dishes and bowls as I helped clean up after supper last night and it didn't result in any disasters." I felt smug when I said it, but the smugness quickly turned to embarrassment when I realized I was bragging about the ability to move a half-full bowl of peas from the table to the sink without causing a messy catastrophe. Not exactly like boasting about winning the Nobel Peace Prize, or graduating from law school. But Paula blew it off as she did everything else I'd ever said to her.

"Okay. Just don't pick up anything you might have trouble carrying. I don't want you to drop anything on the floor. I spent a lot of time making all these side dishes to go along with the catered barbecued meat," Paula told me. I could have guessed it wasn't my well-being she was worried about when she expressed concern.

I nodded and headed inside to the kitchen. Paula came in through the sliding glass door right behind me. To the right of the refrigerator was a built-in desk. On top of the desk were a laptop computer, a couple of loose pieces of paper, and several opened envelopes. I assumed they were unpaid bills and the desk was used for that purpose.

I was bending over to pick up a large bowl of macaroni salad when Paula brushed past me, straight to the desk. She snatched up the loose papers, folded them quickly and stuck them inside one of the envelopes. She then opened the top right drawer of the desk and shoved the envelopes into the back of the drawer. I got the impression she wanted to make sure nobody saw what was on those papers, especially me.

Was she afraid I would look at them when I made one of my trips into the kitchen to retrieve bowls of food? I was a little bit offended by the notion. Yes, I probably would have looked at the papers, but that didn't give her the right to assume I'd do such a thing. Some people could be so rude. My opinion of Paula went down a notch or two, and it hadn't been that good to begin with.

And now I *really* wanted to see what was on those papers. I'd have to contrive a way to come inside without Paula seeing me. Right now, however, numerous people were filing in and out of the house, and I had to get all of the food out to the table on the patio. I found I could grasp one side of the bowls with my right hand and balance the other on the cast on my left. I started making one trip after another, carrying cole slaw, pitchers of tea, baked beans, an assortment of condiments, a variety of desserts, and a pump thermos full of coffee. Once the task was completed, I pumped myself a Styrofoam cup full of coffee, and a cup of tea for Stone.

With everything that used to be on the kitchen table and counters now outside on the large table, I glanced around for Stone. I spotted him talking to Perry Coleman and another one of the church elders, as they stood beside a flower planter full of petunias. I joined them and handed the cup of tea to Stone while greeting the other two gentlemen. They inquired on the condition of my wrist before resuming their conversation with one another.

"I still can't believe he's gone," Perry said to Stone. "This all seems so surreal."

"It sure does," Stone replied. I listened quietly while I sipped at my coffee.

Looking around, I could tell it was going to be a huge gathering. People were still swarming in, and more were driving up the street looking for parking spots. Apparently, everyone Paula had spoken with at the visitation and funeral had been invited.

It was a sunny and mild day, with temperatures hovering in the mid to upper sixties. I was thankful I'd chosen to wear a sweater because I had a tendency to be cold-blooded, sometimes in more ways than one. Perry, however, was dabbing at sweat above his brow with a cloth handkerchief. I suggested he take off his suit jacket. I assured him I'd be happy to run it inside and hang it up on the coat rack I'd noticed just inside the double sliding glass door into the dining room.

Perry agreed and removed his jacket, thanking me and handing over the black striped coat. As I walked toward the house I saw Paula chatting with the caterers who'd just arrived with several large tin containers full of barbecued beef, pork and chicken. This might be the only chance I'd have to get a look at the papers Paula had stashed away in her desk drawer.

Damn, I thought to myself. Teddy was standing at the kitchen sink, running tap water into a glass as I opened the glass door, and walked inside. He looked up at me with an astonished expression. "I saw you at the funeral," he said. "I was surprised the county sent their grief counselor to the funeral, and I'm even more surprised to see you here at the luncheon. You are really devoted to your job, aren't you?"

"Well, Teddy, it just so happens I also went to your dad's church, so I knew him personally. I'm kind of wearing two hats at once to this function."

"Oh, I see." I could tell he was just being polite. He probably still felt a certain degree of gratitude toward me for convincing the goons to give him a reprieve, albeit a short one. I stood up for Teddy when most county grief counselors might not have.

"How are you doing?" I asked.

"Okay, I guess."

"Are you going to be able to pay off Harley by Friday like you promised him? In both my professional and personal capacities, I'm worried about your welfare."

"Thanks," he said. Teddy seemed completely sober to me, but very jittery and uptight. "I don't know yet if the money is going to come through by then or not. I sure hope so."

"For your sake, I do too. Those thugs aren't the sort of people you want to piss off, you know."

"Yes, I know. Been there, done that! And I'm lucky to still be here to talk about it. I guess I'm just a slow learner."

My chance to check out the hidden papers was thwarted, so I walked over to the coat rack and hung Perry's jacket over one of the hooks. As I turned to leave I saw Teddy put a pill in his mouth and swallow it with the glass of water he held in his hand. He was either taking something to calm his nerves or quell a headache, or he was taking some kind of narcotic, and his sobriety would be short-lived. I hoped, for his sake, he had a blinding headache.

Once outside, I stopped at the beverage cart and poured myself another cup of coffee. At this rate I would need to use the restroom soon, which would present another opportunity to enter the house. Of course, I could use this excuse whether or not I actually had to pee. Unless Paula had x-ray vision, she had no way of knowing how full my bladder was. And, truth be told, I had a bladder akin to that of a camel. For a reasonably petite person, I was fortunate enough to be able to hold cup after cup of coffee on a long road trip without visiting every rest area on the way.

I rejoined Stone and Perry. They were discussing the benefits of starting a Bible study class for the younger generation at the church. Perry was indeed passionate about his cause. He didn't feel today's youth knew enough about the Bible, and he thought the class was a way of keeping them off the streets and out of trouble. He stated that when he was much younger the church has saved him from a life of petty crime, and he saw this project as a way of giving back. When he brought up the questionable finances at the church, neither Stone nor I remarked on what we'd discovered about Betty Largo and the two sets of ledgers. We both felt we should keep this observance close to the vest until the authorities had investigated the situation further.

Stone listened to Mr. Coleman politely, nodding his head on occasion. I could tell he was tiring of the conversation as he glanced around for someone else to chat with. At his first opportunity, when Perry took a break to draw a breath, Stone excused himself to go speak to Harold and Bonnie Bloomingfield. I excused myself to run inside and use the restroom.

On the way into the house I asked Paula if I could use her restroom and she told me where to find it. She was in the middle of an argument with the caterers about the amount of pulled pork she'd ordered, so I figured I had a few minutes to spend in the kitchen without her presence.

Double damn, I thought. Now Quentin Steiner was in the kitchen. He was sitting at the dining room table, just ending a conversation on his cell phone. We greeted each other, and then I asked him if he'd gotten an opportunity to speak with his old coach, Buck Webster, at the funeral. He shook his head and replied. "No, and I was hoping to catch up with him. I see him at the high school football games sometimes but rarely get the chance to talk to him. And, unfortunately, he told Paula they'd be unable to attend the luncheon."

"That's too bad. I'm sorry you didn't get an opportunity to visit with him. Where do you live, Quentin?"

"I live with my girlfriend in Lawrence. She's taking some post-graduate courses at Kansas University. She's trying to earn her doctorate. I work at the Indian college there, Haskell University, as a biology professor," he said.

"Yes, I know exactly where it's located. Lawrence is not all that far from Shawnee, where I used to live. I've passed by Haskell on my way to Clinton Lake before. My fiancé, Stone, likes to fish for walleye and crappie at that lake."

"Oh, sure. I've had good luck fishing there too. We also take our jet skis to the lake a lot during the summer."

"That sounds fun," I said to Quentin. "Well, it's nice to see you again. I've just come in to use the restroom."

"Down the hall, on the left. It was nice to see you again too."

Despite multiple cups of coffee, I still didn't have to go, which, naturally, did not surprise me. But I took my time in the restroom, hoping Quentin would have headed back outdoors by the time I walked back into the kitchen. I waited several minutes to no avail. Quentin was still sitting at the table when I came back through. He was talking on his cell phone again, so I just waved and went back outside to the patio.

I pumped another cup of coffee from the thermos, and walked over to where Stone was conversing with the Bloomingfields. I noticed he was using the same line I'd used with Teddy.

"We are actually members of the Baptist Church, so we also knew Pastor Steiner on a personal basis, as well as being involved with the crime scene investigation," he said to Harold. Harold nodded, and greeted me rather coldly as I joined the group.

Bonnie looked a little dazed, but she greeted me in a friendly tone. I asked her how she was doing. She just smiled and looked down at the ground. I could tell she didn't recognize me, and was embarrassed that she couldn't remember my name. I just patted her on the shoulder and reintroduced myself as if we'd never met before.

Harold was telling Stone about the B-2 Stealth Bombers at Whiteman Air Force Base in Knob Noster. I stood quietly and sipped on my coffee as the topic of their conversation switched over to the ongoing war in Afghanistan. After about twenty minutes of listening to the two men discussing war strategies, there was a lull in the conversation and I told Stone I was going to go see if Paula needed any more help. People had begun filling their plates, and were sitting down at an array of card and picnic tables. A few set on lawn chairs with their plates resting on their laps. Some were situated on the steps leading up to the upper deck of the two-story home. A few of the younger men sat cross-legged on the stone patio, holding their plates with one hand and their forks with the other, leaving room for their elders at the scattered tables.

I found Paula, rearranging brownies on a platter, and asked her if I could further assist her in any way. She replied that everything was in order and thanked me for my earlier help. I then walked over to pump another cup of coffee, as if I needed another shot of caffeine, and found that the thermos was nearly empty. I think I'd drunk the biggest part of it myself.

I walked back over to the dessert table to inform Paula of the shortage of coffee and asked her if I could go brew another pot in the coffeemaker inside to pour into the thermos. I assured her I knew she was busy and I didn't mind making the coffee at all. She agreed, telling me where to find the Folgers and filters.

Hot damn! This time I found myself alone in the kitchen. Before anyone else walked in I hurried to the desk, pulling out the drawer and picking up the three envelopes. One was from the electric company, another from a carpet-cleaning company, and the third one was from a regional life insurance company, called Full Faith Insurance. This one caught my interest. As I slid the papers out of the envelope, I knew this was the one Paula had tried to hide.

Reading as fast as I could, I realized it was the official documents of a whole-life insurance policy on Paula's father, Thurman Steiner, and the coverage was for five hundred thousand dollars. Further down the page it showed Paula was listed as the sole beneficiary. This was interesting. I wonder if she'd informed the investigators of this fact. Having the papers loose on her desk indicated to me she was in a hurry to collect on the policy. Was she in a financial bind as others in her family seemed to be? Had Teddy hit his sister up for a loan to pay off Harley, his bookie? Is that from where he was hoping the money would come through before Friday? Or did he also have an insurance policy on his father? I knew they all had equal shares coming to them off the proceeds of the policy the church provided for the pastor, but knew it wasn't a substantial amount, and I didn't know how soon beneficiaries generally collected in a situation like this. I thought Friday would be pushing it, if Teddy was depending on his inheritance from his father to save his scrawny neck from Harley's two goons.

Just as I started to fold the papers back up I heard the back door sliding open and Paula's sultry voice telling someone she'd be right back. I didn't have time to get the papers in the envelope and the envelopes back in the drawer. Acting on instinct, I flung open the door next to the desk and, still holding the papers I'd extracted from the envelope, stepped inside as rapidly as I could. I had thought it was a pantry or closet, but it turned out to be the door to the basement. I didn't have time to shut the door before Paula entered the kitchen, so I quickly and quietly made my way down the stairs. Hopefully she'd assume I had revisited the restroom, as I was starting to actually need to do.

As I reached the bottom of the stairs I heard the low growling of one dog, and the high-pitched yapping of another. It was not a walkout basement, and there was only one small window well so it was nearly pitch dark. I didn't know whether I wanted to be at the mercy of two angry, protective dogs, or one ticked-off Paula Bankston. In a moment of pure insanity I chose the dogs.

"Tiny! Moose! Shut up down there!" I heard Paula shout from the top of the stairs. I'm sure she was wondering why the basement door was open, but she was on a mission and too pre-occupied to walk down the stairs and check out the situation. Instead, she just closed the door. Then I heard the sound of a dead bolt sliding shut. She had locked me in the basement with her dogs, who didn't appear to want to share their space with me.

Now I decided I'd rather be at Paula's mercy. Was it too late to change my mind? I ran back to the top of the steps and banged on the door with my cast, calling out Paula's name several times. She must have just grabbed something quickly and gone back outside. No one came to my rescue.

Moments later a small bundle of energy rushed up the stairs toward me. My eyes were beginning to adjust to the darkness. With what little light was coming in through the one recessed window, I could tell it was a Chihuahua, a pint-sized monster who thought he was a Doberman pinscher. This must be Tiny, I thought, as he latched on to the bottom of my jeans leg and began thrashing his head back and forth. I backed down the stairs as I tried to shake the miniscule dog off me. "Down Tiny! Let loose! Get off me, you little shit!"

As I backed across the floor of the basement, still trying to free myself from the Chihuahua, I began to hear deep growling behind me, which soon turned into snarling. I could tell from the low timber of its voice it was a large dog. Then I heard the whining of puppies and knew I was in a world of trouble. A mother of nearly any species would fight to the death to protect her young. God knows I'd do the same for Wendy.

As I saw a huge dark dog approach me I, fortunately, also saw a wooden table out of the corner of my eye. It was right behind me, a couple of feet to my right. I could now see clearly enough to realize a huge mastiff was pursuing me. Just as she lunged at me with her gnashing fangs bared, I jumped backward on to the table with the Chihuahua still dangling from my pants leg, its back feet now off the ground as it was swinging back and forth like the pendulum on a metronome.

"Get off my leg, Tiny! Back off Moose!" I yelled, with a violent shaking of my leg that was attached to the small dog's incisors. Just then I heard the ripping of fabric as the Chihuahua dropped to the floor. I quickly lifted my leg up onto the table.

Tiny continued to yelp and Moose continued to bark and snarl. I was trapped up on the table in the extremely dark basement, and I was terrified. I'd always had a healthy fear of dogs, and now my heart was racing at full throttle. I really did have to pee now, too. Naturally, the coffee would wait to go through me until getting to a restroom was impossible. I hollered out for help as loudly as I could but my cries apparently went unheard.

Back in the corner of the basement I could just make out the sight of four or five squirming puppies, whimpering for their mother. The mastiff puppies were already as big as, or bigger than Tiny, who was now jumping up and down like a kid on a trampoline, easily clearing the height of the table. Moose had her massive head draped over the top of the solid wooden table as I stood at the very rear of it. Slobber was running down both sides of her mouth. It was only a matter of time before one of them got a hold on me again.

When my breathing finally slowed down enough for me to speak coherently, I pulled my cell phone out of my pants pocket and dialed Stone. When he answered,

I spoke loudly to be heard over the dogs, who hadn't forgotten I'd trespassed onto their territory. Neither one of the dogs showed any indication of backing off.

"Where are you, Lexie? When you didn't come back after a few minutes, I asked Paula where you were. She said you'd gone to the kitchen to make a fresh pot of coffee and she hadn't seen you since. Are those dogs I hear?"

"I went into the kitchen to make a pot of coffee, and now I'm in the basement, and, yes, I've got two dogs anxious to rip me to shreds. How can I get out of here without Paula knowing I've been down here? She locked the deadbolt on the door when she came into the kitchen and I had to hide."

"Why did you have to hide?" Stone asked. "Or do I really want to know?"

"I've got something in my hand I think the authorities need to know about, and I didn't want her to catch me snooping in her stuff."

"Oh, boy. Well, we'll get into that later. Right now I need to get you out of the basement. I'll just go in the kitchen and unlock the deadbolt for you. No problem."

"It's not that easy, Stone. I have an ankle-nipping Chihuahua and a mastiff the size of a musk ox, who have me cornered up on a table. I can't get by them to get to the top of the stairs and escape. Moose, who I assume is the mastiff, has a litter of pups down here too, so she's even more aggressive than she'd probably be otherwise."

"How do you get into these situations with such regularity?"

"I'm sorry."

"Okay, I've got an idea," Stone said. "Andy just called, and he and Wendy are going to stop by here for a few minutes. They should be here shortly. If you hear voices at the top of the steps, try to get somewhere out of sight until you can make a safe escape. Okay? In the meantime, stay put where you're at."

"Of course. Please hurry."

Stone rang off, and I balanced precariously on the very back edge of the table, still clutching the papers I'd removed from the envelope sent to Paula by the insurance company. In all of the commotion, I had clung to the papers like a life raft in the middle of the Pacific Ocean. Even in the midst of pure terror I couldn't be distracted from trying to find Pastor Steiner's killer. I don't know what that said about me, but it probably wasn't an enviable trait.

I waited for what seemed like eternity, when finally the basement door opened and the lights came on. I heard Paula's voice at the top of the stairs. "Tiny and her pups are down here," she said. "Tiny is an English mastiff, probably the largest breed of dogs in the world. She weighs a hundred and ninety pounds. The male pups could end up weighing up to two fifty, but that's at the upper limit for this breed."

Tiny and her pups! I had presumed wrongly. Moose was the Chihuahua and Tiny was the mastiff. At least the names she'd chosen for her pets showed Paula had a sense of humor.

Then I heard Andy's voice as he responded, "I was so excited to hear you bred mastiffs. I prefer the temperament of the English mastiffs to the bullmastiffs. I've wanted one for so long, especially now that I'll be living out on some ranch property. It will be good company for Sallie, the golden retriever I've inherited."

The dogs switched their attention over to the new invader at the top of the stairs. The Chihuahua started up with his incessant yapping. I used the noise as a cover-up for the sound of rustling papers as I folded up the insurance document and shoved it into my back pocket.

"Shut up, Moose!" Paula shouted from the landing at the top of the basement stairs. The Chihuahua snorted in obvious discontent, and then continued its yapping as Paula and Andy began to walk downstairs to the basement.

While the dogs were distracted I stepped off the table and crouched down behind a workbench. I was hidden from view as Paula and Andy descended the steps. Peeking around the bench, I watched Andy brush Moose off as if he were an annoying gnat. The Chihuahua immediately stopped yelping, as if realizing he wasn't intimidating the intruder.

Andy walked straight up to Tiny and held out his hand. The English mastiff sniffed his hand and let Andy caress her head. I wondered why the dogs reacted so differently to him than they did to me. Perhaps it was true that animals could sense fear. Andy obviously had none where Tiny and Moose were concerned.

As he bent down to inspect the puppies, Paula stood behind him, with one hand on Andy's shoulder, while she related all the details of their heritage and birth. When asked, she stated a hefty price for each puppy. It was a figure that staggered me. Wouldn't a free dog at the local pound be just as good at keeping Sallie company?

I was surprised when Andy replied, "Okay, fine. I'll take this one, the runt. He seems to have taken to me the quickest."

I saw this as an opportunity to escape, but knew I couldn't ascend the stairs without being noticed and heard. Instead, I walked up behind Paula, and greeted both her and Andy. The dogs were now more interested in Andy than they were in me.

"Oh, my!" Paula said, startled. "Where have you been, and how did you get down those stairs so silently?"

I laughed, and said, "Everyone tells me I walk like a cat."

Paula didn't look convinced. I knew she was trying to visualize me being as graceful as a cat after having seen me fall through the stage curtains at the church and knock down an entire display of spaghetti sauce bottles at the grocery store.

Before she could respond, I turned to Andy, "Are you sure you want another dog? Two might be a handful for you."

"Yes, I really would like a puppy. It will give Sallie another dog to pal around with on the ranch. With all the animals I've got now, what's one more to feed and take care of?"

I agreed with him, but hoped he wasn't taking on the responsibility of a puppy that could soon turn into a two hundred and fifty pound eating machine just to help me out of a messy situation. The pup would probably eat his weight in Puppy Chow every day. I felt better seeing that Andy seemed genuinely fond of the puppy he was holding in his arms.

"When can I pick him up, Ms. Bankston?"

"Please call me Paula, Andy. Don't be so formal," she said, brushing Andy's arm in a feminine gesture of flirtation. *Hey, he's taken*, I wanted to say to her. *Keep your hands off my future son-in-law! Besides you're a good ten years older than he is.*

Paula giggled like she was fifteen, and said, "The pups are a month old, so should be weaned in a couple of weeks. I'll get your number and give you a call so we can arrange to get together then."

I'm sure you would love to get together with Andy again, Paula. I'm sure you'd like to get together with any good-looking young man who had that kind of disposable cash to spend on a puppy, you money-hungry cougar!

I was still ruminating about Paula's obvious attraction to Andy and the insurance policy she stood to gain a hefty amount from due to the death of her father, when Andy, said, "What do you think, Lexie? Would you pick this little one, or one of the others?"

I would pick a kitten, a gerbil, or some other pet that couldn't take my arm off with one bite. The last thing I would pick was an English mastiff puppy who would be the size of a Shetland pony within a year or so.

"Whichever one appeals the most to you, Andy, is the one you should get," I said.

"This runt's a male, and that's preferable to me since I don't want to breed them or have any litters of pups. I'll get him neutered, and he should get along fine with Sallie."

"What will you call him?" Paula asked Andy. I noticed she couldn't seem to speak to him without touching his arm at the same time.

"I think I'll let my girlfriend, Wendy, name him. She's outside on the patio."

Paula took a step back, as if offended by his reference to Wendy. I couldn't have been prouder. He'd even referred to my daughter as his girlfriend, a fact that would surely thrill Wendy when I told her about the incident later on that evening. *That's my boy, Andy! Now if Wendy can just be as fortunate to snag Andy, as I am to marry his uncle, Stone.*

CHAPTER 11

Stone greeted me at the top of the steps as the three of us went back upstairs to the kitchen. I was beyond relieved to see daylight again. With a worried expression, Stone whispered, "Are you okay? Were you bit or hurt in any way?"

I shook my head in response. "Only my favorite pair of jeans was damaged, I'm happy to report."

I took hold of Stone's arm and led him outside. Andy followed us to the far corner of the large patio. "How did you end up downstairs?" Andy asked.

I recounted the sequence of events that caused me to be trapped in the basement with Tiny and Moose. Stone and Andy's eyes met, and they exchanged a look that spoke volumes. Then I looked around and spotted Paula and Wendy at the beverage cart. Paula was filling a Styrofoam cup with lemonade. She leaned over and spoke to Wendy. I saw Wendy nod in agreement with something Paula said to her. I could tell Paula was sizing up the competition. I was glad Wendy had taken extra time with her hairstyle that morning. Knowing Paula was preoccupied, I pulled out the papers, unfolded them, and explained their significance to Stone and Andy.

After scanning the document briefly, Stone asked, "Did you notice this policy was just purchased a month ago? That seems like quite a coincidence to me. Could she have had a premonition of her father's impending death?"

"Or could she have precipitated it?" I added, dramatically. After all, I could be a real drama queen when the situation allowed for it. "Could she have purchased the policy as an investment in her future, and then made sure she cashed in on it as soon as possible? Could she be behind Thurman's death, either causing it herself, or paying a hit man to do it for her?"

Stone looked at me as if seeing me for the very first time. Was he wondering what he'd gotten himself into by asking me to marry him? I wasn't sure, but I felt admonished when he went on to say, "Let's not jump to conclusions."

"Well, Wyatt did say money was a great motivator, a common motive for murder."

"Yes, Lexie, but still we shouldn't be presumptuous. We can't assume Paula killed her father just because she bought a life insurance policy in his name a short time ago. It could very well be a coincidence, an extraordinarily lucky case of good timing."

Even as Stone said this, I felt more and more sure I had discovered the killer. After all, *presumptuous* is my middle name. "But don't you think we should show these papers to Wyatt?" I asked.

"Of course I do," Stone said.

"Then we need to get a copy of this document and get the original back inside in Paula's desk drawer so she won't know we're on to her," I replied.

Stone flashed me that odd look again. Wendy, who

had rejoined us, had the exact same expression on her face. I felt like I had the word *presumptuous* tattooed across my forehead.

"Why don't Andy and I go back to the inn and make a copy on your all-in-one fax machine?" Wendy asked. "We'll hurry and get back here as quickly as possible. This luncheon doesn't look like it's going to end any time soon. I can sneak the papers back into the desk drawer while Andy keeps Paula occupied outside with questions about his new puppy. She'll give him her undivided attention, I'm sure, because I can tell she thinks he's the best thing since dark chocolate Milky Ways."

Stone and I both agreed with her plan. Andy was always willing to go with the flow, so he fell right in line with Wendy as they rushed back to his truck.

Stone and I mingled with the guests while waiting anxiously for Andy and Wendy to return with the insurance papers. I wouldn't breathe easily until the original document was back inside the envelope and back in the desk.

I introduced Stone to two of Steiner's sons, Teddy and Quentin. Teddy now seemed a little out of it. He wasn't interested in chatting, so I turned to Quentin instead. "Quentin is a biology professor at Haskell University, Stone. He's the son who played football in high school for Coach Webster. He told me he and his girlfriend like to ride their jet skis at Clinton Lake."

"Oh, really?" Stone asked. "My friend, Wyatt Johnston, and I, have been there several times to go crappie fishing. We plan to go walleye fishing there this spring too. We've heard they like to hang around that little island in the middle of the lake."

"I've heard that also," Quentin said. "We don't just go there to ride jet skis. We swim at the little beach, camp out in the state park, and I occasionally fish there too. Do you use worms or crank bait when you fish for walleye?"

I left them to discuss the benefits of using different kinds of bait, while I walked over to approach Bonnie and Harold Bloomingfield.

"Hello again, Bonnie. Are you enjoying the luncheon?" I asked.

"Yes, the barbeque is delicious, isn't it?"

I hadn't taken the time to eat, or even given food a second thought since arriving at the post-funeral gathering. "Yes, I think her potato salad is the best I've ever eaten."

"Me too," Bonnie said. "And we just had a slice of the lemon cake, which is divine."

"I'll have to try it." I was happy to see Bonnie so much more lucid than earlier in the afternoon. It was almost like dealing with a schizophrenic. I never knew what personality she'd display when I spoke to her. I'd seen it change three times already on that day alone. The shock from having found her neighbor dead in his home must have subsided some. She was obviously having a better day now. Harold hung on to her arm protectively, but it was probably just a habit.

"How are you today, Harold?" I asked.

"Fine," he said. He obviously was not going to elaborate on how fine he actually was, or make any further comments to me, so I excused myself after telling them it was nice to see them again and hoped they were enjoying the luncheon.

I headed to the beverage table for another cup of coffee. I'm not sure who had ended up making a fresh pot. Most likely Paula had made it herself. My nerves were still a little frayed from my experience in the basement. I wasn't sure another hit of caffeine was going to help any, but decided to have some more anyway. Paula, who was still standing near the beverage table, stopped me as I turned to walk away. "Lexie, have you seen Andy?"

"No, not recently. I think I heard him tell Wendy that he needed to go pick up something at the inn. They should be back shortly."

"Oh, good," Paula said. "I forgot to tell him I registered Tiny's litter with the American Kennel Club, but he'd have to complete an individual registration form for his new puppy. I have some of the forms in my desk, and I want to have him remind me to give him one when he picks up the pup in a couple weeks."

"When I see him, I'll tell him to remind you."

"Oh, no, that's all right. I'll tell him myself. There are actually a few other things I want to speak to him about too," she said.

I'll bet there are, you brazen hussy!

Wendy and Andy were back at the luncheon within minutes. Paula spotted Andy the second he stepped back on to the patio. Wendy had no trouble returning the insurance papers to their rightful place while Paula flirted shamelessly with her boyfriend. I felt much relief knowing I'd barely squeaked by without being caught. I vowed to be more cautious in the future. I might not be as lucky the next time around. Instead of munching on lemon cake, I could just as easily be on my way back to the Heartland Memorial Hospital with lacerations sustained in a mauling by a mastiff. The very thought made my wrist begin to throb again.

As we pulled back into the drive at Alexandria Inn, Wyatt pulled in behind us in his patrol car. I was instantly glad Wendy had thought to whip up a batch of chocolate-chip cookies that morning. She and Andy had driven off in the opposite direction when the four of us left Paula's house. They were heading back to Andy's new property.

"How was the luncheon?" Wyatt asked as he took a seat at our kitchen table. He sat down in what I'd begun to think of it as "Wyatt's chair" since he was about the only one who ever sat at the rear of the table with his back to the wall. He claimed it was a cop thing—they never liked to sit with their backs to the door. The guests were all served at the larger table in the dining room, so only Stone and I ever actually ate meals at the small table in the kitchen.

"The luncheon was fairly uneventful," I said. Stone glanced up at me as I continued. "The food was delicious and a lot of people attended. Andy is planning to purchase one of Paula's mastiff puppies."

"Oh really? For how much?"

After I told him what I thought was an exorbitant amount, Wyatt shook his head and responded. "That much, huh? I knew there was a good reason I don't own a dog. I can't afford one on a police officer's salary. I couldn't afford to buy a mastiff puppy, much less feed one."

"I think my nephew has taken leave of his senses," Stone said. "But at least his new dog will have a lot of land to run around on."

"Yeah, sounds like he will," Wyatt agreed. "Wendy told me all about the property Andy just bought. Sounds impressive. Having gotten to know Andy a little, I think he'll really enjoy his time at the ranch."

I sat the platter of cookies down in the middle of the table, and said, "Yes, it really is very impressive. Some day when you're off duty, we'll take you out to see it. Here, Wyatt, have some cookies."

"Don't mind if I do."

While Wyatt gobbled down several cookies, I told him about the insurance policy papers I'd discovered at Paula's house. I was very evasive about how I'd come to have a copy of Paula's personal insurance document. I reached around to grab the copy of the policy, set it down in front of Wyatt, and said, "Do you think this is odd, or merely a coincidence? Check out the amount of the payoff and the date the policy was purchased."

As I scurried about the kitchen, straightening up and wiping off counters, Wyatt studied the papers with an intense look on his face. He brushed some cookie crumbs off the front of his shirt before responding. "I suppose it could be a coincidence, but what are the odds of cashing in on a half million dollar policy just a month after securing one on an extremely healthy parent? I wonder if the chief, or any of the other investigators, know about this. They may want to give Paula a second look. Can I take this copy back to the station with me?"

"Of course."

"I actually stopped by to tell you some news too," Wyatt said.

I instantly pulled a chair out with my good hand and sat down at the table. I didn't want to appear too over-anxious, so I brushed away a few cookie crumbs, straightened up the napkins in the napkin holder, and when I couldn't contain myself any longer, asked, "What's up?"

"I showed the chief the photos of those ledger sheets you forwarded to my phone. He sent me over to Betty Largo's house to pick her up and bring her in for questioning. She was whimpering in the back seat of my patrol car all the way down to the station."

"Did you handle the interrogation?" I wanted to know. "Was she booked?"

"Well, no, Lexie," Wyatt said with a sigh. "She wasn't booked. There will be charges coming down, no doubt, but she hasn't been officially charged with anything yet. And she wasn't exactly 'interrogated.' It was another detective who questioned her, but I listened in. It was very interesting. The investigation has taken on an entirely new twist. Your pastor had a whole different side to him that most, if not all, of his parishioners might not realize."

I have a tendency to munch on snacks when I'm excited and distracted, so I was shoving in chocolate-chip cookies even faster than Wyatt was. Suddenly I didn't care how anxious I appeared. Around a mouth full of cookie, I said, "Tell us about it!"

"Betty came clean about her involvement in 'cooking the books,' and claimed she wasn't alone in the scheme. In fact, the idea to embezzle money from the church wasn't even her idea. According to Betty, she was asked to participate in pilfering the money by no other than the deceased pastor himself, Thurman Steiner."

"To pay off gambling debts?" I asked.

Both Wyatt and Stone turned to stare at me in amazement. I was so giddy, I was on the edge of my chair when Stone asked, "What makes you say that?"

Then Stone turned his astonished expression toward Wyatt when the detective asked me, "How did you know he had gambling debts?"

"Just a hunch," I responded. No way was I going to offer up the story of going alone to Teddy's motel room and having a run-in with Harley's goons. I had gotten into enough trouble the last few days without stirring up even more for myself.

"Well, yes," Wyatt said. "You're right, Lexie. Steiner had been betting on horses and also spending a lot of his spare time down at the riverboat casinos. He'd gotten in too deep and asked Betty if she'd agree to skim twenty-five percent off the top and split it with him fifty-fifty. She told the detective she balked at the deal and refused to be involved in his swindling for a long time, but he finally wore her down and she relented. They'd been embezzling the money for about six months when the pastor was killed. Betty was hoping she'd be able to cover up the crime by destroying the second ledger that held the actual figures in it. She said she'd kept that book only for her own records and never meant for anyone else to ever see it, but I think that goes without saying. Betty Largo may have been too efficient for her own good."

"Did the investigators tell Betty where the photos of the ledger sheets came from?" I asked. If Betty was willing to go along with an agreement as she had with the pastor, what else was she willing to do to the individual who had turned her in?

"No, of course not," Wyatt said. "She was left with the impression a detective had come across the ledgers in a routine search of the church property immediately following Steiner's death. She has no idea of your involvement."

Stone let out a sigh of relief. "That's good. I was a little worried about that aspect of it. It's not that I'd worry about an act of retribution by Betty, or anything of that nature. But I don't particularly want word of our snooping in her office to get around. That wouldn't make us look much better than she does as an embezzler."

"Yeah, I don't want word of our involvement getting around either," I said, even though I didn't see that what we'd done was on par with embezzling money from a church.

Wyatt nodded. "I understand, but there's no need to worry."

"Is Betty considered a suspect now in Steiner's death?" I asked. "It seems like she would have a motive to kill him. She might have wanted out of the arrangement before they were caught, and been afraid Steiner might harm her if she tried to back out. On the other hand, she may have gotten greedy and wanted to continue skimming, keeping the entire amount to herself."

"So far there's nothing that ties Betty Largo to the murder. She claims she was at home asleep in bed with her husband at the time of the murder, exactly where one would expect her to be at five in the morning. Mr. Largo will be questioned, too, to corroborate her alibi. Betty claims he knew nothing about the embezzlement agreement, and that she was depositing the money in an account she'd set up in her own name. So far she looks to be guilty of theft but not murder. But she's not out of the woods yet, by any means."

"How about Harley, the bookie?" I asked, "Have you questioned him?"

Again both sets of eyes turned to stare at me in astonishment. I hadn't thought about what I was about to reveal before I blurted it out. If I weren't careful, I'd have myself backed into a corner and have to relate the entire incident that took place at the Sands Motel.

"Who's Harley?" The two men spoke in unison.

"Well, uh, you see—"

"Yes?" Again the question was asked in stereo. I knew I needed to tread lightly with my response.

"I was chatting with Teddy and he told me he owed some money to a bookie named Harley from Topeka. It was money he lost on a bet on the horse races. He told me he was really hoping 'the money,' as he put it, would come in soon so he wouldn't be harmed, or worse, by the bookie's two goons, Rocky and Spike. Pastor Steiner moved to Rockdale from Topeka, and I doubt there are any bookies in the small town of

Rockdale. So it stands to reason he might have had dealings with Harley too. Owing money to a bookie can be dangerous, even deadly." I could tell by Stone's expression he was wondering why this was the first time he'd heard about my conversation with Teddy, and about Harley, Teddy's bookie.

"Do you know Harley's last name?" Wyatt asked.

"No, but Teddy probably does, and being in debt to a bookie could be a strong motive for Teddy to murder his father for his share of the insurance money."

"I'll ask them to bring Teddy back in for further questioning. He never mentioned any gambling debts in his first interview. I'd say both he and his sister, Paula, could use a little more scrutiny. Good job, Lexie."

Wyatt's words meant a lot to me. It's the first time he'd complimented me on my efforts in the investigation into Steiner's death. He'd shown little appreciation for my assistance up to this point. It was certainly a step in the right direction.

I was also pleased to know that Betty had admitted to the embezzlement and that any future theft of the church's money would be thwarted. However, I was shocked and dismayed to hear about the pastor's part in it. I would have never pictured him as either a gambler, or even worse, a thief. I doubt anyone else could have imagined the pastor's secret lifestyle either. Probably the only person who'd be happier than me about this turn of events would be Perry Coleman. Now maybe the church would be able to afford a new youth group at Rockdale Baptist Church.

CHAPTER 12

"What's on your schedule for today?" Stone asked me the next morning when he joined me on the back porch for a cup of coffee. I was reading the *Rockdale Gazette* and momentarily wishing I'd opted to postpone the wedding. Saturday was looming, now only several days away, and our first guests would be arriving in the afternoon.

Sheila and Randy were from Fairway, Kansas, but had planned to spend several days at the Alexandria Inn, visiting, attending the wedding, and generally just taking a vacation from the usual grind of their busy lives. Fairway was only about an hour and a half from Rockdale, but they wanted a change of scenery for a few days. Sheila had been my best friend since seventh grade, but we seldom had the opportunity these days to get together and rehash old times and catch up on what was currently going on in our lives. I was really looking forward to her spending time with us, and I hoped the wedding would go on as planned so my friends wouldn't feel they'd taken this vacation in vain.

Sheila had always been as impulsive and adventuresome as I, which was one of the things that drew us together. I knew she'd be intrigued with this current murder mystery and I was hoping I could get her insight on the situation. A fresh pair of eyes might prove useful in the investigation. I could hardly wait for her to arrive.

She and her husband were due at the inn just after lunch, which would give me time to freshen up their room and do some light housekeeping around the inn. They'd never been here before, and I was anxious to see what their impressions were of both the Alexandria Inn and my new husband-to-be. Sheila and Randy had always gotten along well with Chester in years past, and I felt confident they'd be just as fond of Stone, whom they'd yet to meet.

While Stone and I discussed our plans for the day, we drank several cups of coffee and sifted through the paper looking for any news on the Steiner homicide case. At the bottom of page twelve, we found a short article about an investigation into the financial records at the Rockdale Baptist Church. The article was vague, and without much substance. It didn't mention either Betty Largo or the pastor by name. It didn't say anything about the pastor's gambling debts, or, thankfully, how the financial indiscretions had come to be found out. Basically the article only indicated the church's treasurer had been charged with embezzlement and fraud.

"We did good, didn't we?" Stone asked. "Since the financial status of the church is involved, and we are members of the congregation, this investigation affects us, as well as all of the other churchgoers. As much as I hate to, I have to admit your prying and snooping paid off in this instance."

"Yes, I agree." I wasn't sure I liked the way Stone

referred to my efforts as "prying" and "snooping," but I was pleased to hear him say that those efforts had been successful and beneficial to all the members of the church. I did hate, though, that my discovery implicated the pastor we had held in such high regard. Apparently, not all of our admiration for Thurman Steiner had been totally justified. But, like it or not, those implications were well founded, and we'd have to put the good of the church before all else.

"The Davidsons are due here in a few hours," Stone said. "I don't know whether to use the next few hours weed-eating, and sprucing up the grounds, or resting up on the hammock."

"You just got out of bed, dear. Why would you need to take a nap this early in the morning?"

"Well, I know how exhausting it can be just trying to keep a handle on you when there's a murder investigation going on. I can only imagine the chore it will be when you have your sidekick here to encourage and spur you on. I wonder if Randy knows what he's getting in to. More importantly, I wonder if I do."

"Lexie has been impulsive and unpredictable for as long as I've known her," Randy told Wyatt, as the four of us sat around the kitchen table, visiting and drinking coffee laced with Kahlua. "Sheila isn't much better, particularly when she's in Lexie's company."

"I figured as much," Stone replied. "Lexie has a knack for dragging unsuspecting individuals into her strategic plots and schemes."

Randy gave me an apologetic look as he continued. "Yeah, I know. And I don't mean to say there's anything wrong with having traits like impulsiveness and unpredictable behavior, but it can, and has, led to some sticky situations."

Wyatt nodded, with a wry grin on his face. "So I've noticed."

"Hey—" I interjected, but was quickly cut off by Randy.

"Stone, as much as I'd like to tell you these impulses will fade away with time, I'm afraid I can't. Where Sheila and Lexie are concerned, they never have and undoubtfully never will. But, don't worry. You'll soon get use to having to bail Lexie out of...unfortunate mishaps, I'll call them, but you will never rest easy again, for as long as you both shall live. God knows I haven't!"

Randy was being dramatic and chuckled at his reference to our upcoming wedding. He had a tendency to exaggerate when he was on a roll, but he soon had us all laughing as he related some of the stories he'd heard involving Sheila's and my past shenanigans. Even I had to laugh at most of them, like the time we got booted out of Girl Scouts for starting a food fight at camp, or the incident where I fell through the ice while we were skating on a small farm pond. Sheila had gingerly walked over and helped me get out of the icy cold water. Then when she asked me what had happened, I showed her how I had stomped my foot down to check the depth of the ice, and this demonstration caused me to fall through the thin layer again. This time I was on my own, for Sheila was laughing too hard to even help me out.

Sheila went on to tell Stone about the time we'd moved her trampoline to her front yard so we could see how high we could bounce by jumping down on it off the roof of her house. Naturally, I was the guinea pig who got to attempt it first. The trajectory of my jump sent me flying through the upper limbs of a tree, crashing down in the middle of the street that ran in front of her childhood home.

"Do you remember what you said to me after ensuring I was okay?" I asked my friend.

"No," she said between giggles. "What did I say?"

"You said, 'This time when you jump off the roof try to come down straight on the trampoline instead of at an angle so you'll bounce up and not out.'"

"Oh yeah, now I remember," Sheila said. "I was very interested in seeing how successful the stunt would be, but there was no way I was going to try such an idiotic trick after seeing what happened to you."

"I realize that now," I said. "And do you know what, guys? I really was stupid enough to do it again! Obviously, I was a very slow learner, and Sheila was very persuasive. I won't go into details, but suffice it to say, the second jump involved one of my many trips to the emergency room."

"And I got grounded for a week," Sheila lamented.

"And with good reason. See this scar?" I asked, as I pulled up my right pant leg. "It has 'Sheila' written all over it!"

Stone nodded at Randy, and said, "Just since I've been with Lexie there have been numerous trips to the emergency room. Believe me, I know all about the E.R. and all the people who work there by name."

After several cups of coffee, and a lot of shared laughter, Sheila helped me peel potatoes and carrots for supper to go with the seven-bone roast I had in the oven. The men retired to the den to watch a baseball game on television while I explained the current situation with the death of our pastor to my dearest friend. As expected, she agreed that carrying on my own low-key investigation into the murder was reasonable. "I can't get off work again next week, and I can't miss your wedding for anything in the world. I'll help you do whatever is needed to solve this crime as soon as possible so the wedding can go on as planned, without causing you any feelings of guilt or discomfort."

"Thanks pal, but we've only got a couple of days until Stone and I are scheduled to tie the knot."

"Between us, we've accomplished more than that in less time. If we put our two heads together we can surely come up with a plan. A fresh set of eyes never hurts, you know," Sheila said.

"No, I don't know about that," I said. "Remember when we climbed a ladder and fell off the roof trying to capture a June bug to win the 4-H scavenger hunt? Remember when the people who owned the house we fell off came outside to find us lying in a pool of blood in their driveway, and we had to explain what we were doing up on their roof? It's no small wonder we didn't both end up in a home for juvenile delinquents."

"Yeah, it was hard to convince them it was a June bug we were after, wasn't it? But we're older now. What possible harm can we come to just doing a little investigating?"

Wasn't that the same question I'd asked myself several times before? Hadn't I nearly come to great harm on each of those other occasions? What were the chances this time would be any different—especially with Sheila as my accomplice?

"Exactly what I thought," I agreed. "What harm could possibly come from the two of us working together to solve a crime?"

Sheila laughed, but I wondered if this might end up being fodder for another story of our disastrous impulsive decisions in the future. A decision we might both end up regretting.

"Randy and I are going to watch an old western on

TV," Stone said as Sheila and I cleared off the dinner table. The Davidsons were our only guests at the time, but more guests would be arriving the next morning, the Friday before our Saturday wedding.

After loading the dishwasher and retiring to the back porch with our ever-present cups of coffee, Sheila turned serious and she gently said to me, "Lexie, you do realize, I'm certain, that it is really too late to call off the wedding, whether a murder suspect is apprehended or not?"

Sheila leaned over and patted the cast on my left wrist, and continued, "I know how much you hate to risk offending anyone at your church, or even in the town of Rockdale, but you can't disappoint and inconvenience all the many people who would be affected by postponing your wedding at the last moment. I'm sure members of your congregation will understand this terrible tragedy occurred at too late a date for you to reschedule everything. And if some old biddy is upset with you, well, so be it. She'll just have to get over it."

I nodded and looked her squarely in the eyes, "I know you're right, but I so hoped this could all be settled before we exchanged vows in front of a substitute pastor. I just don't feel right brushing off Thurman's murder as if it was inconsequential. But I also know there's very little I can do about it."

"That's right, Lexie, if you could do something about it, you would, and you are trying to, but you also have to be reasonable when it comes to all the arrangements that have already been made by you and also by those guests planning to attend."

"I know I do," I agreed. "I don't think I really seriously let myself consider postponing the wedding because I knew the ramifications of such a decision. I believe in the back of my mind, I always planned on going ahead with the wedding this Saturday, no matter what happened with the murder case. I tried to convince myself the wedding would have to be canceled if a suspect weren't apprehended, even though I knew it wasn't feasible. I just hoped and prayed the killer could be caught quickly and make it all a moot point."

I'm not sure if I was admitting this to my friend or to myself, but I realized it was true. Stone had told me the decision of whether or not to cancel the wedding was up to me, and that he'd back me no matter what I decided. In the back of my mind I wouldn't even let myself dwell on the idea of postponement from that moment on.

Our conversation was a reminder of how much joy Sheila had brought to my life. She always knew what to say to bring me out of a blue funk, and exactly when to say it. She stood by me no matter what happened in our lives, and we'd never had a cross word between us. I marveled now at how youthful she looked, as I did nearly every time I saw her after several months apart. Despite the fact she was the same age as me, she managed to keep her body lean and fit, and had the kind of face that never seemed to age.

Sheila, who was four or five inches taller than me, at about five-foot-seven, had dark brown hair that had been somewhat frizzy as a child, but now hung straight and silky to her shoulders. The only concession to her age was a small silver patch of hair, about a half-inch wide, running down the right-hand side of her head. I found it totally endearing and was glad she didn't opt to keep it colored, as I might have done out of pure vanity.

"I guess it's settled then?" Sheila asked, bringing me out of my reverie.

"I think it probably has been all along."

"So, what's on our agenda for tomorrow?"

"We'll have a busy morning. We need to pick up the flowers at the florist's shop in the afternoon. I've got to purchase all the miscellaneous groceries, as well, such as the ingredients for the punch, the nuts, butter mints, and other refreshments, and the paper products we'll need. I should have had the grocery shopping already done, but I've been too preoccupied."

"Are we spiking the punch?" Sheila asked with a sly grin.

"Is there any other way to serve punch? I think we might all need a healthy dose of rum by Saturday afternoon."

"Amen to that! The wedding is scheduled for three o'clock. What all will we have left to do on Saturday morning?"

"Not too much," I assured her. "We'll just have to get the final details worked out and the gazebo and back patio all decorated and ready. The rental tables and folding chairs will be delivered around nine Saturday morning, and Stone and Randy can probably help out by getting them set up. Then there will be some minor details to take care of, but all in all, the day shouldn't be too hectic or time-consuming. But this is your vacation, and I don't expect you to work the entire time you're here. You've been pitching in since you got here."

"Well, we came a couple of days early so I could serve as your minion, as you have done for me on several occasions. I'm willing and able to do anything I can to help, so you can forget the vacation nonsense," Sheila said as she stood up and motioned for my coffee cup. "Sit out here and relax, and rest your bruised and battered body while I go in and pour us a refill."

"Thanks, pal! I'm so thankful you're here!" I handed her my cup and settled back into the cushion on my outdoor lounge chair. I felt better knowing the wedding was going to take place as planned, with the blessings of my dearest friend. I was sore and exhausted, but having Sheila here helped give me the burst of energy I'd needed. With her assistance, getting everything ready would be a lot of fun, not a taxing chore like it would be under other circumstances.

When Sheila returned with fresh cups of coffee, we turned the conversation toward more light-hearted topics. She told me what her two sons were currently doing, and how her job as a financial consultant was going. I told her about Wendy's job as the county coroner's assistant, and about her budding romance with Stone's nephew, Andy. Then we reminisced about our younger days and all the hair-raising experiences we'd shared, and some more of the predicaments we'd found ourselves in.

Finally, we got back to the subject of Pastor Steiner's death. I related everything I could remember to her about the case that I hadn't already told her, and all about my on-going amateurish involvement in the investigation. It was nice to have someone to talk to who wouldn't chide me about the risks I took in order to obtain as much information as I could. Sheila had seen me take a lot of foolish risks before, and was not above doing the same. I knew no matter what situation might arise, I could trust her to go along with my hair-brained ideas and still have my back.

CHAPTER 13

"I have always maintained there is no such thing as a coincidence," Sheila said as we sat on the back porch the next morning. "Even though you've decided definitively to go ahead with the nuptials, I still think we should look further into the murder investigation. Don't you? If nothing else, I know having the killer arrested, or just a suspect in custody, would make you feel better about the whole situation."

"You bet it would!" I answered enthusiastically. I couldn't help but feel some excitement at Sheila's comments. I was hoping she'd feel enthusiastic about my investigation because I'm not one to give up easily, and I still wanted nothing more than to see the killer brought to justice. Despite his shortcomings, I still considered Pastor Steiner a friend, and a fine gentleman, and I wanted justice served on his behalf.

Stone and Randy were establishing a fast friendship and shared an interest in fishing. Hoping for a mess of crappie, they'd gone to Smithville Lake with Detective Johnston, so Sheila and I would be left to our own devices for most of the morning. That was scary. The very thought sent a shiver up my spine, and I'm sure it gave Stone and Randy reason to pause, as well.

I set my cup down as I listened to Sheila thinking out loud. "I find it extremely odd that Steiner's daughter, Paula, would take out a five-hundred-thousand dollar insurance policy on her father just weeks before his death. I also find it strange his son, Teddy, would need money so desperately right at the exact time of his father's death. Don't you?"

"Yes, the timing in both instances seems almost too coincidental."

"Didn't you tell me that Stone's nephew is buying a mastiff puppy from Paula?"

"Yes. As I told you, Andy is purchasing a cattle ranch and inheriting a golden retriever named Sallie. He's buying this pup from Paula to be a companion for Sallie on the ranch. Why do you ask?"

"Well, I was just thinking. Who's to say I'm not in the market for a mastiff puppy myself?"

"You? You've got to be kidding! You've never owned a dog in your life, Sheila. You don't like being tied down to a pet because it interferes with your traveling. You wouldn't own a goldfish, much less a two hundred pound mastiff!"

"True, but Paula Bankston doesn't know that. I thought we could drop by her house on the pretense I'm interested in purchasing one of her pups. After asking some benign questions about the dogs, we can bring up the death of her father. Who knows what we might learn that has been overlooked by the authorities? And I might even be persuaded to ask some rather blunt questions about the insurance policy, because, after all, I don't really care if I piss her off or not. I have nothing to lose."

Sheila seemed very pleased with herself for coming up with this idea, and I had to admit it had a lot of promise. I wasn't particularly concerned whether I pissed Paula off either. If she had anything to do with her father's death, then she deserved to be upset, and if not, she shouldn't hesitate to tell us what she knew and be glad to help in any way she could.

"I'll give her a call," I said. "Maybe we can stop by her house on our way to Pete's Pantry."

"Good Morning Paula! Are you doing okay?" I asked, as the door opened at the Bankston residence. "I know how tough a week this has been for you, so I really appreciate you letting my friend come over and take a look at the puppies."

Paula nodded. She had very little emotion in her voice and an almost vacant expression on her face, as if nothing going on around her was even registering. I introduced Paula to Sheila, and she took Sheila's outstretched hand and gave it an unenthusiastic shake.

"Please come in," Paula said. "Tiny and her puppies are in the basement."

Unfortunately Moose wasn't in the basement and bypassed Paula and Sheila to make a beeline for me. He growled and firmly grasped the bottom of my jeans with his teeth. He then began to snarl as he thrashed his head back and forth, tearing at the denim fabric. At least I'd come prepared this time and worn an old pair of raggedy jeans I'd accidentally tie-dyed with Clorox bleach while cleaning all the toilets at the inn.

"Get down, Moose," Paula said, with what sounded to me like resignation. It was almost as if the sounds the dog was emitting were wearing on her nerves, and she had no concern for my clothing or my personal welfare. Paying no attention to his master's command, Moose continued his attempt to shred my jeans. I considered slinging him across the living room with my foot, and would have gladly done so if not for Paula standing right next to me.

"Wow! Moose has really got it in for you, doesn't he?" Sheila asked. "Whatever did you do to make him dislike you so much?"

"I really don't know," I replied. Perhaps referring to him as a "little shit" the last time we met had offended him, I wanted to say. Any five-pound dog, named Moose, must surely have a size complex. But I kept my thoughts to myself since Paula was not aware of my previous encounter with her dogs during the luncheon. She was still under the impression I'd only descended the stairs to her basement after she and Andy had gone down to check out the puppies.

Paula finally extracted the tiny Chihuahua from my leg and set it out on the front patio, closing the screen door behind him. "You two can go on downstairs. I'll be down in a minute. I need to visit the bathroom. I guess you remember where the basement door is, Lexie."

I assured her I did and motioned for Sheila to follow me. As we walked through the kitchen, I pointed out an envelope lying on the built-in desk. I silently tapped on the return address, which indicated the Full Faith Insurance Company of Independence, Missouri, had sent it to Paula.

Sheila glanced at it quickly and nodded. I had shown her an extra photocopy of the document I'd found in an envelope like this one earlier. I assumed it was the same envelope but couldn't be certain. Perhaps the policy had paid off, and this was a new envelope containing a check for a half a million dollars. I don't know if I could have left a check for that amount lying casually on top of a desk in my kitchen, however. I certainly wouldn't have used it as a bookmark. More likely I'd have duct-taped the check to my abdomen underneath a shirt and a sweater, and hightailed it to the bank thirty seconds after I'd retrieved it from the mailbox. Sandy Webster, the teller at my bank, would have already deposited the half million in my account, or possibly in two or three separate accounts so the entire amount would be FDIC insured. I didn't take any chances when it came to huge sums of money, nor was it a problem I dealt with on a regular basis.

Paula headed back toward the rear of the house as I opened the door to the basement. This time Tiny didn't raise much of a fuss as we descended the steps. I motioned Sheila back toward where I knew the mastiff and her litter were, and laughed as Sheila's eyes widened at the sight of Tiny nursing her pups.

"Good Lord," she said. "Are the puppies going to be that large too one day?"

"Yes," I replied. "They are full bred pups. The males, of course, will grow even larger than Tiny. Are you sure you don't want two or three of them?"

"I've been known to be a pretty good actress at times, but I'm not sure I can even pretend to want a dog, much less one the size of a Jersey cow!"

"Oh, sure you can! You're a very believable actress. I've seen you in action! Remember? Shhhh, here she comes."

"Tiny is gorgeous," Sheila said as Paula walked up behind us. "And the puppies are so cute and healthy looking. How old are they now? Are they nearly weaned?"

"A month old tomorrow. It will just be a couple weeks before they're weaned and ready to go to their new homes. All five have been given clean bills of health by the vet."

"I can tell by looking at them they're full bred," Sheila said. Before two minutes ago I wasn't sure if

Sheila could tell the difference between a mastiff and a St. Bernard, but she'd just heard me say they were full-blooded and nothing slipped by her when she was in her acting mode.

"Yes, you're correct. Are you partial to any of them?" Paula asked wearily.

"I think if I decide to purchase one, it'd have to be the one with the small white patch on its chest."

"Oh, sorry," Paula said, with no pretense of regret in her voice. I was initially surprised at how much more chipper she suddenly sounded. "That one has already been spoken for. Speaking of which, Lexie, do you know when Andy is stopping by again? I'd really like to see him! And I also have the American Kennel Club form to give him."

"I'm not sure when Andy plans to stop by. But I'd be happy to take the registration form and give it to him for you," I offered.

"Thanks, but I'd much rather give it to him myself," Paula said cheerfully. "There are some other things I wanted to speak with him about."

Bristling at her sudden change of mood, I couldn't help but stab a tiny dagger into her heart with my next remark. "Then Andy will have to make some time to come over, as he is spending every spare moment with my daughter. They are very tight, you know."

"Humph!"

I could tell my comments had left a mark, so I couldn't resist one more little plunge with the dagger. "But then, I imagine Andy will bring Wendy with him as he is seldom very far from her side."

With a subtle nudge of her elbow, Sheila brought me back to the subject of the puppies, as she said, "Darn! I had my heart set on that particular one. I'm really fond of mastiffs with the white markings on their chests. I'm not sure I'd be happy with any of the other ones at this point. I'll have to give it some serious thought, and discuss the matter with my husband. I'll get back with you soon."

"Whatever," Paula said, as she turned to lead us back upstairs. Her cheery mood had dissipated. Obviously, finding homes for the mastiff pups was not the foremost thing on her mind right now. But I wasn't sure if it was the death of her father, or the notion of stealing Andy away from Wendy that had her preoccupied.

Knowing we had to work up to a conversation about Pastor Steiner's death before she showed us out the front door, Sheila took on an apologetic tone, and said, "I probably shouldn't have bothered you about the puppies at a time like this. I was so sorry to hear what happened to your father. How dreadful for you and your family. I'd like to offer my sincere condolences to you and, of course, your husband. I assume Mr. Bankston is as distraught as you are about the death of his father-in-law."

"Thank you. Yes, Bruce was very upset when I called him with the news. He's overseas on an important business trip right now, which is why he was unable to attend dad's funeral. Bruce felt bad about that, but there wasn't much he could do about it."

"I understand. I'd feel bad if I missed his funeral too. I've attended the Baptist Church with Lexie on several occasions and was very impressed with your father's sermons and dedication to his faith." Sheila had never stepped foot in our church, but, like me, she was not above telling little white lies when the situation called for it. "And I was absolutely stunned by what I read in the paper about the church's finances, and that Largo lady teaming up with your dad to embezzle money from the church. I'm so happy she's been arrested and will be held responsible for her actions."

Sheila did not usually beat around the bush, but even I was a little taken aback by her brashness this time. I knew she felt she had nothing to lose and didn't care what Paula thought of her. I looked down, a bit embarrassed myself, and concentrated on a tiny stain on the carpet, but not before noticing the flush on Paula's face, following Sheila's statements.

"Alleged embezzlement. Nothing has been proven yet," Paula retorted. "I don't believe for a second my father knew what Betty Largo was doing behind his back. Dad would have never stolen from the church, or from anyone else for that matter!"

"Yes, of course. I'm sure you're right," Sheila said. She had struck a nerve with Paula, who was now more animated than she'd been since we'd arrived. "I didn't mean to offend you, Paula. I was just repeating what I read in the paper, but you know how dramatic and sensational the media can be at times. I'm just concerned about your welfare, and that of your siblings. I assume you all inherited enough to cover his final expenses and won't be left in a financial bind."

Paula only nodded with a scowl on her face. She didn't appear willing to share any information about her finances with us, which didn't surprise me in the least. Maybe I'd have better luck if I took over and approached the subject from a different angle. I was afraid if Sheila uttered one more word she'd get us tossed out on our cans. Before she could speak again I joined in the conversation.

"I spoke with Teddy a few times the last couple of days. He told me he was in debt to a bookie—"

"What else is new? He likes to gamble now and then. What of it?"

"—and he mentioned that your father had also dealt with this bookie in the past."

"And? Your point is—"

"Well, it stands to reason that finances might be a problem when it comes to getting your father's final affairs in order."

"There's no problem. And our finances are a personal matter!" Paula was livid now, and it looked as if I might get us thrown out of the house even quicker than Sheila was on the track of doing.

"I apologize, Paula. We don't mean to pry, and I didn't intend to upset you, but a lot of the church members were wondering if they might need to take up a collection to help cover the funeral expenses. If you all need some help, I would be more than willing to step in and take charge of setting up a fund at my bank in order to solicit donations." This was an even whiter lie than the ones Sheila had been spouting, but it seemed to do the trick.

"No, that won't be necessary," Paula said, somewhat pacified by the idea we were only trying to offer our help. "It's really no one else's business. But I guess it doesn't hurt to tell you that my father recently gave me money to purchase a life insurance policy on him. He knew he'd gone through most of his savings, with the gambling and all, and he was afraid he might possibly leave some unpaid bills if something were to happen to him. I still don't believe he'd steal from the church. But, anyway, he felt bad about his financial situation and wanted to leave us enough to cover any debts he might leave behind, and to take care of his final expenses. He also told me he hoped there was quite a lot of money left over after his final expenses were covered following his death. So I purchased the policy as he requested. It must have been prophetic on his part, with him being killed just a month later."

"Wow, what are the chances?" Sheila asked. She didn't sound convinced that greed didn't play a factor in the pastor's death. Paula certainly had motive. "It was awfully thoughtful of your father. Did he do the same for his other children?"

"Well, actually, this policy was for all six of us. Because I work as an accountant, he listed me as the executor of his estate, and I'm to split the proceeds among my siblings and myself, which of course is what I intend to do. After all the final expenses are taken care of, whatever remains will be split six ways," Paula explained. Her voice had taken on a defensive tone again. Of course, Sheila's questions would have made me defensive too.

"Did he leave you a lot of unpaid debts to cover, as he feared he might do?" Sheila was like a dog with a bone now. She wasn't going to let up, but I feared her invasive questioning might cause Paula to shut down completely. I was wrong.

"I really don't know yet," Paula replied. "I haven't had time to sort everything out. But the policy was for five hundred thousand dollars, so I'm sure there will be plenty to pay for whatever debts he might have left. Still, I fear if he owes money to a bookie, it might have had something to do with his murder. I know the detectives are looking into the possibility after I told them about his gambling problem when they questioned me."

Sheila shot me a smug look as I asked, "If your brother Teddy had gambling debts too, do you think that could've figured into your father's murder?"

"Well, I'm sure Teddy had nothing to do with Dad's murder, but I can't say for sure what a bookie might do to get repaid for any debts Teddy might have. Teddy is a screwed-up mess, but he'd never do anything to intentionally hurt Dad. Of that much, I'm sure."

"Well, I know for a fact from speaking with Teddy that there are bookies right now trying to collect from him," I said. "Teddy told me he had money coming in by today that would cover those debts. Was he referring to his share of the insurance money?"

"I doubt it. He spoke to me about it during the luncheon, and he knows it might be awhile before that money comes through, with the killer at large and the murder case still up in the air. Teddy told me he owes ten thousand bucks." Paula ran her fingers through her hair several times. Her eyes welled up. It was obvious she truly cared about her brother and was nervous and upset about his situation.

"He told me the same thing," I said. I patted Paula's shaking shoulders as a tear ran down her cheek and she continued to speak.

"Well, I told him I could come up with eighty-five hundred to lend him but he'd have to somehow come up with the other fifteen hundred. He said he thought he could come up with it if he hocked a few things he'd brought with him, like a Cartier watch, a diamond and sapphire ring he'd inherited from our grandfather, a couple of handguns, and maybe a few other things. Still, I'm worried about him. I've heard owing money to a bookie can be really dangerous."

I didn't want to upset Paula any more than she already was, but I knew for a fact that two goons had already threatened her brother with great bodily harm if he didn't come up with the ten thousand dollars today. I hoped for his sake he was at the pawnshop right now, hocking his eyeteeth if he had to, to come up with the money he owed.

Like Paula had said, Teddy was a total screw-up, but he still seemed like a nice enough guy. I didn't know if I could live with myself if I just stood by and let Teddy get badly injured or worse, if there was anything I could do to help him out. I took out a pen and a gum wrapper from my fanny pack, wrote down my cell phone number on the scrap of paper, and handed it to Paula. "Give this to Teddy if he contacts you and have him call me. I might be able to help him. Just tell him I'm the county grief counselor, and he'll know who you're talking about."

"Grief counselor?" Paula asked. I could tell she was thinking I must be a piss poor counselor, considering how little I'd done to assuage her grief.

"Long story," I said. And one I had no intention of sharing with her. "Just make sure he gets the number."

"Well, okay. Thanks for trying to help him out. I'm really worried, and I appreciate anything you can do for him."

"I'm concerned too, Paula! This bookie is no one to mess with. And neither are the guys who work for him. There's a reason they aren't accountants like you, or library assistants like I am. They are thugs because that's the only thing they know how to be."

We said our goodbyes, and Sheila promised to get back with Paula if she decided to purchase one of the mastiff puppies. That'd be on that cold day in hell when pigs flew over the house wearing ballerina shoes and pink tutus.

CHAPTER 14

"We learned a lot in there," I said as I started up my little blue sports car. "It was definitely worth the trip! Thanks for coming up with such a worthwhile idea, and also for getting Paula to talk."

"No problem," Sheila replied. "I enjoyed the challenge."

"It amazes me that even though Paula's married, and her father was just murdered, she is still able to flirt so openly with Andy. Paula is under a lot of stress right now, and I almost feel sorry for her that she's never going to get her slutty little claws in my future son-in-law."

"Oh, congratulations, Lexie! You never told me that Wendy and Andy were engaged." Sheila's face lit up, and then her expression of delight faded away as I continued.

"That's because they aren't. Their relationship is still a work in progress. The engagement is just a figment of my imagination and perhaps a little wishful thinking on my part. But it will definitely come to pass if I have anything to do with it."

"I wonder if Andy has any idea what kind of force he's up against," Sheila said.

"No, he doesn't, and don't you be the one to tell him!"

"I hope an engagement comes to pass too. I'd love to see Wendy find the man of her dreams after the ordeal she went through with her first husband, Clay. Now let's go pick up those sheet cakes at Pete's Pantry while we think about what to do with all that information we just gathered."

"Okay. I have a list of other supplies we need to pick up there too."

"Are we going to lash the cakes to the roof of this tin can, or are you going to lash me to the roof so you can fit everything you purchase at Pete's inside this thing?" Sheila asked.

"Well, the back seat won't accommodate a normal sized human being, but I think the cakes will ride okay back there. We might have to make a second trip for all the other stuff we need. Let's pay for the cakes, take them home and get them stored in that large refrigerator in the pantry, and then go back for the rest of the groceries. We've got time before we need to pick up the flowers. I was told they wouldn't be ready until two this afternoon."

I paid the older lady behind the bakery counter for the cakes after making sure they were designed in the fashion I had ordered. I motioned for Sheila to pick up the vanilla sheet cake. Holding the chocolate cake with my right hand, and balancing the other end of it on top of the cast on my left wrist, we headed back to the front of the store where the exit doors were located. Just as we reached the end of the condiment aisle, I spotted Edward, the store manager, coming our way. He was the last person I wanted to see inside the store after the spaghetti sauce fiasco.

I quickly held out my right arm, as best I could, to stop Sheila in her tracks. She looked at me in puzzlement as I glanced away from Edward who was approaching us rapidly.

"Can I help you, ladies?" I heard Edward ask.

"No, thanks," I muttered, turning to shield my face from his view. As I did so, I felt the cake shift slightly and I made a sudden lurch to right its balance. As I shifted my weight, I felt my cast tap the edge of a towering display at the end of the aisle, and gasped as I saw numerous rows of peanut butter jars, separated by cardboard, begin to tilt and tumble.

"You again!" Edward spat out, above the clatter of thirty or forty plastic jars bouncing across the floor. I watched his face crumble into a look of pure disgust, as he tried in vain to stop the rest of the display from crashing to the floor. I noticed that the expression on Sheila's face never wavered. She'd known me long enough now that nothing could faze her.

"Oh, Edward! I'm so sorry! I didn't mean to knock your display down. Let me set this cake down and reassemble it for you. I can't believe this has happened again. I guess I was concentrating too hard on balancing this cake in my arms. It's this darned cast, you see," I rambled on. "I still haven't gotten quite accustomed to it, and, well, uh, you know, shit happens!"

"It certainly does when you're in my store!" Edward retorted. "Step aside, lady. I don't want you causing any further destruction by trying to clean up this latest mess you've made. I'll have the stock boys come out from the back room—again—and fix the display. Let me carry this cake to your car for you in order to prevent another incident."

"Look on the bright side," I said, handing him the

cake. "At least with these plastic jars, there's no breakage or sloppy liquid to mop up this time."

"Thank you for your consideration," Edward said, with more than a little sarcasm in his voice. "Do you think you could stay out of my store until you get 'accustomed' to that cast on your wrist? Would that be too much to ask?"

"Actually I need to return in about an hour to pick up a few more supplies for a wedding tomorrow."

"Oh, swell," the manager replied. "I'll keep my stock boys on standby."

"I'm getting married tomorrow afternoon. That's what these two cakes are for," I said, trying to veer the conversation away from my unfortunate mishaps at the store.

"My condolences to your fiancé."

We'd just gotten the cakes situated in the miniscule back seat when my cell phone rang. I answered it and was surprised to hear Teddy's voice on the other end. I hadn't truly believed his sister would give him my number, or that he'd call if she did. I enabled the speakerphone feature on my new mobile so Sheila could listen in on the conversation.

"What's up, Teddy? Is everything okay?"

"Not entirely," Teddy said. "I've rounded up all but two-fifty of the ten grand I need to pay off Harley. I borrowed most of it from Paula, and pawned everything I had with me that was worth anything, and am still running a little short. I remembered you telling Rocky and Spike that you had two hundred dollars, and I wondered if I could borrow it, and maybe fifty more, until I get my next paycheck, which will be Friday, a week from today. I don't have anything left to put up as collateral, but I'm sure my sister will vouch for me and co-sign for me on a written I.O.U."

"Yeah, I guess I could do that, but I'll trust you to repay me without a written I.O.U. if you'll promise me you'll get some help for your gambling addiction. This current situation with Harley's henchmen should convince you to give it up," I said. "Maybe the death of your father is a sign you should clean up your act in honor of his memory and attempt to turn your life around. It's never too late to make a fresh start."

"I will, I promise. I think I've finally seen the light. I've never been this scared before in my life. Thank you so much, ma'am! I don't know how to tell you how much this means to me. Today was the deadline to pay back the bookie, as you might remember from the day you came to counsel me. I'm not sure what they'd do to me if I didn't show up with the entire ten grand, but I doubt it'd be pretty."

"I doubt it too, Teddy. Where are you at right now?"

"I'm just leaving the pawn shop, but I'm to meet Rocky and Spike at that abandoned warehouse on Locust Street, right across from the Dairy Queen. Can you meet me there at twelve? Do you know where the building's at?"

"Yes I have an addiction myself, to chocolate ice cream. I've been to Dairy Queen several times, and I vaguely recall a run-down vacant building across the street. My friend and I will meet you there at noon," I said.

"That would be terrific! And thank you so much for helping me out. You've got to be the very best grief counselor in the county," Teddy said, with a very relieved tone to his voice. Sheila just rolled her eyes at me and climbed into the passenger seat.

Stone and Randy were still out on their fishing trip with Wyatt when we returned to the inn. I really didn't expect them to come back from the lake until early afternoon. I hoped they were all having a good time together and catching a lot of fish. I was really pleased with how well Stone and Randy had clicked. They were both about the same height, just a couple of inches taller than Sheila, and they had similar interests. Randy was a retired police officer, and Stone enjoyed listening to the stories he told about his days on the force. Stone, having served as a reserve officer in Myrtle Beach, could relate to these tales and responded accordingly.

Randy and Sheila were an adventuresome couple and enjoyed snow skiing and scuba diving, among other outdoor activities. Randy also played golf occasionally and promised to give a few lessons to Stone, who still wanted to take up the game but hadn't quite gotten around to playing. He knew he needed to acquire a hobby or two to keep busier when he wasn't working around the inn.

Sheila and I discussed their budding friendship as we refrigerated the two cakes in the walk-in pantry, and made ourselves a couple of turkey sandwiches for lunch. I added a handful of potato chips to each plate and placed them on the kitchen table. Sheila set down two cups of freshly brewed coffee. She extracted a bottle of hazelnut-flavored creamer from the door of the fridge for her own coffee and pulled up a chair at the table.

"The day has been eventful already, and it's only eleven-fifteen," Sheila said. "What do you have in mind to do after we drop off the money with Teddy and pick up the rest of the groceries at Pete's Pantry?"

"I thought we'd play it by ear."

"I was afraid you'd say that, because in most cases nothing good has followed that statement," Sheila said. "Would it be okay if I just stayed behind and rearranged the can goods in your pantry into alphabetical order?"

I'd always teased Sheila about being organized and systematic to an almost obsessive-compulsive degree, but I knew she was kidding, because she'd always been game for anything I suggested, no matter how dangerous or idiotic the suggestion had been.

After consuming several cups of coffee, we placed our cups in the dishwasher and tossed our paper plates into the trashcan. I knew the first of the guests checking in that afternoon wouldn't be arriving until around four, so I didn't feel pressed for time. I'd enjoyed catching up with my dear friend and assumed the rest of the day would be relaxing and just as pleasant. Once again, I assumed wrong.

CHAPTER 15

As I pulled my car into the alley that ran behind the abandoned warehouse on Locust Street, Sheila asked, "This is it?"

"Yeah, I believe so."

"It's kind of spooky and ominous looking," Sheila said. "What did it used to be?"

"I'm really not sure. I think it's just been a falling down vacant warehouse for many years. The front of the building has a faded out sign that says Midwest Manufacturing, which could be just about anything."

"Where in this warehouse are we supposed to meet Teddy?"

"I don't know that either. I didn't think to ask him."

"It's a three-story building that takes up half the block. Perhaps you should've asked. Do you think we should just wait for him in this alley?" Sheila asked.

"What if he parks on the other side, off Cherry Street? I have no idea what kind of car he drives," I said. "It's still only ten until noon. Maybe we should wait here for a few minutes, and if he doesn't show up by five or six after, go in that back door and look around."

"Okay. But I hope he shows up soon. I have a bad feeling about going inside this building for some reason."

"Don't be silly," I said. I had a bad feeling too, but didn't want to frighten Sheila. Anyhow, I knew it was too late to back out of the deal I'd made with Teddy.

After waiting about twenty minutes in the alley, we reluctantly walked through the warehouse's back door, which hung open on broken hinges. With most of the windows boarded up, it was dark and eerily quiet inside the building. It was obvious the warehouse had been looted and that teenagers were now using it as a meeting place. There were cigarette butts and beer cans littered all over the floor. I almost tripped over an empty bottle of Jose Cuervo. Perhaps Perry Coleman was right. We did need more youth programs established in this town to keep kids off the streets.

Sheila flipped up a light switch she saw on the wall beside us, but nothing happened. The electricity had probably been turned off many moons ago. She then shivered violently as she swatted spastically at the cobweb she'd just become entangled in. I knew she'd never been particularly fond of bugs and other creepy crawlers, and I couldn't say I didn't feel the same way. I reached up to flail wildly at imaginary cobwebs in my own hair.

"I don't think he's in here," Sheila said in a whisper.

"We've only stepped ten feet into the building. We need to make our way to the front to see if he's up there. He very likely came through the front door."

"Oh, all right."

"Teddy!" I hollered out. My voice echoed across the vast empty room. Only a few dilapidated crates and broken down pallets could be seen from where we stood. Very little light was filtering into the room from outside. "Where are you? Teddy! Can you hear me?"

There was complete silence as I paused to listen for a response. After hollering several more times, I led Sheila to the front of the building. We wandered around in vain for ten minutes or more. "I can't imagine he would have gone upstairs, can you?"

"I shouldn't think so. And I'm not anxious to go upstairs to find out," Sheila answered. "I think he's just running late. Maybe we should go back out and wait in the car. Or maybe you can wait in the car and I'll stand in front of the building and watch for him."

I could tell Sheila was uncomfortable and wasn't much more excited about waiting in the alley than she was about wandering around in this dark and dank building. I was about to suggest I give Teddy a call to verify his whereabouts when I had the crap scared right out of me.

"Hey!" I yelled out in terror, as a hand reached out of the darkness behind me and grasped my shoulder. I saw Sheila's eyes widen, her pupils as large as elephant-egg marbles, and I nearly fainted and fell to the concrete floor beneath me.

"Fat chance, sister! You'll wait here with us, and so will your friend." I recognized Rocky's voice immediately. "If Teddy wants to see his girlfriend alive again, he'll show up with the ten thousand bucks he owes our boss! He promised he'd be here at noon. What time is it, Spike?"

I turned to see the glow of an indigo light on a cheap plastic watch. I could barely make out Spike's lips move on his face in the dimly lit room. "Twelve twenty-three."

"I'm sure he'll be here at any minute. Maybe he's looking for a parking spot," I said.

"This is a vacant warehouse, lady. There's enough

parking in back for the hundred or so employees who used to work here. I don't need to hear any more excuses out of you, covering for your boyfriend. We'll give Teddy seven more minutes," Rocky said. "If he ain't here by then, he can say hasta la vista to his woman. And who's to say we might not opt to have a little fun with her and her girlfriend in the meantime?"

"Please don't hurt us," I begged. "I'm not his girlfriend. Remember? I'm just a county grief counselor who decided to loan him a little money so he could pay you the money he owes. That's all. I swear."

Rocky was not moved by my remarks. He grabbed the front of my jacket and shook me roughly. "Where is he? I know you know. Did he send you to do his dirty work and have you ask us for more time? If so, you made a grave mistake by agreeing! I really don't think he's planning to show."

"No, Rocky, please trust me," I said. "He'll be here! He promised!"

"Rocky?" Sheila asked. "You two are on a first name basis? My, you've really come up in the world, haven't you, Lexie?"

I knew she meant to be funny, because we both had a tendency to resort to humor when we were scared spitless. But no one was laughing. It was all I could do to keep from wetting myself. All the coffee I'd been drinking all morning picked a fine time to want out of my bladder.

"Listen, Rocky. Teddy is on the way. He has all but two hundred and fifty of the ten grand, and I have the rest. Here, let me get it for you," I said to the two men, as I dug into my fanny pack for the wad of bills. Even when being threatened with my life I have a tendency to be polite. While digging for the cash, I came up with an open pack of Dentyne. "Gum anyone?"

Ignoring my offer, Spike asked, "What time did he tell you he'd be here? He told us to meet him here at noon."

"He told us noon also, but he may have run into a traffic jam or something."

"In Rockdale? A traffic jam here is when two cars are trying to pull into the post office at the same time. I told you I didn't want to hear any more excuses for your boyfriend."

"Please, trust me, he'll be here any minute. And quit calling Teddy my boyfriend. I find it very insulting," I said. I handed the money I'd taken out of my fanny pack to Rocky, who snatched it and shoved it into the front right pocket of his jeans. When he did so, I saw the glint of a large knife hanging from a sheath attached to his belt. I prayed he wasn't planning on using the imposing weapon on Sheila and me. His next statement convinced me that he might.

"For your sake, he better be! He's got about five more minutes before I get very angry, and you won't like it very much when I'm angry!"

Sheila, who had yet to utter a word, opened up her purse. Spike leapt toward her, grabbing her arm in case she was searching for a weapon. She shook off his hand, and spoke. "My name's Sheila. I'm glad to meet you, Rocky and Spike. Lexie's my best friend, and has been for most of my life. You can take my word for it when I tell you she's not Teddy's girlfriend. In fact, I'm only here in Rockdale because my husband, Police Sergeant Randy Davidson, and I, have come to attend her wedding tomorrow—to a man named Stone, not Teddy. Her fiancé is a former cop too, by the way."

I knew Sheila thought if she could keep chattering she might distract them long enough for Teddy to arrive. I knew she also hoped to make them think twice before harming us because her husband and my fiancé were former police officers. And if they injured us, or worse, Randy and Stone would surely track them down and either kill them or see them put them behind bars for life. It was an interesting strategy, but one I thought might have an adverse effect if they'd had a lot of run-ins with the law and had an ax to grind with cops. It might even give them more incentive to do away with us.

I think Sheila probably also thought if she were extremely pleasant and the two men felt like they knew us personally, it would be harder for them to kill us or hurt us in any way. I prayed her strategy would work, although I wasn't betting on it. I watched her open up her billfold and extract all the bills it contained. "Here's another hundred and thirty seven dollars to hold you until Teddy arrives. I would gladly give you more if I had it. I really would."

Rocky reached out and took it and added it to the stash already in his pocket. I couldn't believe Sheila thought a hundred and thirty seven bucks would impress these jerks enough to spare us our lives. Still, I couldn't blame her for trying. If I had any more money on me, I'd be forking it over right about now too. But since the creation of debit cards, I rarely carried a lot of cash any more. I wondered if my Black Hills Gold engagement ring would carry any weight with these dudes. It wasn't particularly valuable, even with the small diamond and rubies but I doubted either of these dudes had much experience in evaluating jewelry. I considered handing the ring over for a moment, but then changed my mind. They didn't appear to me to be Black Hills Gold kind of guys. And damn it all, I was getting married tomorrow and was not going to show up without my engagement ring, assuming Sheila and I showed up at all.

I could feel my heart beating in double time, and I looked at Sheila who was white as the sheet cake she had recently carried into the inn. I felt terrible for getting her into a situation that might cost my best friend her life. I mouthed, "I'm sorry," but she just waved my apology off, as if to remind me that it wasn't over until it was over, and with any luck at all, we might somehow come out of this intact.

"One more minute and you're going to be sorry you ever met Teddy," Spike said, pushing the button to light up his watch again. "We're going to take you and—"

"Hello?" I heard a deep voice call out. "Anybody here?"

I was never so happy to hear a voice in my life as I was to hear Teddy's just then. If I wasn't so pissed off at him, I'd have run up and kissed him. How could he ask us to meet him here at the exact same time he was due to meet these goons, and then have the gall to be a half hour late? I wanted to threaten him with his life, the way Sheila and I had just been threatened with ours.

"Where in the hell have you been?" I demanded to know. "You are thirty minutes late!"

"Well, I got to the warehouse on time," he replied. "But when I saw the Dairy Queen across the street, I realized I hadn't had a bite to eat all day, so I swung in for a pork tenderloin sandwich, fries, and a chocolate malt."

"Why you worthless piece of—" I began.

"Sorry, Lexie. I didn't think a few minutes could matter all that much."

"We were being held as collateral until you showed up and threatened with great bodily harm. If you hadn't finally shown up when you did, there's no telling what these guys might have done to us!"

"Well, I'm here now, so relax," Teddy said. He reached into his jacket pocket and withdrew a large stack of bills, held together with a rubber band. "Assuming Lexie already gave you the other two-fifty, it's all here. Paid in full, just as I said it would be."

"Lucky for you, and also for your girlfriend and the other broad," Rocky replied.

I glanced over at Sheila and could tell instantly she was as insulted at being called "the other broad" as I was being called Teddy's girlfriend. I swallowed hard when she demanded the return of her hundred and thirty seven dollars, and was surprised when Rocky counted out that amount and handed it back to her.

We followed Teddy toward the back of the building and outside to the alley, as Rocky and Spike headed in the opposite direction. Teddy apologized again for being late and the fact we'd been threatened and were terrified by the thought of what might happen to us had he not appeared right in the nick of time. "I don't really think they'd have hurt you two. They were all bark and no bite with you, I'm sure. It's me they were after. You were in no real danger whatsoever."

I wasn't so sure myself, and I could tell Sheila wasn't either. Those two didn't get and keep the jobs they had by being all bark. I pulled an index card out of my back pocket that I'd written my name and address on. I handed it to Teddy, and he promised to mail me a check for two-fifty when he got paid the following Friday. He thanked me one more time and got into an older model white Monte Carlo, with t-tops, and red stripes down the sides, and a spoiler across the back bumper that was held together with duct tape. I knew it to be a 1987 model, because I'd once owned one nearly identical to it. If Teddy drove a car built in the eighties, he truly couldn't afford to lose ten grand gambling. He was lucky his dad's insurance policy stood to pay off in a big way.

Pulling out onto the street in the sports car, I slowed down as I watched Rocky and Spike leave through a broken window in front of the building. When Rocky walked up to the driver's side door of a faded green Chevy van, I handed my phone to Sheila. "Get a photo of them getting in that van if you can."

Fortunately, Sheila's phone was very similar to mine and she wasted no time snapping a photo. After she studied the picture she'd just taken, she assured me it was in clear focus. Both men were recognizable, and she could read the number on the license tag of the van. I didn't know if this photo would prove to be useful, but I knew it couldn't hurt to have it available.

It took very little discussion between Sheila and me to decide it'd be better not to mention the day's activities to Stone and Randy. We chose self-preservation over full disclosure, as I've been known to do in the past. By the time we were closing in on Cedar Street, we'd begun to calm down. "Would you like to see where Thurman Steiner lived?" I asked Sheila.

"Sure."

As I drove slowly down the residential street, I pointed out the blond brick ranch house the pastor had lived in. A man walking at a rapid pace down the sidewalk turned to look at us as we drove past. With a start, I recognized Harold Bloomingfield and wondered at the exasperated expression on his face. I stopped the car and backed up until we were alongside the gentleman. "Is everything all right, Mr. Bloomingfield?"

"Oh, hello, Lexie," he said wearily. He didn't sound

pleased to see me. "I can't find Bonnie. She must have wandered off again while I was taking a shower. I've been looking for her for almost an hour. I've spoken with most of the neighbors and none of them have seen her."

"Can we help you look?" I asked. I liked Bonnie and felt sorry for both her and her husband. I knew how sad and scary Alzheimer's could be. I was concerned about the elderly woman's welfare. "We can drive around the neighborhood and speak with anyone we see out and about. Maybe one of them has seen her walk by. It wouldn't hurt to have a couple more pairs of eyes out looking for her."

"Yeah, you're probably right. Well, thank you. I would appreciate the help. This is the longest I've ever spent looking for her. She's only wandered off twice before, and she didn't leave the immediate area either time."

We spent the next forty-five minutes driving up and down the adjoining streets, broadening our search as we went along. We saw relatively few residents outside their homes, and none of those claimed to have seen an older woman walking alone, appearing lost and confused. Finally, we went back to the Bloomingfields' house to see if Harold had located her or she'd returned to the house on her own. No such luck.

As we stepped outside the car, I'd heard what sounded like the whimpering of a kitten. "Do you have any pets Harold?"

"No. Why?"

"Did you just hear a whimpering sound, Sheila?" I knew she was more apt to have heard the sound than Harold, who wore a hearing aid in his right ear.

"Well, I thought I did hear something, but I can't put a finger on where it came from."

"Me either. Let's split up and do another thorough search around the house and the next-door neighbor's yards," I suggested.

We each headed off in a different direction. I found myself heading toward the Steiner home. Calling out Bonnie's name, I stopped every few feet to listen for a response. As I approached the back patio of Thurman's house I heard the whimpering sound again. I felt sure it had come from his back yard.

The only thing in the back yard, aside from a couple of large oak trees, was a small garden shed. Sure enough when I headed in that direction and called out Bonnie's name, I heard a muffled reply. As I opened the door I saw Bonnie, squatting in the corner of the shed behind an ancient lawn mower that appeared to be on its last legs and an old-fashioned metal gas can. Glancing around, I saw a nearly empty bag of grass seed, a rusty rake, a spade with a wooden handle that was split down the center, and a few cans of old paint. That was the extent of the shed's contents. I could understand why it was left unlocked and Thurman had apparently not been worried someone might break in and steal his stuff. There wasn't anything in there worth stealing.

"It's okay, Bonnie," I said, as I crouched down beside her. She had a wild-eyed expression and looked at me as if she'd never seen me before in her life. I got back up and went to the door to shout out to Sheila and Harold, and they soon joined me.

Bonnie was incoherent and very befuddled. All we were able to make out of what she said was that she was looking for Pastor Steiner to see if he wanted any radishes from her garden. I glanced over at the Bloomingfield's back yard and shrugged my shoulders. The back yard was well manicured and very lush, but no garden could be seen from my viewpoint.

"We haven't had a vegetable garden in about thirty years," Harold said sadly. "It became too much for us to take care of, so we started buying our produce at the farmer's market that's held at the old drive-in theater every weekend."

The speakers and concession stand had been removed from the outdoor movie theater east of town and the site used for local flea and farmer's markets for many years, he went on to tell us. I was consumed with sadness for Bonnie and Harold, but pleased to know there was somewhere I could buy locally grown fresh produce for use at the Alexandria Inn. I always strove to prepare healthy meals for our guests. Even though my cooking wasn't always up to snuff, it was hard to screw up a tossed salad full of colorful veggies.

We got Bonnie settled back into the recliner in the Bloomingfields' living room. Harold thanked us for our help, and for the first time since we'd met he didn't look at me with either mistrust or dislike, or a combination of the two. He was relieved and sincerely grateful for our assistance.

Harold told us it was the worst condition he'd ever seen Bonnie in since the onset of Alzheimer's. He felt certain she was having a reaction to the emotional impact of discovering Steiner's body. He likened it to PTSD, post-traumatic stress syndrome. "It's like a light in her brain switched off when the situation occurred," he said. "I'm taking her to see the doctor on Monday, and I hope he can help her. Her meds do not appear to be working. She may benefit from a higher dose."

We agreed with his assessment and wished him luck. Before we left I pulled out my phone and showed Harold the photo Sheila had taken. "Do you recognize this vehicle?"

"No, sorry."

I knew if Rocky and Spike had anything to do with Steiner's murder, it would more likely be Bonnie who had seen the green van, but I also knew asking her about it would be a futile effort. Not only would she not remember seeing any particular car, she probably had no recollection of finding her neighbor dead in his house, since she still believed him to be alive and craving radishes she'd grown in her garden three decades ago.

Sheila and I said our goodbyes and went outside to the car. As we opened the car doors simultaneously, Sheila asked, "Do you think there's any chance that the Larry Blake you told me about might recognize this van? If he heard Steiner calling out for someone to please help him, it stands to reason the van, or at least the killer's vehicle, was parked in or around the area at the time of the murder. Which house does he live in?"

I pointed out the white two-story house adjacent to the Steiner home, and agreed that it couldn't hurt to ask him if, by some slim chance, we could catch him at home on an early Friday afternoon. I backed the car out of the Bloomingfields' driveway, and pulled in to Blake's.

There was no doorbell, so I rapped loudly on the wooden door. After waiting awhile and knocking again several times, we headed back to the car. I hadn't really expected to find him home. I knew he had a full-time job.

"I figured it was a long shot," I said. "He works as a janitor at the community college here in town. You probably remember me telling you about him."

Sheila nodded and stepped into the car. Just as I opened the driver's side door, I heard a whistle and looked up to see Larry standing in the doorway in silk pajamas. He looked hideous wearing a pair of white furry flip-flops that matched the floral design on his purple pajamas. The hair on his toes resembled that of an orangutan. He had more hair there than on his head. I motioned for Sheila to get back out of the car and join me.

"Good morning," Larry said as we walked back up his front walkway. He then sarcastically asked, "Are you here on a personal visit or in your official capacity as the Witness Statements Records Collector, Natalie?"

Sheila looked at me in confusion, as I'd not gone into a lot of detail about my previous visit with Larry Blake or the watering, swollen eyes that had resulted from my trip to the college to meet with him. I just shrugged noncommittally at her and turned to Larry.

"I'm sorry about that earlier misunderstanding, Larry. My real name is Alexandria Starr, but please just call me Lexie."

"Oh, well, okay, Lexie. But before you tell me what you've come for, please introduce me to your lovely friend." Larry licked his lips and then flashed a brilliant smile at Sheila, or at least as brilliant a smile as one can accomplish with only three teeth. His face held a comical expression, like that of a jack o'lantern, and my friend laughed in response as she took a step backward.

I introduced the two and noticed one of Larry's eyes was fixated on Sheila's breasts. The one I assumed was made of glass stared straight ahead. I was rather annoyed he hadn't given my breasts a second look. Sure, Sheila always had been better endowed than me, but I still found his indifference a bit rude. I almost felt betrayed. Sheila pulled her windbreaker tighter around her waist and spoke to Mr. Blake.

"It's a pleasure to meet you, Larry. We didn't really expect to find you at home," Sheila said. Her eyes darted back and forth. She obviously didn't know which of his eyes to try to make contact with. She eventually gave up and concentrated on a disposal truck picking up a trashcan on the curb across the street. "Lexie told me you worked as a janitor."

"Yeah, well, I should be at work right now. But I woke up with some kind of bug this morning," Larry said. "So I called in sick, thinking I'd be fine by Monday, after a three day weekend at home. I reckon by then all the vomiting and diarrhea should be over with."

Sheila took another step backward. I'm not sure if her reaction was an aversion to the man himself, or just to the germs he was harboring. I think Larry was pleased with this as it gave him a better angle in which to stare at her breasts. She folded her arms across her chest.

"Larry?" I said.

"Yes?" He replied without evening lifting his good eye up to meet mine. "What can I do for you ladies?"

"We've got a photo of an older green Chevy van on my phone we'd like you to take a look at and tell us if you recognize it."

Larry forced himself to look away from Sheila long enough to glance at the photo. He shook his head, and said, "Can't say that I do. Why do you ask?"

"We have reason to believe this vehicle could be connected to the death of Thurman Steiner. We had rather hoped you'd seen it in the neighborhood the morning of his death—or at any other time for that matter." Disappointed in his response, I placed the phone back in my fanny pack.

"No, sorry. I told the authorities about the little red truck I saw in Steiner's driveway the evening before and numerous times before that, but it was nowhere to be seen the next morning. I think the only vehicle I saw that morning was a dark colored muscle car flying up the street, quite a bit over the residential speed limit. I'd come outside to leave for work when I heard that strange sound coming from the direction of Steiner's house, and noticed his flood light had been turned off, which, like I said, he normally didn't do until he went outside to get his morning paper around seven or so. It was about five-thirty, which is the time I leave for work every morning. Then I remembered I'd left my sack lunch inside on the kitchen table. When I came back outside, I saw the vehicle gunning it down the street. It was picking up speed as it passed me. I probably should have mentioned it to the crime scene detectives."

"Did you see the driver?" I asked. I couldn't believe he'd thought this information was not worthy of sharing with the cops. "Could you tell if the car had just left Thurman's house?"

"I don't think so. It seemed to have come from farther up the road. It was going too fast to have just pulled out of Steiner's driveway. And, no, I didn't pay attention to the driver."

It stood to reason someone wouldn't park directly in front of the house, or in the driveway of someone they intended to kill. They'd park further up the street, a block or two from the pastor's house, so as not to draw attention to his vehicle. Had the detectives given Buck Webster enough scrutiny? He drove a dark colored muscle car. I wondered if it was just a coincidence. "Was this car a black Ford Mustang by any chance?"

"Could've been. It was still dark outside, and I wasn't paying a lot of attention to the traffic on the street," Larry said. He still had not averted his eyes from Sheila as he conversed with me. "I reckon it could've been a Chevy Camaro or a Dodge Charger, or one of any number of models. I do sort of recall the car had a bright colored bumper sticker on the front left bumper. Maybe yellow with red writing, or the other way around, but I can't say that for certain, so I never even mentioned the car or the bumper sticker to the cops. I didn't reckon, at the time I was questioned, that it was related in any way to the killer."

"I understand. I don't reckon I would've thought so either," I said. I was talking like Larry Blake again, after only speaking with him for a minute or so. What did it say about me that I could pick up someone else's mannerisms or speech impediments so quickly?

We thanked Larry for his time and told him we hoped he felt better soon. It was time to head back to Pete's Pantry, so we could purchase the groceries and get them home in time to head to the floral shop around two. I'd considered traveling to a nearby town to pick up groceries at a store besides Pete's Pantry. I didn't particularly want to risk another disaster, or have any more run-ins with Edward, the manager. Then I decided I might as well bite the bullet, because I'd surely see him again some time. I wasn't about to start driving an extra thirty miles every time I had to pick up a few items at the store. And did I really care what Edward thought of me? I had better things to do with my time than worry about things like other people's impression of me.

CHAPTER 16

We managed to fill our basket, and pay for the groceries without causing another scene at the grocery store. After returning to the inn and stashing away all our purchases, we headed back out to the floral shop in town. There was only one, and it was small, but it did appear to have good quality flowers and decent prices. I'd ordered a half dozen pink and white lily and baby's breath arrangements for the table centerpieces, and a bouquet in matching colors for my maid of honor, Wendy, to hold. Wendy and I would wear white orchid corsages, and Stone and Andy would wear matching boutonnières. An elaborate multi-colored spread for the table that held the cakes and the punch completed my order.

When we arrived at the shop, the florist was running a bit behind, so we had to wait about fifteen minutes for her to finish up with another customer and put the final touches on Wendy's bouquet. While we were waiting, Wendy called me on my cell to verify everything was on tap to go off on Saturday as scheduled. She'd just spoken with Detective Johnston and wanted to relate what she'd learned.

According to Wyatt, all of the people I'd talked to had also been questioned by the police and cleared of any suspicion. I had to agree there was no substantial evidence that pointed to any one of them and assumed we'd all been barking up the wrong tree all along. Wyatt told Wendy the detectives would be widening their search to take in all the people associated with the church, Steiner's neighborhood, and his friends and relatives who'd not already been questioned. They also intended to make another thorough investigation of the crime scene in case some small clue had been overlooked, or a bit of trace evidence had not yet been discovered.

It sounded to me as if the investigating team was stepping up their search for the perpetrator, and I was happy to hear this was the case. I'd pretty much come to the conclusion my efforts were at a dead end, and I'd be forced to leave it entirely in the hands of the detectives, where it no doubt should have been left in the first place. Investigating murders and other crimes was their forte, not mine, and I had other important matters to concern myself with right now.

After the wedding the next day, Stone and I would have a relaxing day at the inn on Sunday to recuperate from the effects of a busy weekend. All of our guests, except the Davidsons, would be departing that day and no one else was scheduled to arrive for nearly ten days. Sheila and Randy would head home to Fairway on Monday morning, and Stone and I would have one more night before taking off on our much-deserved honeymoon.

We had booked a flight to Jamaica where we'd spend a week of touring, trying out some Caribbean cuisine, and enjoying the sunshine and beautiful beaches. We'd climb up Dunn's River Falls one day, if

I was still able to do that with a waterproof cast on my left wrist, and take a raft ride down the Martha Brae River on another. We planned to take in some reggae music and sample some fried plantains and jerk chicken. We hoped to see all the sights that Kingston and Ocho Rios had to offer.

I was really looking forward to our honeymoon, and to spending quality time with Stone that didn't revolve around the responsibilities of running the Alexandria Inn. I was tired from the events that had followed Pastor Steiner's death, and sore from my recent falls. I could use a little rest, relaxation, and good times, all in the company of my new husband.

Stone and Randy had returned from their fishing trip with Wyatt by the time we'd made it back from the floral shop. They were excited about a successful day of fishing and were planning a fish fry for Saturday evening. They assured Sheila and me they'd be responsible for frying the crappie and preparing all the fixings to go with it. They'd be serving green beans stewed in bacon fat, and Stone didn't think a person could eat fish without fried potatoes to go with it. I was happy to leave them in charge of Sunday's supper. I would be exhausted from the wedding activities, packing for our honeymoon, and taking care of an inn full of guests.

For tonight's meal, which would have to serve a dozen people, Stone was smoking barbecued ribs and chicken on the oversized grill he'd recently purchased at Home Depot. Randy was outside sweeping off the back patio and decorating the gazebo for tomorrow's festivities.

Sheila and I spent the afternoon welcoming guests to the inn. My Aunt Carol and Uncle Joe came in from Deadwood, South Dakota, and several of my closest friends arrived from various locations that included Gardner, Kansas, and St. Charles, Missouri. One old high school friend of mine, Kylie Schoelanker, traveled to Rockdale from south Texas. A cousin from down around the Lake of the Ozarks rounded out the array of guests checking in that evening. She showed up just before supper was ready to serve.

All the other guests were due in Saturday morning, planning to be in Rockdale just long enough for the wedding and reception. They all lived close in and around the Kansas City Metro area and would not be staying overnight with us. Still, I would enjoy showing the Alexandria Inn off to them. I was proud of all the hard work Stone and I had put in to restoring the historic mansion and bringing back the elegance and grandeur it once had. Sheila stayed busy in the kitchen while I took guests on tours of the inn.

Sheila helped me prepare supper's side dishes for all the guests. She fixed a macaroni salad and some baked beans to go with the barbequed meat Stone had smoking on his grill. Together, Sheila and I made up a vegetable and dip tray for appetizers, and a large blueberry cobbler for dessert to be served with vanilla ice cream. While we were in between tasks we sat down at the kitchen table to chat over coffee.

"Do you think we'll have time tomorrow morning to run by the Websters' house?" Sheila asked. "We might be able to get a glimpse of Buck's Mustang. I'd like to see if it has a sticker on the front."

"Good idea. I know there are other black Mustangs in the county, but I can't imagine a lot of them having colorful bumper stickers. People rarely put those on cars these days. I'll get Buck's address out of the phone directory, and we'll just plan on driving by his house."

"What are we going to tell Stone and Randy as an excuse to leave the inn?" Sheila asked.

"We might need some more paper plates and plastic forks," I said. "We might even need a few extra Styrofoam cups for the coffee and punch."

"Oh, are you running short on all of those things?"

"No," I said with a laugh. "I have enough for a royal wedding, but the men don't know that. I don't think Stone even knows there's a walk-in pantry off the kitchen, much less ever stepped foot in to it. As long as food somehow shows up on the table, he's content."

An hour later we served supper and everyone ate heartily. Stone's barbeque was a huge success. Following supper, all the ladies helped clear the dining room table and clean up the kitchen. Then everyone gathered in the parlor as Aunt Carol played the piano and Kylie sang popular tunes while others joined in. Stone was mixing drinks at the bar he'd built for just such an occasion. It was a fun evening and everyone appeared to enjoy themselves. Once again I was glad I'd opted not to cancel the wedding and reschedule it at a later date.

While getting ready for bed Friday evening, I told Stone what Wyatt had told Wendy about the detectives clearing everyone they'd interviewed. I also told him I'd thrown in the towel and was leaving the investigation entirely up to the investigators. I had too much to do now to concern myself with it any longer. Stone appeared very relieved.

"I can't say I'm sorry to hear you say that," he said. "I spoke with the Methodist minister at Wyatt's church, Tom Nelson, yesterday and he's planning to be here at about one-thirty tomorrow. I told him about your reservations in going ahead with the wedding, and he thought that was pure nonsense. He agreed it would be nice if the killer had already been apprehended and arrested, more for the sake of the family and congregation at the Baptist Church than anything else, but he thought it would have been silly to postpone our wedding when all the details had already been planned and arranged. He didn't think anyone would think less of us for going through with our nuptials as scheduled."

"That makes me feel a little better," I said.

"And it makes me feel better hearing you say you're backing off your desire to help track down a suspect. I've seen your life and well-being endangered more than once because of your impulsive actions, and I really don't want to see it happen again."

He and Randy knew nothing of our encounter with Rocky and Spike earlier in the day, and if I had my way, they never would. There were just some things that were better left unsaid. "Don't worry, Stone. I've been cautious and totally in control this time around. Nothing is going to happen to me. You needn't worry so much."

"Good," he said. "Because I love you more than life itself, and I couldn't stand to see anything happen to you. You are my life, and about to become my wife. I can't tell you how happy I am right now!"

We fell asleep in each other's arms, exactly where I wanted to fall asleep for every single night from that moment on.

CHAPTER 17

I woke up in the midst of a nightmare about three o'clock in the morning. In the dream, I'd been standing in front of Tom Nelson, who held an open Bible in his hands, and I was surrounded by all my family and friends. I was wearing my lovely pink silk dress, and my hair, recently permed and highlighted, looked as good as it was ever going to look. My nails, all manicured and painted, also looked terrific. The cakes, punch bowl, and flower arrangements were all positioned perfectly. The guests were all smiling in anticipation. Even the pair of doves that had been delivered an hour earlier, as planned, were cooing quietly in their cage and waiting patiently for their chance to fly free after the vows had been exchanged. Everything was in perfect order for a picture-perfect wedding.

The only thing missing was the groom. Stone was nowhere to be found. Neither Randy nor Wendy knew where he was, and he hadn't mentioned being late to Detective Wyatt Johnston or to his nephew, Andy, either. The grandfather clock just inside the back door struck half past the hour of three, and there was still no sign of Stone. He had skipped out and left me standing at the proverbial altar. I'd been afraid he'd take a long, hard look at all my inherent faults and weaknesses and come to his senses before the big day, but I hadn't expected him to change his mind at the very last moment. I hadn't expected him to humiliate me this way.

I looked around at the crowd who were now all laughing at me as they began to realize what was happening. Even Paula Bankston's dogs, Tiny and Moose, were perched on chairs in the back row, snickering as only a tiny Chihuahua and a massive mastiff can do. This should have clued me in that it was only a dream, but it didn't. Nor did the dancing clown with the creepy makeup, or the fact that Sheila had morphed into my late, great-grandmother and was serving hot dogs and peanuts to the crowd. I hadn't remembered inviting Joe Namath to the wedding either, but there he sat in the third row.

It was only when Frieda, the vocalist from church, began singing "For He's a Jolly Good Fellow" that I woke up, bathed in sweat. I was relieved to discover I'd only been having a nightmare, and that my fiancé was lying in bed next to me. I tried to go back to sleep, but only managed to doze off a few times, while spending the rest of the night tossing and turning. It was a wonder I didn't wake Stone up with all the thrashing I was doing trying to find a position that would put me back to sleep.

With my mind racing in numerous directions, I knew the chances of me falling back to sleep were remote. I was worrying about every little aspect of the wedding to be held tomorrow, afraid some critical detail had slipped my mind. I was also wondering if driving by the Webster's house in the morning was a good idea. It had been very important to me to see Pastor Steiner's killer apprehended before another minister stepped in to officiate our wedding, but all my efforts so far had been fruitless, causing me nothing but grief, embarrassment, fear, and humiliation, not to mention a broken wrist. Wasn't it better to leave well enough alone, whether the killer was ever brought to justice, or not? I flipped over in bed for at least the hundredth time while I mulled it over.

At six o'clock I gave up and went downstairs to brew a pot of coffee and have a few moments to myself out on the back porch before the inn became a beehive of activity. There I reflected on how my life was about to change. I would never make a major decision on my own again without talking it over with Stone. It would never be just "me" again, for I would soon form a partnership and be half of "we." I knew I could never give up my independent nature, and I knew Stone would never ask me to, or even want me to. But I also realized I wasn't the type to be selfish, and would always take his best interests into consideration before I acted on any impulse.

The impulsiveness would never fade entirely from my personality, but it might be tempered some. For both of our sakes, I hoped so.

"Are you ready for a refill?" Sheila's voice behind me startled me awake. After my fitful night of rest, I had dozed off in the lounge chair on the back porch.

"Oh, my, I fell asleep," I told her. "I didn't sleep well last night."

"Worried that everything wouldn't go smoothly today?"

"Well, yes, that's one of the things I've been fretting over."

Jeanne Glidewell

"Well, there's no need to worry at all," Sheila assured me. "Wendy is due here any moment and she and I are in charge today. This is your wedding day, and you shouldn't be burdened with all the mundane responsibilities you normally have. While you rest back here on the porch, she and I will prepare bacon, eggs, and French toast for all the guests, then we'll freshen up the guest rooms, pass out clean linen, clean up after breakfast, and make sure everything is in order.

"Oh, Sheila. You two don't need to do all that."

"Maybe not, but we're going to. Now hand me your cup. I can see you need a warm up."

After Sheila refilled my cup I stood up to give her a big hug, "I love you, my friend. I am so lucky you are in my life."

"I love you too. Always have, always will. Now sit down and relax and leave everything to Wendy and me."

"Thank you."

"You're most welcome," Sheila said. "By the way, we really do have a valid reason to go out this morning. I just noticed we are running low on coffee. We had it on our shopping list but somehow forgot to put any in our basket yesterday."

"Oh, that's right! I remember we got distracted by the old man and woman arguing about their cholesterol levels at the meat counter."

"That's right, we did. Well, we'll plan on going to Pete's after breakfast. Wendy can hold down the fort while we're gone, I'm sure. And, of course, we can cruise by the Webster's house on our way home."

"But Sheila, you don't think Wendy will wonder why I can't make the trip to the grocery store by myself?" I asked. We really did need to go out to purchase coffee, I realized. The thought of running out of it sent a chill up my spine. I needed coffee nearly as much as I needed oxygen. Surely nothing bad could come of driving by the Webster's house while we were out and about anyway. I could feel my recent resolve to leave the murder case well enough alone begin to slip out of my grasp.

"We haven't seen each other in ages," she replied. "It's only natural we'd want to spend every spare minute we can visiting with each other."

"I guess that's true enough. Well, don't let me keep you from working while I'm back here lounging around like a lazy slug. Are you still going to do my hair for me before the wedding?"

"Of course!" Sheila said, as she turned to go back into the inn. "I am your slave for the day. Just don't get too accustomed to it!"

CHAPTER 18

"Should we stop and pick up the coffee first, since it's on our way to the Webster's house?" I asked.

"Good idea," Sheila said. "Why don't you let me go in and get the coffee? I don't think the manager wants to start his day off by seeing you walk into his store. Besides, like I said earlier, I'm your slave for the day, and you don't want to waste an opportunity like this. It may never happen again."

"Okay. I'll wait here for you."

It was only about five minutes later when Sheila walked out of Pete's Pantry with a bag in her hand. The plastic bag was bulging.

"Folgers was on sale today," she said, as she opened the passenger side door. "So I bought three big containers of their Gourmet Supreme Dark Roast. I know you like your coffee strong and thick as motor oil."

"Thanks, pal!"

I pulled the car out of the parking lot and turned left toward Mulberry Street, which was about five or six blocks east of the store. It wasn't long before we located the Webster house, a tan, very nondescript house with absolutely no landscaping, about halfway down the block. I didn't think it was a good idea to pull right into their driveway, or even right in front of the house. "Let's park a couple houses up and walk down there so as not to be too obvious."

"Before we get out, I want to call Wendy," I said. "I forgot to tell her that Andy called right before we left and said he'd be over around eleven to help out in any way he could. I know my daughter, and she'll want to freshen up her makeup and comb her hair before he gets there."

I spoke briefly with Wendy, and told her we'd be gone a little longer than expected because I was going to show Sheila a few things around town, which was technically the truth. I then stowed the cell phone in the pocket of my jacket and got out of the car.

It was still fairly early in the morning and, despite the beautiful weather, there was no activity on the street. It was quiet and serene with a soft breeze blowing. I was pleased that no one was outside their homes to observe us walking up to the Webster house.

The garage door was closed, but the door leading into the garage from the side yard was standing wide open. I doubt this would be considered an open invitation to enter the garage, but I hoped walking through that open door would not be construed as breaking and entering. It was not my goal to get arrested on my wedding day.

"What do you think?" I asked, pointing toward the side door.

"Well, I would take that as an indication they're home. I'm not sure it would be wise to go into the garage though. It's a good way to get shot as intruders. What if Buck is actually messing around in there? Then what would we say?" Sheila asked.

"We could say we were going to knock on the door until we heard a racket inside the garage, and figured he wouldn't be able to hear the doorbell ring, so we decided to join him."

"Join him in the garage for what reason?"

"I don't know. We'll just have to play it by ear."

"Oh, boy—"

"Come on, it will be okay. Follow me," I said. I really wasn't convinced it would be okay, but we'd come this far and I hated to give up now.

Approaching the house from the next-door neighbor's property line, we could hear Sandy's voice coming from the back deck. I peeked around the corner of the house and saw her resting comfortably in a chaise lounge, holding a glass of tea and talking to someone on the phone. She appeared to be quite involved in the conversation and I didn't think she'd be standing up and going into the garage any time soon.

Buck was even farther away, digging a hole on the opposite property line. A balled up Blue Spruce was lying on its side near him. I was happy to see him showing a little interest in the landscaping of the yard, which was bare and unattractive. The back of his t-shirt as he leaned into the shovel was soaked in sweat. He was deeply engrossed in his work.

"They are both in the back yard, and involved enough in what they're doing to give us a few minutes in the garage. Let's hurry in there and get out quickly," I whispered to Sheila.

She nodded her head and followed me to the side door. She stepped back and let me enter first, perhaps afraid there was a dog resting in there. That thought had crossed my mind too, but I was relieved when we were met by silence as we stepped over the threshold.

Sure enough, the black Mustang was parked inside.

I motioned for Sheila to follow me around to the front of the car, and when we got there I pointed at the red and yellow bumper sticker on the front of the car.

"Is prayer your steering wheel, or just your spare tire?" The sticker read.

"If I remember right, that's a quote by Corrie Ten Boom," Sheila said quietly.

"Who?" I was always amazed by the treasure-trove of fascinating, and sometimes useless, information Sheila carried around in her brain. I'd often encouraged her to try out for Jeopardy, hoping some day her knowledge of little-known trivia would pay off.

"Corrie Ten Boom was a Dutch holocaust survivor who spent time in a couple different concentration camps. She helped a lot of Jews escape the Nazis during World War Two. I remember she wrote an autobiography which was later turned into a movie," Sheila explained.

"You really do need to get out more," I told Sheila. I liked to read too, but memorizing the Encyclopedia Britannica was not my cup of tea.

"Hey, it's interesting stuff."

"It is interesting, I'll admit. I'm just blown away by how much you're able to remember. I can't remember if I brushed my teeth this morning."

"You did. Now let's get out of here. We've accomplished what we came to do."

"Okay. I'll call Wyatt and let him know what we've discovered after we get back in the car. We should probably just tell him we saw Buck's car on the road, not in his garage, because that would involve a lot more explaining than I'm prepared to do."

Walking back around the side of the car, I happened to glance inside the cab of the Mustang. My eye caught a reflection of light glinting off an object in the little cubbyhole located in the center console of the car. Out of curiosity, I leaned over to take a closer look. Among other small items in the compartment, including a paper clip, a lighter, and about a dollar's worth of change, was a Black Hills Gold ring, very similar to my engagement ring, except for the absence of a diamond with flanking rubies.

"Sheila! I can't prove it, but I'm almost positive that ring belonged to Pastor Steiner. He had it on his right ring finger as he lay in the casket at his funeral. I assumed it was his wedding band because it was such a close match to the ones Stone and I bought. We wanted something different, and I was surprised at how much Thurman's ring looked like ours."

"But if he had it on at his funeral, how can Buck be in possession of it now?" Sheila asked. "Could he have removed it from Steiner's hand before they closed the lid on the casket?"

"I don't know," I replied. "I remember seeing Buck and his wife at the funeral. I guess it's possible he slipped it off the pastor's finger when he walked up to view the body, and nobody noticed it was missing when they closed the lid to lower the box into the ground."

"Yeah, I guess that's possible. Ballsy, but possible."

"Do you think there's any significance of this discovery? Or could Buck just have coveted the ring, and wanted to steal it to make it his own? I'll have to run the matter by Wyatt when I call him about the bumper sticker. I think it's an odd coincidence, don't you?"

"Well, you know how I feel about coincidences."

Just as we stepped around the car toward the side door, six fluorescent lights on the ceiling of the garage flicked on. Sheila gasped behind me. I froze in my tracks.

"What are you two doing snooping around my wife's car?" Buck asked, clearly angry. "I heard voices in here as I was coming to get a spade. What are you even doing in our garage?"

"Uh, well, we're just, uh—"

"Yes?"

"We knocked on the front door and no one answered, but we could hear voices so we thought you might be in the garage when we saw the door was open." It wasn't much, as excuses go, but it was the best I could come up with. I could hear Sheila breathing heavily behind me.

"What did you want to see me about?" Buck asked.

"Actually, I just wanted to ask Sandy if she remembered me depositing a check from my former bank last week. I can't find it and thought maybe I'd already deposited it, and then forgotten I'd done so in my haste to get everything ready in time for my wedding this afternoon," I explained feebly. "Oh, my, look at the time! The ceremony is at three, so we'd better get going. I'll speak with her next time I'm at the bank. Sorry for the intrusion, Mr. Webster."

"No, just stay right here," Buck demanded. I wasn't sure if he believed my flimsy story, but the stern expression on his face had softened some. "Sandy is right out back on the patio. I'll get her. It will only take a few seconds. Since you're already here, you might as well speak to her."

When Buck walked out the door, Sheila exhaled noisily. "Oh, my God! I knew this was a bad idea. I don't suppose we could make a run for it now without looking suspicious. Did you really deposit a check at the bank?"

"Yes, fortunately I did. I recently closed my account at my bank in Shawnee and the check was for the balance of that account. I was transferring it to my new account at the bank where Sandy works. She was the teller at the drive-through window that day."

"Oh, good, then maybe your story will ring true."

Within seconds Buck re-entered the garage, followed by his wife. I greeted her warmly, and introduced her to Sheila. I then explained to Sandy my plight about having misplaced my check, and she replied, "Yes, you brought the check to my window to deposit. I remember you telling me you were somehow involved with investigating the death of Thurman Steiner."

The tone of Sandy's voice alerted me. Just then a light bulb went on in my brain. "Buck, did you say this Mustang was Sandy's car?"

"Yeah, I hardly ever drive it. Only on days like today, when my pickup's in the shop. My truck's at Boney's Garage getting a new fuel pump put in it."

"Why did you want to know whose car it is?" Sandy asked. She sounded suspicious of me, and my interest in her car, and now I was suspicious of her, as well. If this was her car and not her husband's, was it Sandy who had sped off down Cedar Street shortly after the estimated time of Steiner's murder? Did she have a connection to the pastor, and if so, what was it? I didn't recall ever seeing her at the church, or any of the church-related events.

"Oh, no reason, really. I just think it's an awesome-looking ride, and I was wondering what kind of fuel mileage you got in it. I drive a sports car myself, but I get amazingly good mileage with it."

"That's nice," Sandy said. I could tell she really didn't give a damn if I got two miles to the gallon, or ninety, but I pretended I really believed she was being sincere.

"I also noticed you have a ring very similar to mine lying in the storage compartment in your console.

See?" I held my left arm out for her to admire my ring, which I'd picked up at the jewelers on Thursday after it had been sized. Even though my wrist was in a cast, my fingers were exposed. "I just love Black Hills Gold, don't you?"

Buck glanced at my ring, and then peered into the cab of the car to look at Sandy's. "They are a lot alike, aren't they?"

"I suppose," Sandy said. She glared at me, and then turned to glare at Buck, as if suddenly convinced we were involved in a conspiracy against her. She never blinked once as her husband spoke again.

"Isn't that the ring you used to always wear around your neck all the time? Why'd you stop wearing it all of a sudden?"

"Don't know. Just did."

"That's funny," Buck continued. "I never saw you take it off even once for four or five months, and now you're not wearing it at all. Where did it even come from?"

"I got it from a friend," was all Sandy said in response to his question.

"Want to know what's even funnier?" I asked. "Pastor Steiner had a ring just like it too. Same two-toned gold colors, and same floral pattern. Isn't that odd? He was actually wearing it in his casket at the funeral. I assumed it was his wedding ring and his children wanted him buried with it out of respect for him and their mother."

"That really is funny," Sandy said. She was not laughing, or even smiling. She appeared to catch on to the fact I was putting two and two together. "Hang on a second, Lexie. I have something in the house I want to give you."

I watched her turn and walk through the doorway that led from the garage into the house. That bad feeling I'd had when we'd entered the vacant warehouse the day before had come back. I didn't much like the look in Sandy's eyes when she'd said she had something she wanted to give me. But there was little I could do but stand there and wait.

I glanced from Sheila to Buck. Sheila looked alarmed, and Buck looked perplexed. I would have loved to know what was going through his mind. Before I could dwell on it, however, Sandy rushed back out the door brandishing a very large handgun. I didn't know if it was a forty-five, a nine-millimeter, or what, only that it reminded me of the pistol Clint Eastwood had carried in the Dirty Harry movie Stone and I had watched recently on HBO.

"What the hell—?" Buck said, as he took a step backward and stumbled over a water hose lying on the floor of the garage. Sheila fell to the floor behind me and began to crawl behind the front right wheel of the Mustang in an attempt to put a ton or two of metal between her and any flying bullets.

"Listen, Sandy," I said, as calmly as I could manage under the circumstances. "Please put the gun down. Whatever's bothering you can be discussed and dealt with accordingly. There's no need to hurt anyone. I'm sure there's a good reason for whatever you've done. I'm going to step over there, and you can hand me the gun. You don't want to do anything you'll later regret, and make matters even worse for yourself."

I took one timid step toward her. She waved the gun at me, and with steel in her eyes, said, "Stand back! If you get any closer to me, I'll shoot you right between the eyes!"

I had no reason to doubt her. I took a step backward and looked behind the car to see if there was room next to Sheila for me.

"What's going on?" Buck asked hysterically. "Talk

to me, Sandy. Why are you holding my gun?"

Sandy waved the gun my way. "She knows what's going on. Ask her!"

"No, I don't know, Sandy," I confessed. "Please put the gun down and we'll all pretend this never happened. No one else needs to know."

"It did happen. And there's no way you'll pretend it didn't, Lexie," Sandy said. "All three of you, stand together next to that back wall while I think about what I'm going to do with you. Make any sudden moves and I'll start shooting!"

"But honey—" Buck began.

"Don't honey me, Buck! I'm sorry, but when you started caring more about winning the state football championship than you cared about me, I decided to have an affair. I met Thurman Steiner at a non-denominational prayer meeting. He was kind and gentle, and not hard on the eyes. He showed a genuine interest in me, and in what I had to say. I decided then and there to make a move on him. He was not opposed to my advances, I might add."

Buck gasped in pure shock. It suddenly occurred to me that Sandy was about to confess to her part in the death of the pastor, and that Buck, Sheila, and my lives were in imminent danger. I reached in the pocket of my jacket and pressed the "send" button twice on my phone. This would cause it to dial the number from the last call I'd made, which had been to my home phone to speak to Wendy. Hopefully, she or Stone would pick up the phone, figure out where we were, and what was happening, and notify the police.

"I have never cared more for football than you, honey, I swear—"

"Shut up!" Sandy replied. She brushed her long, beautiful red hair back off her shoulders using the barrel of the gun, and then flipped it back around to point at us, aiming it at each one of us in turn. "Anyway, we were having an affair until Thurman tried to break it off with me a couple of weeks ago. He suddenly felt remorseful, and as if he had turned away from God by 'coveting thy neighbor's wife,' being involved in an adulterous affair, and all that crap! He told me he was going to confess his sins to the congregation at church this Sunday. I couldn't let that happen. It would soon have been all over town, and I'd have ended up jobless, divorced, broke, and desperate. Our marriage wasn't ideal, Buck, or even particularly happy, but at least it was comfortable financially, and I wasn't anxious to see it end unless I could've convinced Thurman to marry me after the divorce. He refused to even consider it."

"My God, Sandy!" Buck exclaimed. "What are you saying? Did you kill Pastor Steiner?"

Sandy just stared at her husband as if she were talking to a moron. What part of "I couldn't let that happen" didn't he understand? I decided I better get involved in the conversation in case someone was on the other end of my phone call, waiting for a clue to where we were. I was holding the phone in my hand, aimed right at Sandy, because she was too wound up to notice, and I wanted her words to be as clear as possible on the other end of the line. I was praying somebody would be listening to them and send help before it was too late.

"Look, Mrs. Webster, Sheila and I didn't come over here to your house on Mulberry Street to confront you or accuse you of anything. I'm sure whatever it is you did, a good lawyer will be able to get you off on an insanity plea. It was obviously a crime of passion, and you went temporarily insane. Please put the gun down. If you were to kill all three of us off now, you'd never see the light of day again. In fact, I would be terribly surprised if they didn't just give you the needle."

Sandy stopped swaying the gun back and forth from one of us to the next and seemed to reflect for a moment. "You're right," she finally said. "My life as I know it is over no matter what I do now. There's no point in even living."

She looked down at the gun in her hand for a few seconds and then pointed it at her own temple. She wore an expression of resignation.

"Sandy! Wait!" Buck and I yelled out in unison. Sheila had closed her eyes and placed her hands over her ears. She was probably hoping Sandy would pull the trigger before she changed her mind again and aimed the gun back at us.

"No," Sandy said. "There's nothing left for me to do but to end it all. I killed the man in cold blood. I parked my car a couple of blocks away and walked to his house in the dark, wearing my driving gloves. All I could think about was the humiliation and embarrassment it would cause you and the entire town of Rockdale when you found out about my affair with Thurman. I truly loved him, but he'd already made it clear we weren't going to end up together, and I couldn't bear to let him confess his sins in church, and bring my world crashing down around my feet."

"But, honey," Buck pleaded. "I would have been there for you. I would have forgiven you. I love you more than anything in the world."

"Yeah, right," Sandy said, sarcasm dripping off her tongue. She had started her story and was determined to finish it before she committed suicide right in front of us inside the garage. "So, anyway, I knocked on Thurman's back door and after he'd let me in the house, I hit him on the head with the tire iron out of my trunk. He hollered out, and then staggered a bit before falling to the floor. After he lost consciousness, I held a sofa cushion over his face until he stopped breathing. I turned off the outside floodlight and looked out the kitchen window. I saw a car running in the driveway across the street. A man started to get in the car, but then walked back into his house. I didn't see a sign of anyone else who might witness my departure, so I raced out of the house with the tire iron and back to my car to make a quick get-away. Until now, I actually thought I was going to get away with it and no one would be the wiser. I hadn't counted on a nosy bitch like you, Lexie, interfering in my business."

"So where does Steiner's wedding ring fit into all this?" I asked. After all, I'd already been classified as a nosy bitch, so why not delve even deeper into the situation. I was still confused about the ring and how it ended up in the console of Sandy's car. "Did you wear it around on a necklace for a while and then give it back to him when he called off the affair? Then, for some reason, you removed it from his finger at the funeral? Didn't it feel a little weird to you to wear his wedding ring from his marriage to Stella?"

"It wasn't his wedding ring. He bought us matching rings to wear as a symbol of our love. He found them at a crafts fair when he attended a religious conference in Montana. His wedding ring from his marriage to Stella is in his lockbox at the bank, I think, to pass down to one of his daughters some day. He was wearing his ring like mine when he was buried. I don't know why he continued to wear it even after he broke it off with me. I stopped wearing mine that day, and it's been in my car ever since."

"Where was I during all this?" Buck asked. I could tell he was trying to find a broken link in her story, making it all a gory and vivid figment of her imagination.

"The affair or the murder?" Sandy asked.

"Both, I guess."

"Well, as far as the affair was concerned, you were at ball practice, sporting venues, or other after-school events. You were golfing, you were fishing, you were hunting, you were bowling, and you were anywhere else you could go to get away from me. Basically, you were gone more than you were home, so running around on you was pretty easy."

"I'm sorry," Buck said. "I never realized how unhappy you were. I should have stayed home more, spent more time with you and the kids. Please forgive me. Put the gun down and we'll talk it over and work things out."

It pained me to watch Buck grovel for forgiveness when it was his wife who'd had the affair and committed murder. He might have not been the best husband, but he provided for his family, and he professed to love Sandy. And, as far as I knew, he was loyal to his wife. He wasn't attentive, perhaps, but he most likely wasn't abusive, a cheater, or a cold-blooded killer either.

"What about the murder?" Buck asked, his voice having dropped several octaves. "Where was I when that took place?"

"It was early and you were still asleep. I was home and back in bed before you even woke up. I was sweating and shaking like a leaf, but naturally you didn't notice because you pay almost no attention to me these days. I could have been lying there dead myself, and you'd have gone right on about your day without giving me a second thought. "

"Sandy, you know that's not true! I would have gone back to the bedroom to check on you when you didn't come into the kitchen and fix me breakfast like you've done every morning of our married life."

That's not what I think Sandy wanted to hear. It only stood to remind her of her depressing life with Buck as a husband, and what might have been had she and Thurman eventually ended up together.

With renewed resolve, Sandy pressed the gun firmly against her temple and squeezed her eyes shut. I knew the moment had come. Sandy was concentrating hard, lost in the moment. I was the nearest person to her, and seeing her eyes were tightly closed, I made a lunge for her right arm, the arm that held the gun.

Ka-Boom! A loud explosion reverberated through the garage. I watched the large pistol bounce off the concrete floor. I grabbed the gun mid-bounce as a mounted jackalope fell off the wall and down on to the workbench below. The fur was flying and the left antler was broken off right above the bottom spike from the fall. There was a ghastly-looking hole where the animal's nose used to be. If the jackrabbit hadn't already been dead, it would be now.

Sandy collapsed to the floor. She was emotionally and psychologically spent, but not injured from the accidental firing of the weapon. As she began to sob into her hands, several uniformed policeman rushed through the side door into the garage with their weapons drawn. Wyatt Johnston was in the lead. I knew they thought they were walking into the middle of a massacre when they heard the gunshot as they were approaching the house.

"Don't shoot!" I yelled. "Everything is okay!"

"Is anyone injured?" One of the cops asked.

"No, although the jackalope didn't fare well," I said. I quickly explained what had just happened. Wyatt told me that Wendy had been vacuuming when my call came in, drowning out the ringing of the phone. Because of this, the answering machine picked up and captured nearly the entire conversation that had taken place inside the garage. Sandy's recorded confession would no doubt be valuable evidence in court. Wyatt said he didn't really want to know how Sheila and I had ended up in the Webster's garage, but was thankful I'd had enough wits about me to dial home. Wyatt went on to explain that Stone had walked into the kitchen and heard the voices being picked up by the answering machine. He'd let the machine keep recording and dialed Wyatt on his cell phone. Wyatt, who was in his patrol car just a couple of blocks from the Webster's house, called for back up, and he and his partner were on the scene within a minute or so.

"As you can imagine," Wyatt said, "Stone, Randy, Wendy, and everyone else at the inn are frantic. Please ring the house again and let them know you two are all right. My partner is cuffing Sandy right now, and we'll take her to the station and book her."

"Okay, good. I'm so glad this turned out the way it did. My entire life was passing before my eyes for the second time in the last few days. It was really annoying me that I was about to get killed on my wedding day," I said. Sheila echoed my sentiments. She claimed she wasn't wild about getting shot on any day.

Wyatt smiled, and went on to say, "I don't know how you two figured out Sandy was the killer, but she was totally off the radar as far as the investigators were concerned. We had questioned Buck, because of the black Mustang reported to have been seen in the area at the time of the murder, but never even considered speaking with his wife. We didn't even know Sandy and Steiner were acquainted."

"Well, I'll tell you all about it later," I promised. "Right now we need to get back to the inn so Sheila can style my hair for me and we can get ready for the wedding ceremony. You're still planning on being at the inn at three, aren't you, Wyatt?"

"I wouldn't miss it for the world. After what's taken place here this morning, Stone might need someone to hold him up while he repeats his vows."

"And I might need someone to drag him to the altar!" I replied. Flashbacks from my wedding nightmare were going through my head. It wasn't too late for Stone to change his mind and leave me standing at the altar. I just hoped the clown, Paula's dogs, my late great-grandmother, and a long-retired NFL quarterback didn't show up this time!

CHAPTER 19

"With this ring, I thee wed, with all I am, and all I have," I spoke softly, looking directly into Stone's watering eyes, with all our family and friends looking on from their chairs in front of the gazebo, where Tom Nelson stood in his flowing robe, holding his open Bible. "I offer this ring to you as a symbol of my love, and my commitment to love, honor, and respect you, from this day forward. As this ring has no end, neither does my love for you. I ask you to wear this ring as a reminder of the vows we have spoken today."

As I finished speaking, I smiled at Stone. As much as I had adored my first husband, Chester, Stone was my one true love, and I couldn't wait to begin our married life together. My eyes began welling up too as Stone read his vows out loud to me. I could hear Wendy sniffling beside me, and looked up at Andy just in time to catch him wink at my daughter. I hoped the next wedding we attended would find Stone walking Wendy up the aisle to marry his nephew.

"I now pronounce you husband and wife. Stone, you may kiss your bride," the minister said. As Stone kissed me tenderly on the lips I heard the flapping of wings as two doves flew out of their cage and around the gazebo twice before heading skyward. I'd always heard having it rain on your wedding day was a sign of a successful and happy marriage to come. At that moment I could have sworn I felt moisture dropping from the sky. I hoped it was coming out of the single fluffy cloud above us, and not one of the doves.

"Congratulations, Mrs. Van Patten!" Wyatt said, kissing me on the cheek. "The wedding was perfect, and you look beautiful. I can't tell you how relieved I am to see this day turn out so wonderfully. I had my doubts about it for a while."

"Me too," I said. I knew exactly what he was referring to. The day could have ended in tragedy, but instead, Sheila and I were unharmed, and Pastor Steiner's killer had been apprehended and charged with first-degree murder just in time for our wedding to take place exactly as scheduled. I couldn't be any happier. "Thanks, Wyatt. But actually, Stone and I have discussed it, and he's content with my decision to keep my last name. We aren't young adults anymore, and going through the hassle of having it changed on my driver's license, social security card, bank accounts, credit card accounts, passport, and all that, seems a little unnecessary. We feel we're just as married whether or not we share the same last name."

"Well, as long as you two are happy, that's all that matters to me," Wyatt said. "I'll be glad when all of your guests get their fill of cake and ice cream, and head home. You've had an eventful day and I know you can't wait to get out of that dress and back into your jeans and t-shirt."

"Stone invited you and Veronica to the fish fry tonight, didn't he?" I asked in amusement.

"Well, yes, but that's not the reason I'm anxious for the crowd to clear out. I can hardly wait to hear your story about how you came to find out Sandy Webster was the killer we've been trying so hard to find. But I realize you have a lot of wedding guests who want to congratulate you, and that you need to mingle and visit with them right now. So the story can wait until later during the fish fry."

"Well, it might be a couple of hours, Wyatt. Would you like some leftover blueberry cobbler in the meantime? There's some in the fridge you can have to tide you over until supper," I offered.

"I thought you'd never ask!"

THE LEXIE STARR MYSTERIES

Leave No Stone Unturned
The Extinguished Guest
Haunted
With This Ring
Just Ducky
Cozy Camping
The Spirit of the Season (a novella)

Turn the page for an

excerpt from

JUST DUCKY

A Lexie Starr Mystery
Book Five

Jeanne Glidewell

"Name's Reliford," he answered, although it came out sounding more like "really bored" because of his current condition.

"Hmm, I knew a lady whose last name was Reliford before she got married a few years ago. Her name was Bertha. Poor lady was found dead in the library a couple days ago. Was she any relation to you?" I asked, innocently.

"Yeah, she was my old lady for a long, long time. Went by Bert, and now I hear she goes by Ducky. Always hated the name her mama give her. Too bad about the dying thing; heard she hung herself."

"Yeah, that's what the investigators said. She didn't seem like the suicide type to me, though. Did she to you?" I asked.

"Dunno. Never could figure that broad out, myself."

"Were you two still on good terms? When was the last time you saw her?"

"Ain't talked to Bert since the divorce was final," Bo said. He had drained his last beer in two or three gulps and opened up another bottle. He seemed in somewhat of a stupor, as he continued, "But I think I might have seen her in (hiccup) town a couple weeks ago. I pulled up behind a (loud juicy belch) VW bug at a light, and the driver looked like that old (very graphic adjective) bitch, so then I (incoherent muttering) so I could teach her a lesson."

"You must be very angry about the divorce. I'm sure you didn't deserve to be dumped that way," I said, hoping to get him stirred up and elaborating, no matter how crudely, on how he, in a drunken rage entered the library after I left, got involved in a heated argument with Ducky, or Bert, as he called her, and decided to drag her up the ladder and hang her from one of the log beams. Afterward, to save his own hide, he typed up a suicide note on one of the computers designated for library patrons to use, printed it out, and left it on the chair at her desk. That's what I hoped to hear and be able to decipher, amid all the hiccupping, belching, cursing, and even, occasionally, noxious farting. With all the sounds emitting from him, this old fellow was a one-man band.

If I could get him started confessing his sins, I would activate the voice recorder app on my smart phone, and then drive his recorded confession straight to the police station. I was very proud of the plan I'd developed, and was mentally patting myself on the back for a job well done. So naturally, I was then terribly disappointed when instead of reciting a detailed description of how he'd murdered his ex-wife, he merely passed out cold on the couch, dropping his nearly full beer on the linoleum floor.

Watching the beer flow out of the bottle onto the dark, grimy floor, creating a large puddle, the urge to urinate became more than I could control. As much as the thought disturbed me, using this man's *new-fangled crapper* had become a necessity. I'd used enough gas station restrooms in the past to perfect the art of peeing without one inch of my flesh ever touching the toilet seat, and I would have to utilize that talent again now.

When I was done relieving myself, I'd head home and leave Bo to sleep it off in his chair. There'd be no more conversing with him until he sobered up, and I needed to get home shortly anyway, to avoid worrying Stone.

I found the bathroom behind the second door down the hallway. The restroom was every bit as nasty as I'd imagined, but I'd have to risk untold germ and bacteria exposure, and use it. I locked the door behind me in case Bo woke up and came looking for me. Evaluating the toilet in front of me, I tried to imagine what bell or whistle it had that the old one might not have, and came up with nothing. Unless, I thought, it was the black mold under the lid, or the ring around the bowl a jackhammer couldn't chip off.

After peeing while performing a world-class balancing act, I realized there was no toilet paper on the holder. There was not even an old Sear's catalog in the john. Thank God I carried a small pack of Kleenex in my fanny pack just for emergencies such as this one.

After completing the task at hand, I grasped the doorknob only to find it wouldn't unlock. I shook the rusty knob as violently as I could, jammed my fingernail file in the key opening, and wiggled it frantically. I then hollered out as loudly as I could, hoping to raise Bo. When those attempts failed, I looked for door hinges to remove the bolts from, but for some odd reason the door opened outward instead of inward, putting the hinges on the other side of the door.

My next thought was to crawl out the window, but

was forced to accept the fact that, although I might be able to squeeze my arms and head out the tiny window, the extra junk in my trunk was going nowhere. Even if I busted out the window, and greased the window frame with oily residue off the floor, there was no hope of squeezing my rump and thighs through the opening.

Damn that Wyatt Johnston! If I didn't always have to keep so many fattening treats on hand to satisfy his sweet tooth, and then feel obligated to taste-test them before serving them to him, there might have been a prayer of escaping Bo's utterly disgusting privy.

I tried messing with the doorknob again, while intermittently calling out Bo's name, to no avail. Glancing at my watch, I knew it was Stone calling as soon as my phone rang. I could be evasive, or even downright lie about my situation, but what good would that do me at this point? It wouldn't get me out of the slimy, stinking bathroom anytime soon. I decided to bite the bullet and explain to him what had happened. I knew it would result in a lecture about my appalling disregard for my personal safety, and my lacking the sense God gave a lemming, on Stone's part, and a lot of shameless crying and pleading on mine, but it had to be done.

Apparently, Stone was getting accustomed to my impulsive nature, and the unfortunate and sometimes dangerous, predicaments this bad trait sometimes landed me in. He was angry, disgusted, and bitterly disappointed with me, but he didn't sound at all surprised. He sighed and asked for directions to Bo's place. Before he hung up, he asked, "This dude actually bought your story of being interested in buying his harrow?"

"Well, sure, I was very convincing. He even believed I might want to purchase his old toilet, since he done went and bought himself one of those new fangled crappers."

Stone didn't laugh, comment, or even sigh again. He just rudely hung the phone up in my ear. I could tell it was going to be a long, long night.

JUST DUCKY

**available in
print and ebook**

Jeanne Glidewell and her husband, Robert, live in Bonner Springs, Kansas. When not traveling or fishing in south Texas, Jeanne enjoys reading, writing, and wildlife photography. She's the author of Soul Survivor, and five Lexie Starr mysteries. A member of Sisters-in-Crime, she's working on more Lexie Starr mysteries. You may contact her through her website, www.jeanneglidewell.com.

Jeanne is a pancreas and kidney transplant recipient and volunteers as a mentor for the Gift of Life program in Kansas City. The promotion of organ donation is an important endeavor of hers. Please be an organ donor, because you can't take your organs to heaven, and heaven knows we need them here.

CPSIA information can be obtained at www.ICGtesting.com
Printed in the USA
LVOW10s1329030615

PP9648900001B/1/P